MORE TALES OF
PIRX THE PILOT

ALSO BY STANISLAW LEM

STANISLAW LEM

MORE TALES OF PIRX THE PILOT

TRANSLATED BY LOUIS IRIBARNE
WITH THE ASSISTANCE OF MAGDALENA MAJCHERCZYK,
AND BY MICHAEL KANDEL

A Harvest/HBJ Book
A Helen and Kurt Wolff Book
Harcourt Brace Jovanovich, Publishers
San Diego   New York   London

Requests for permission to make copies of any part of the work
should be mailed to: Permissions, Harcourt Brace Jovanovich,
Publishers, 757 Third Avenue, New York, N.Y. 10017

The translation of "The Hunt" originally appeared in *Mortal
Engines* by Stanislaw Lem. English translation copyright © 1976
by The Seabury Press. Reprinted by permission of The Con-
tinuum Publishing Corporation, New York.

Library of Congress Cataloging in Publication Data

Lem, Stanislaw.
  More tales of Pirx the pilot.

  (A Harvest/HBJ book)
  Translation of: Opowieści o pilocie Pirxie.
  "A Helen and Kurt Wolff Book."
  I. Title.
PG7158.L390613 1983   891.8'537   83-6172
ISBN 0-15-662143-6

Printed in the United States of America

First Harvest/HBJ edition 1983

CONTENTS

MORE TALES OF
PIRX THE PILOT

PIRX'S TALE

Sci-fi? Sure, I like it, but only the trashy stuff. Not so much trashy as phony The kind I can dip into between shifts, read a few pages at a time, and then drop. Oh, I read good books, too, but only Earthside. Why that is, I don't really know. Never stopped to analyze it. Good books tell the truth, even when they're about things that never have been and never will be. They're truthful in a different way. When they talk about outer space, they make you feel the silence, so unlike the Earthly kind—and the lifelessness. Whatever the adventures, the message is always the same: humans will never feel at home out there. Earth has something random, fickle about it—here a tree, there a wall or garden, over the horizon another horizon, beyond the mountain a valley . . . but not out there.

People on Earth can't imagine what a pain the stars are— what a drag it is to cruise the cosmos, even for a year at full thrust, with never a change of scenery! We fly, sail around the world, and think: So that's what outer space is like! But there's just no comparison.

Once, on my way back from a patrol, I was tuned in to a pilots' argument somewhere up around the *Arbiter*—the usual scuffle over who had landing priority—when I happened to sight another homeward-bound ship. The guy must have thought he was alone, because he was tooling around as if in an epileptic fit. All pilots know the feeling: you're space-borne only a few days, when, wham, it hits you—that goofy urge to pull something, anything, to rev to full, hang a U-turn, and let your tongue stick out.

I used to think it was bad business to get so freaked out. But you're driven to it—by the despair, by the urge to stick out that old tongue at the cosmos. The cosmos is not a tree; maybe that's what makes it so mind-boggling. The good books talk about that. And we don't care to hear the truth about the stars when we're out there, any more than a dying man likes to read about death. What we want then is something to distract us; as for me, I'll take sci-fi, the corny, easy-to-read stuff, where everything, the cosmos included, is so tame. But it's an adult tameness, full of calamities, murders, and other juicy horrors, yet all quite harmless, because it's bull, from A to Z: scariness to make you smile.

The story I'm about to tell is just such a spook tale. Only this one actually happened. Never mind that, though. It was during the Year of the Quiet Sun, during a routine circum-solar round-up of the scrap revolving parallel to Mercury's orbit—space hulks junked during the six-year construction of a giant space station at the perihelion, to be recycled for scaffolding, according to the Le Mans System, instead of being sent to the scrap yard. Le Mans was a better econo-mist than an engineer; a station constructed of recycled scrap may have been three times as economical, but Operation Mercury had caused such tribulation that eventually nobody gave a damn *what* the cost savings would be. Then Le Mans had another stroke of genius: why not move this morgue back down to Earth; why let it wheel around till doomsday when it could be melted down? But to keep it profitable, the job of towing went to ships not much healthier than the hulks.

I was a rookie pilot at the time, meaning a pilot only on paper and once a month on payday. I was itching to fly so badly that I'd have flown a kiln if it had some thrust, so no sooner had I read the want ad than I was making application at Le Mans's Brazilian office. Now, I wouldn't go so far as to call those crews hired by Le Mans—or, rather, by his agents—a kind of cosmic foreign legion. The days of space adventurers were over, because for the most part there weren't any more adventures to be had. Men were driven to work in space either by a fluke or by some personal hang-up—not the best qualifications for a profession that demanded more on-board grit and stamina than the merchant marine.

I'm not trying to play psychologist but to explain how I came to lose half of my crew on the first trip out. The technicians were the first to go, after they were turned into boozers by the radiotelegraph operator, a shrimp of a mestizo who knew every trick of the bootlegger's trade—sealed plastic pouches hidden inside canisters, that sort of thing. The early space pioneers would have been shocked. Beats me how they could have believed that any man placed in orbit automatically became an angel. Or was it just a subconscious effect of that brief, blue, paradisical sky that faded so abruptly during blast-off? But why quarrel with the dead. The Mexican, who was in fact Bolivian-born, peddled marijuana on the side and loved to bait me. A mean customer, all right, but I've flown with worse.

Le Mans was a big man; he didn't fuss over details, simply handed his agents a budget, and that was that. So not only did I wind up with a skeleton crew, I also had to sweat every kilowatt of thrust and to scrimp on every maneuver, because the uranographs were audited after every trip to see whether—God forbid!—ten dollars had gone up in neutrons. Never had I commanded such a ship, nor, I venture to say, had there been one quite like mine since old tramps plied the seas between Glasgow and India. But I wasn't about to complain, and I even look back on my *Pearl of the Night*, I'm ashamed to say, with some nostalgia. What a name! A ship so weather-beaten that more time was spent tracking down leaks and shorts than at the helm. Every lift-off or landing was a violation of the laws of physics. And not just physics. Le Mans's agent must have had a lot of pull in the Mercurean port, because any self-respecting controller would have padlocked the *Pearl* right away, from controls to pile.

As soon as we got within range of the perihelion, we'd start radar-stalking, round up the hulks, and form a train. What a time I had *then*: hassling with the technicians, jettisoning liquor overboard—thereby putting gallons of London dry gin into perennial orbit—and agonizing over the mathematical hell of finding approximate solutions for the problem of too many bodies. But worst of all was the idleness. Of time and space.

That's when I would hole up in my cabin and read. Don't remember the author's name (it was an American) or the title (something with the word *Stardust* in it). Don't remember the beginning, either, because I started it somewhere in the middle—where the hero is in the reactor chamber, talking to the pilot on the phone, and suddenly hears, "Meteoroids astern!" All this time they're in free fall; suddenly he notices that the reactor, a huge colossus with dials like yellow eyes, is coming at him—the engine burn had caught him in zero-g. Luckily, he meets it feet first, but the acceleration yanks the receiver out of his hand; for a second he hangs on to the wire, then falls, flattened to the deck, with the receiver swinging overhead; he makes a superhuman effort to grab it, but, weighing a ton, he can't budge a finger; finally he gets it between his teeth, just in time to give the saving command.

A memorable scene, but even better was the part describing their passage through a swarm. A dust cloud, lo and behold, big enough to blanket a third of the sky, and so thick that only the brightest stars could pierce it. And the best is yet to come, because suddenly our hero spots something on the scanners: from out of this yellowish typhoon there looms a blinding swirl with a black core. God only knows what it was, but I almost died laughing. What a per-

fect set-up! All that cloud business, the typhoon, the receiver—because, need I say it, at the time that guy was
dangling on the telephone wire, a woman was waiting for
him in his cabin. A stunner, of course. The secret agent of
some cosmic tyranny—or was she one of the freedom fight-
ers? A looker, in any case.

But why the long preamble? Because that book was my
salvation. Meteoroids? In all the weeks I spent hunting down
hulks in the twenty-to-thirty-thousand-ton range, I must have
missed at least half of the meteoroids on the radar. Oh, yes.
Once, while we were in free fall, I had to grab my half breed
friend by the neck—which was a lot trickier than grabbing
that receiver must have been, and a damned sight less glam-
orous. I'm rambling again, I know. But the whole thing began in just such an unglamorous way.

When the two-month round-up was over, I had between
a hundred twenty and a hundred forty thousand tons of scrap
in tow, and was Earthbound along the ecliptic plane. Was
that against regs? You bet. Like I said, I had to scrimp on
fuel, which meant I had to coast for over two months without thrust. Then doomsday struck. Not meteoroids—this
wasn't a novel, after all—but the mumps. First my nucleonics engineer, then both pilots at once, and so on down the
line. The whole bit—swollen pusses, slits for eyes, high fe-
ver. Soon everybody was on the sick list. Ngey, a black, the
Pearl's cook, steward, and chief something-or-other, had
brought the wicked virus aboard ship. He was sick, too, of
course! Say, don't kids in South America ever get the mumps?

So there I was, commander of a ghost ship, or almost: I
still had a radiotelegraph operator and a second engineer.
Never mind that the operator was stinko from breakfast on.
Not altogether gone: whether he was a sipper or he had a
cast-iron stomach, the fact is he never stopped bustling, especially when we were weightless (which was most of the
time, not counting a few minor course corrections). But the
stuff was in his eyes, in his brain, so that every order, every

errand, had to be checked and rechecked. I had fantasies of getting even the moment we touched down—because how could I cripple him up there? Sober, he was a typical rat, gray, sneaky, always unwashed, with a charming habit of calling certain people by the worse obscenities during mess. In Morse. That's right, in Morse, tapping it out on the table with his finger and almost triggering a few fistfights in the process (naturally, all were fluent in Morse), claiming it was a nervous tic the moment he was cornered. When I told him to keep his elbows at his sides, he'd tap with his foot or his fork—the guy was a real artist.

The only really able-bodied man was the engineer—who turned out to be a civil engineer. No fooling. Signed on at half pay, no questions asked, and it never crossed my mind to quiz him when he came aboard. The agent had asked him whether he knew his way around construction sites and machines, and of course he said yes. He neglected to mention what kind of machines. I told him to stand watch, though he couldn't tell the difference between a planet and a star. Now you know why Le Mans made such huge profits. For all his agents knew, I might have been a submarine navigator. Oh, sure, I could have deserted them for my cabin. I *could* have, but I didn't. That agent wasn't so dumb. He was counting, if not on my loyalty, then on my instinct for self-preservation. On my desire to get back in one piece. And since the scrap, more than a hundred thousand tons' worth, was weightless, uncoupling it wouldn't have boosted our speed by a millisecond. Besides, I wasn't a bastard. Not that I didn't flirt with the idea as I made my morning rounds with the cotton, baby oil, bandages, rubbing alcohol, aspirin. . . .

No, that book about cosmic romance and meteoroid typhoons was really my only escape. I even reread passages, some of them a dozen times. The book fairly brimmed with space hijinks—a rebellion of electrobrains, pirates' agents with microtransmitters planted in their skulls, not to mention that beauty from an alien solar system—but not a single word about the mumps. Which was fine by me, obviously. I was sick of the mumps. Of astronautics in general.

During off hours I hunted high and low for the radiotelegraph operator's liquor stock. Though I may be giving him too much credit, I suspect he deliberately left a trail just so I wouldn't waver and give up the crusade. I never did locate his supply. Maybe he was a sponge and kept it stored inside. And I *searched*, my nose to the deck the way a fly hugs the ceiling, sailing around back aft and midships the way you do in dreams. I was all by my lonesome, too—my swollen-jawed crew quarantined in their cabins, my engineer up in the cockpit learning French from tapes, the ship like a funeral parlor except for the occasional wail or aria traveling through the air-conditioning ducts. The latter came from the Bolivian-Mexican, who every evening routinely suffered an attack of *Weltschmerz*. What did I care about the stars, not counting those in my book, of course, the juicier parts of which I knew by heart (mercifully forgotten by now). I was waiting for the mumps epidemic to end, because my Robinson Crusoe existence was beginning to tell.

I was even ducking the civil engineer. He was an OK sort of guy in his own way, but he swore he would never have signed on if his wife and brother-in-law hadn't got him in debt. In short, he belonged to that species of man I can't stand: the excessively confiding type. I don't know whether he was gushy only with me. Probably not. Most people are guided by a sense of discretion, but this guy would confess anything, to the point of making my insides crawl. Fortunately, the *Pearl*'s twenty-eight-thousand-ton rest mass offered plenty of room to hide.

As you might have guessed, it was my first and last trip for Le Mans. Ever since, I've been much the wiser, which doesn't mean I haven't had my share of adventures. And I wouldn't be telling you about this one—perhaps the most embarrassing of my career—if it weren't for that other, fairytale, side of astronautics. Remember, I warned you this story would sound like a sci-fi tale.

The alert came when we were about even with Venus's orbit. But either our operator was napping on the job or he forgot to record it, because it wasn't until the next morning that I heard the news on Luna's daily meteoroid forecast. At first, frankly, I thought it was a false alarm. The Draconids were far behind us and things were quiet except for the usual swarms, nor was it Jupiter up to its perturbational pranks, because this was on a different radiant. Besides, it was only an alert of the eighth degree—a duster, very low density, the percentage of large-sized particles negligible—although the front was, well . . . formidable. One glance at the map and I realized we'd been riding in it for a good hour, maybe two. The screens were blank. A routine shower, I thought. But the noon bulletin was far from routine: Luna's long-range trackers had traced the swarm to another system!

It was the second such swarm in astronautical history. Meteoroids travel along elliptical paths gravitationally tied to the sun like yo-yos; an alien swarm from outside the solar system, from somewhere in the galaxy at large, is regarded as a sensation, although more by astrophysicists than by pilots. For us, the difference is one of speed. Swarms in our own system travel in circum-terrestrial space at speeds no greater than the parabolic or the elliptical; those from outside may—and, as a rule, do—move at a hyperbolic velocity. Such things may send meteoritologists and astro-ballisticians into ecstasy, but not us.

The radiotelegraph operator was fazed neither by the news nor by my lunchtime lecture. An engine burn (to low thrust, naturally) plus a course adjustment had given us just enough gravity to make life bearable: no more sucking soup through straws or squeezing meatloaf puree out of toothpaste tubes. I've always been a fan of plain, ordinary meals.

The engineer, on the other hand, was scared stiff. My talking about the swarm as casually as if it were a summer shower he took as a sure sign of my insanity. I gently reassured him that it was a dust cloud, moreover a very sparse one; that the odds of meeting up with a meteoroid large enough to do any damage were lower than those of being crowned by a falling theater chandelier; that we couldn't do anything, anyway, because we were in no position to execute any evasion maneuvers; and that, as it happened, our course in good measure coincided with the swarm's, thus significantly reducing the chances of a collision.

He seemed somehow unconsoled. By now, I'd had it with psychotherapy and preferred to work on the operator instead—that is, to cut him off from his liquor supply for at least a couple of hours, which the alert now made more urgent than ever. We were well inside Venus's perimeter, a heavily traveled zone; traffic, and not only of the cargo variety, was fierce. I kept a four-hour watch by the transmitter, the radiotelegraph operator at my side, until 0600 hours—fortunately, without picking up a single distress call. The swarm was so low in density it took literally hours of squinting to detect it: a mass of microscopically small greenish phantomlike dots that might easily have been an illusion caused by eyestrain. Meanwhile, tracking stations on Luna and on Earth were projecting that the hyperbolic swarm, already christened Canopus after the radiant's brightest star, would bypass Earth's orbit and abandon the system for the same galactic void whence it had come, never to menace us again.

The civil engineer, more anxious than ever, kept nosing around the radio room. "Go back and man the controls!" I would bark. A purely cosmetic command, of course, first because we had no thrust, and without thrust there's no navigating, and second because he couldn't have executed the most rudimentary maneuver, and I wouldn't have let him try. I just wanted to keep him busy and out of my hair. Had I ever been caught in a swarm before? How many times? Had there been any accidents? Were they serious? What were the odds of surviving a collision? He kept up a steady stream. Instead of answering, I handed him Krafft's *Basic Astronautics and Astronavigation*, which he took but I'm sure never opened: the man craved first-hand revelations, not facts. And all this, I repeat, on a ship minus any gravity, weightless, when even the soberest of men moved in burlesque fashion—when, for example, the pressure exerted in writing with a pencil could land a man on the ceiling, head first. The radiotelegraph operator, however, coped not by belting up but by jettisoning things: trapped in the space between ceiling, deck, and walls, he would reach into his pants pockets, throw out the first item at hand—his pockets were a storage bin of miscellaneous weights, key chains, metal clips—and allow the thrust to propel him gently in the opposite direction. An infallible method, unerring confirmation of Newton's second law, but something of an inconvenience to his shipmates, because, once discarded, the stuff would ricochet off the walls, and the resulting whirligig of hard and potentially damaging objects might last a good while. This is just to add a few background touches to that idyllic voyage.

The airwaves, meanwhile, were jumping, as passenger ships began switching to alternate routes. Luna Base had its hands full. The ground stations that relayed the orbital data and course corrections were firing away signals at a clip too fast for the human ear to detect. The relays were also jammed with the voices of passengers who, for a hefty fee, were cabling reassuring messages to loved ones. Luna's astrophysics station kept transmitting updates on the swarm's more concentrated areas, along with spectroanalyses of its composition—in a word, a regular variety show.

My mumps-stricken crew, already informed about the hyperbolic cloud, kept phoning in to the radio room—until I switched off the intercom system. I announced they would recognize any danger—a blowout, say—by the sudden loss of pressure.

Around 2300 hours, I went below for a bite to eat. The

radiotelegraph operator, who must have given up waiting
for me, had vanished meanwhile, and I was too tired to hunt
him down, much less think about him. The engineer returned from his watch, calmer and more visibly troubled by
his brother-in-law than by the swarm. On his way out of the
mess, when he wasn't yawning like a whale, he mentioned
that the radar's left screen must have shorted, because it was
showing a sort of green flicker. With these words he made
his exit, while I, who was in the process of polishing off a
can of corned beef, my fork stuck in an unappetizing gob of
solid fat, fairly froze.

The engineer knew radar about as well as I knew asphalt.
A radar screen "shorted" . . . !

A moment later, I was streaking to the cockpit (in a manner of speaking, of course, because I could accelerate only
by shinnying with my hands and by bouncing, feet first, off
the walls and overhead deck). The cockpit—when I finally
reached it—was dead, its dashlights extinguished, its reactor
controls like fireflies, and only the radar screens were still
going, pulsating with every sweep of the scope. My eye was
already on the left-hand one before I was inside the hatch.

The lower-right quadrant showed a bright, immobile dot,
which, when I came closer, became a coin-sized splotch,
somewhat flat and spindle-shaped, perfectly symmetrical and
fluorescent-green in color: a tiny, deceptively motionless fish
in an otherwise empty ocean. If an officer of the watch had
spotted it—not now, but a half hour earlier—he would have
flipped the automatic tracking relay, alerted his CO, and requested the other ship's course and destination. But I was
without any watch officers, a half hour too late, and alone.
I did everything at once: sent out the identification call,
switched on the tracker, and fired up the reactor (it was as
cold as a very old corpse) in order to have instant thrust
ready at hand. I even managed to get the navigational computer going, only to discover that the other ship's course was
almost parallel to ours, with only a marginal difference be-

tween them, so that the chance of a collision, extremely low to begin with, was pushing zero.

But the other ship played deaf. I shifted to another chair and began flashing Morse from my deck laser. It was too close for comfort, about nine hundred kilometers astern, and I could see myself being hauled before the Tribunal for violation of Paragraph VIII: "HA = Hazardous Approach." But only a blind man could have missed my signal lights, I told myself. Meanwhile, that ship sat stubbornly on my radar, and not only did it not alter course, but it was actually starting to lap us—we were moving, as I said, on almost parallel tracks—along the quadrant's outer perimeter. I visually clocked its speed at roughly hyperbolic, or ninety kilometers per second, which was confirmed by two readings taken within a ten-second interval; whereas we were lucky if we were doing forty-five.

Still no response; it was gaining, and it looked splendid, even elegant. A pale-green, incandescent lens, which we viewed sideways; a smoothly tapered spindle. Suspicious about its size, I glanced at the radar range-finder: we were four hundred kilometers away. I blinked. Normally a ship looked no bigger than a comma from that distance. Damn— I thought—nothing works aboard this ship! I transferred the image to a small auxiliary radar with a directional antenna. The same effect. My mind went blank. Then a sudden brainstorm: another of Le Mans's convoys, a string of some forty-odd hulks in tow . . . But why the spindle shape?

The scopes went on sweeping, the range-finder kept clicking away. Three hundred, two hundred sixty, two hundred . . .

I checked the course margin on the Harrelsberg because I smelled a near-collision in the making. When radar was first introduced at sea, everyone felt a lot safer, but ships went on sinking just the same. The data confirmed my suspicions: the other ship would clear our bow by some thirty to forty kilometers. I tested the radio and laser relays. Both functional, but still no response. Until now, I had been feeling a trifle guilty—for leaving the ship on automatic while I sat below and listened to the engineer bellyache about his brother-in-law, snacking on a can of corned beef because I was without a crew and had to do everything myself—but no more. Now it was as though the scales had fallen. Filled with righteous indignation, I knew who the guilty party was: this deaf-mute of a ship, too hell-bent across the sector to respond to another pilot's emergency signals!

I switched on the radiophone and demanded that the other ship display its navigational lights and send up flares, that it report its call numbers, name, destination, owner—all in the standard code, of course—but it kept cruising leisurely, silently along, altering neither course nor speed by so much as a fraction of a degree or a second. It now lay eighty kilometers astern.

So far, it had been situated a little to the port side; now I could see it was lapping me. The angular correction meant that the clearance would be even tighter than the one projected by the computer. Under thirty kilometers, in any case, perhaps as low as twenty. The rules said I should have been braking, but I couldn't. I had a necropolis of over a hundred thousand tons behind me; I would have had to unhook all those dead hulks first. But alone, without a crew? Oh, no, braking was out of the question. Friend, I told myself, what you need now is not astronautical savvy but philosophy— starting with a little fatalism and, in case the computer's projection was high, even a dabbling in eschatology.

At exactly twenty-two kilometers, the other ship began to outstrip the *Pearl*. From now on the values would increase, which meant we were in the clear. All this time my eyes had been glued to the range-finder. I shifted my gaze back to the radar screen.

What I saw was not a ship but a flying island. From

twenty kilometers away, it now measured about two fingers in width. The perfectly symmetrical spindle had become a disk—better, a ring!

I know what you're probably thinking: an alien encounter. I mean, a ship measuring twenty kilometers in length . . . ? An alien encounter. A catchy phrase, but who believes in it? My first impulse was to tail the thing. Really! I even grabbed the stick—then held back. Fat chance I'd have with all that scrap in tow. I heaved out of my seat and climbed a narrow shaft to the small, hull-mounted astrodome atop the cockpit. It was conveniently stocked with telescope and flares. I fired three in quick succession, aiming for the ship's general radius, and tried to get a sighting in the glare. An island, yes, but still hard to locate right away. The flash blinded me for a few seconds, until my eyes adjusted to the brightness. The second flare landed wide, too far away to do any good; the third, just above it. In that immobilizing white light, I saw it.

Only a glimpse, really, lasting no more than five or six seconds, because I was using one of those exceptionally bright flares that fade very fast. But in the space of those few seconds, I saw, looking down at an angle through my night glasses, whose eighty-power lenses brought it to within a few hundred meters, an eerily but sharply illuminated mass of metal. So massive, in fact, it barely fit into my field of vision. Stars showed in the center. A sort of hollow, cast-iron, spaceborne tunnel, but—as I noticed in the last glimmerings of light—somewhat squashed, more tire-shaped than cylindrical. I could see straight through the core, even though it wasn't on the same axis; the monster stood at an angle to my line of vision, like a slightly tipped glass of water.

There was no time for idle contemplation. I fired more flares; two failed to ignite, the third fell short, the fourth and fifth made it stand out—for the last time. Having crossed the *Pearl*'s tangent, it sheered off and quickly widened the

gap—one hundred kilometers, two hundred, three hundred—
until it was completely out of eye range.

I immediately hustled back to the control room to plot its
trajectory, because afterward I intended to sound a general
alarm, in all sectors, such as had never been heard. I already
had visions of a cosmic chase after the alien intruder—a chase
using *my* trajectory—although secretly I was sure it belonged to the hyperbolic swarm.

There are times when the human eye can behave like a
camera lens, when a momentarily but brilliantly cast image
can be not merely recalled but meticulously reconstructed as
vividly as if viewed in the present. Minutes later, I could
still visualize the surface of that colossus in the flare's after-
glow, its kilometers-long sides not smooth but pocked, almost lunar in texture; the way the light had spilled over its
corrugated rills, bumps, and craterlike cavities—scars of its
interminable wandering, dark and dead as it had entered the
nebulae, from which it had emerged centuries later, dust-
eaten and ravaged by the myriad bombardments of cosmic
erosion. I can't explain my certainty, but I was sure that it
sheltered no living soul, that it was a billion-year-old carcass, no more alive than the civilization that gave birth to
it.

With my mind still astir with such images, I computed,
for the fourth, fifth and sixth time, the elements of its trajectory, and, with each punch of the key, entered the data on
the recording machine. Every second was precious; by now,
the ship was a mere phosphorescent green comma, a mute
firefly hugging the edge of the screen on the right, receding
to a distance of two, then three, then six thousand kilometers.

Then it was gone. Why did that bother me? It was dead,
had no maneuvering ability, couldn't run or hide. OK, it
was flying at hyperbolic, but any ship with a high-power reactor and the target's exact trajectory could easily outrun it.

I opened the cassette recorder to remove the tape and take it down to the radio room—and froze. The metal sprocket was empty; the tape had run out hours, maybe even days ago, and nobody had bothered to refill it. I had been entering the data on nothing. All lost. No ship, no trace, nothing.

I lunged for the screens. That goddamned baggage train! Oh, how I wanted to dump Le Mans's treasures and take off. Where to? I wasn't sure myself. Direction Aquarius, I think—but I couldn't just aim for a constellation! Still? If I radioed the sector, gave the approximate speed and course data . . . ?

It was my duty as a pilot, my first and foremost duty, if I could still do anything at all.

I took the elevator to midships, to the radio room. I foresaw everything: the call to Luna Central, requesting priority for future transmissions of the utmost urgency, which were sure to be taken by the controller on duty, not by one of their computers. Then my report about having sighted an alien craft intersecting my course at a hyperbolic velocity and conjectured to be part of a galactic swarm. When the controller asked for its trajectory, I would have to say that I had computed it but was missing the data, because, due to an oversight, the recorder's tape cartridge had been empty. He'd then ask me to relay the fix of the pilot who was first to sight the ship. Sorry, no fix, either: the watch officer was a civil engineer. Next—provided he hadn't begun to smell a rat—why hadn't I instructed my radiotelegraph operator to relay the data while I was doing my computations? I'd have to tell him the truth: because the operator had been too drunk to stand watch. If he was then still in the mood to pursue this conversation, taking place across more than three hundred sixty-eight million kilometers, he would inquire why one of the pilots hadn't filled in for the missing operator, to which I'd reply that the whole crew had been bedridden with the mumps. Whereupon, if he still harbored any doubts, he would safely conclude that I either had flipped or was myself drunk. Had I tried to record the ship's presence in any way—by photographing it in the light of the flares, for example, by transcribing the radar data on ferrotape, or at least by recording all my subsequent calls? But I had nothing, no evidence. I had been too rushed; and why bother with photographs—I recalled thinking—when Earth's ships were bound to catch up with the target, anyway? Besides, all the recording equipment had been off.

The controller would then do exactly what I would have done in his place: he would tell me to get off the air and would inquire of all ships in my sector whether anyone had sighted anything suspicious. None had, of course, because none *could* have observed the galactic intruder. The only reason I could was that I was flying within the plane of the ecliptic, strictly off limits because of circulating dust and the remnants of meteoroids and comet tails. But I had violated that ban to have enough fuel for the maneuvers that were to make Le Mans the richer by one hundred forty thousand tons of scrap iron. Luna's coordinator would have to be told, naturally, in which case word was bound to reach the Tribunal's Disciplinary Board. True, my having discovered the ship might outweigh an official reprimand, and possibly even a fine, but only on condition that the ship was actually tracked down. In short, it was a lost cause, because a pursuit would have meant dispatching an entire fleet into the zone of the ecliptic, twice as hazardous as usual because of the hyperbolic swarm. Even if he wanted to, the Luna coordinator lacked the authority to do it. And even if I did handstands and called COSNAV, the International Committee for Space Research, and the devil only knows who else, there would still be the conferences and meetings and powwow sessions, and then maybe, if they moved with lightning speed, they might reach a decision in three weeks' time. By then—my mind, exceptionally quick that night, had already done its homework in the elevator—the ship would be a hundred ninety million kilometers away, beyond the sun, which it would skirt closely enough to have its trajectory altered, so that in the end the search area would amount to more than ten million cubic kilometers. Maybe twenty.

Such were my prospects as I reached the radio room. I sat down and estimated the probability of a sighting through Luna's giant radiotelescope, the most powerful radioastronomical unit in the system. Powerful, yes, but not powerful enough to pick up a target of that magnitude at a distance of four hundred million kilometers. Case closed. I tore up my computations, got up, and quietly retired to my cabin, feeling as though I had committed a crime. We'd been visited by an intruder from the cosmos, a visit that occurs, who knows, maybe once in a million years—no, once in hundreds of millions of years. And because of a case of the mumps, because of a man named Le Mans and his convoy of scrap, and a drunken halfbreed, and an engineer and his brother-in-law, and my negligence—it had slipped through our fingers, to merge like a phantom with the infinity of space. For the next twelve weeks, I lived in a strange state of tension, because it was during that time that the dead ship returned to the realm of the great planets and became lost to us forever. I was at the radio room every chance I got, nurturing a gradually diminishing hope that someone else might sight it, someone more collected than I, or just plain luckier, but it wasn't meant to be. Naturally, I never breathed a word to anyone. Mankind is not often blessed with such an opportunity. I feel guilty, and not only toward *our* race; nor will I be granted the fame of Herostratus, since fortunately nobody would believe me any more. I must admit that even I have my doubts at times: maybe there never was any encounter—except with that can of cold, indigestible corned beef.

THE ACCIDENT

When Aniel wasn't back by four, no one thought much of it. Around five it started to get dark, and Pirx, more puzzled than alarmed, had an impulse to ask Krull what could be keeping him. But he didn't; he was not the team leader, and anyhow, such a question, harmless and even legitimate in itself, was bound to set off a chain reaction of mutual needling. He knew the symptoms, all the more predictable when, as in their case, the team was a randomly selected one. Three people of widely divergent specialization, stuck in the mountains of an utterly worthless planet, on a mission that all, Pirx included, considered a waste of time.

They had come—their transport, a mini-gravistat so old it was good only for scrap iron, was to be junked afterward—equipped with a collapsible aluminum Quonset hut, a smattering of hardware, and a radio terminal so fatigued that it gave more trouble than service. A seven-week "general recon" mission—what a laugh! Pirx would have turned it down had he spotted it for what it was—a mop-up detail, designed to follow up on probes initiated by the Base Exploration Department, to add one more digit to the raw data fed their memory banks for programming next year's manpower and resource allocation. And for the sake of that perforated figure, they had sat nearly fifty days in a wilderness that, in other circumstances, might have had its attractions—say, for mountain-climbing. But mountain-climbing, understandably, was strictly against regs, and the best Pirx could do was to contemplate the first pitches while he was out doing his seismic and triangulation surveys.

For want of another, the planet bore the name Iota-116-47, Proxima Aquarius. With its small yellow sun, its saltwater oceans shaded violet-green with oxygen-producing algae, and its sprawling, three-shelved, flora-crusted continent, it was the most Earthlike planet Pirx had ever seen. If not for its G-type sun, a recently discovered subspecies of G VIII—hence, one suspected, of unstable emission—it would have been ideal for colonization; but once vetoed by the astrophysicists, all plans for settling this Promised Land had to be scrubbed, even if it took another hundred billion years before going supernova.

Pirx's regret at having been buffaloed into the expedition was not altogether genuine. Faced with being grounded during the three-month suspension of traffic in the solar system, with hanging around the Base's air-conditioned subterranean gardens, glued to a TV and its mesmerizing programs (the shows were like canned preserves, oldies of at least ten years' vintage), he had fairly jumped at the chief's offer. The chief, for his part, was only too glad to be able to oblige Krull, two-man flights being against regs and Pirx being the only one on furlough. Pirx thus came as a godsend.

But if Krull was thrilled, he gave no sign of it, not then or later. At first Pirx thought he might have taken his joining the team as the magnanimous gesture of a chief navigator stooping to the level of a routine surveyor. But what looked to be a personal grudge was merely the bitterness—the kind nourished by wormwood—of a man in the throes of middle age (he had just turned forty). Still, there's nothing like prolonged isolation to bring out a person's foibles and virtues, and Pirx soon understood the source of Krull's character flaw, of this man who was the toughened veteran of more than ten years of extraterrestrial duty. Krull was a case of frustrated ambition, a man unfit for his dream profession, which was to be an intellectronics engineer, not a cosmographer. What tipped Pirx off was Krull's bullheadedness with Massena every time conversation turned to intellectronic—or, in professional parlance, "intellectral"—matters.

Massena was either too insensitive or just plain unmoved, because whenever the cosmographer insisted on some fallacious proof, he was not content merely to refute him, but had to take him to the mat; pencil in hand, he meticulously built his mathematical model and polished Krull off with a glee that seemed motivated less by self-vindication than by a desire to prove the cosmographer an arrogant ass. But Krull wasn't arrogant, only touchy, no more and no less so than anyone whose ambition and abilities were not evenly matched.

Pirx, who was a captive audience for such scenes—unavoidable since they shared a living space measuring forty meters square, divided by partitions with next to no sound insulation—knew he would be made a scapegoat. And he was right. Not daring to show Massena he was a sore loser, Krull made Pirx bear the brunt of his frustration, and in a way that was typical of him: except when circumstances demanded otherwise, Pirx was given the silent treatment.

When that happened, he was left with only Massena for company, and he might have actually become pals with this clear-eyed, dark-haired man, except that Massena was highstrung, and Pirx had always had trouble with high-strung types, deep down distrusting them. And Massena had his tics: his throat needed constant examining, a twinge in his joints meant a change in the weather (not one of his prognostications had ever come true, but that didn't stop him from making more); he complained of insomnia and made a point of scrounging pills every night, pills that he never took but placed beside his bunk, the next morning swearing to Pirx—who read till all hours and could hear the man snoring peacefully away—that he hadn't slept a wink, and apparently believing it. Otherwise, he was a topflight specialist, a whiz of a mathematician, and a born programmer. He was also in charge of the computerized, unmanned surveying program now under way. He even made a hobby of it, working on one of these programs in his spare time, which rankled Krull no end: the man did his job so well and so quickly that he actually had time to spare, and he couldn't be reproached for neglecting his duties. Massena was all the more valuable in that, paradoxically, their planetary mini-expedition included not a single certified planetologist; Krull was anything but.

It was as remarkable as it was distressing, the degree to which, with no special effort on anyone's part, relations between three basically normal, ordinary individuals could become so embroiled in those rocky barrens that were the southern tableland of Iota Aquarius.

To the team belonged one other member, a nonhuman one—the afore-mentioned Aniel, a nondigital robot, one of the latest Earthside jobs to be developed for fully automated land probes. That Massena was there as a cyberneticist was an anachronism—because of a regulation which provided that where there was a robot, there had to be a repairman. Now, regulations, as everyone knows, are seldom updated, and this one was ten years obsolete, since, as Massena himself was often heard to quip, the robot stood a greater chance of repairing *him* than vice versa: not only was it infallible, it was also medically programmed. Pirx had long ago observed that a man could be judged better by his behavior toward robots than toward his fellow man. Pirx belonged to a generation born into a world of which robots were as natural a part as spaceships, though acceptance of robots was tainted with vestiges of irrationality. There were those, for example, more easily infatuated with an ordinary machine—with their own car, say—than with a thinking machine. The era of unbridled modular experimentation was waning, or so it seemed, and construction was now limited to two types: the narrowly specialized and the universal. Only a fraction of the latter were human-shaped, and only because, of all the models tested, those patterned on nature proved the most functional under conditions simulating planetary exploration.

Engineers were never gratified to see their products manifest the kind of spontaneity that grudgingly bespoke an inner life. Popular wisdom held that robots could think but were devoid of any personality. Admittedly, no robot had ever been known to throw a fit, go into ecstasies, laugh, or cry; they were perfectly balanced, just as their constructors had intended them to be. But because their brains were not mass-produced, because they were the product of a laborious monocrystallization susceptible to wide statistical variability and minute molecular shifts, no two were ever created exactly alike. So they *were* individuals, then? Not at all, replied the cyberneticists, merely the products of a random probability—a view shared by Pirx and by just about anybody who had ever rubbed elbows with them, spent years in close quarters with their thinking, with their always purposeful, logical bustle. Though more similar to one another than to humans, they, too, were subject to whims and predilections; some, when called upon to execute certain commands, even practiced a kind of passive resistance—a condition that, if it persisted, was remedied by a general overhauling.

In his attitude toward these quaint machines, so punctilious, at times even ingenious in carrying out orders, Pirx, and probably not he alone, had a not altogether clear conscience, perhaps a throwback to his navigational stint on the *Coriolanus*. In Pirx's mind there was something inherently unfair, something fundamentally wrong, about a situation whereby man had created an intelligence both external to and dependent on his will. A slight unease, difficult to define, yet nagging at his conscience like an unbalanced equation or a bad decision—bluntly put, the sense of having perpetrated a very clever but nonetheless nasty trick. In the judicious restraint with which man had invested these cold machines with his cumulative knowledge, granting them only as much intelligence as was required, and no chance of competing with their creators for the world's favor, lay a perverse subtlety. When applied to their ingenious constructors, Goethe's maxim *"In der Beschränkung zeigt sich erst der Meister"* acquired the ring of a tribute perversely transformed into a mocking condemnation: they restrained not themselves but their own products, and with a mean precision. Pirx, of course, was not about to announce his qualms, knowing full well how preposterous they would have sounded. Robots were not really handicapped or exploited. No, a much simpler method had been found, one that was both more sinister and harder to attack morally: robots were crippled even before they were born—right on the drawing board.

That day—their next to last on the planet—was clean-up day. But when it came time to collate the recorded data, one of the tapes had been discovered missing. They ran a search through the computer, then ransacked all the drawers and files, in the process of which Krull twice made Pirx go through his gear, an insinuation resented by Pirx, who had never laid hands on the missing tape and who, even if he had, most certainly would not have stashed it in his grip. Pirx was itching to pay him back, all the more so because of all the anger he had been swallowing, bending over backward to rationalize Krull's tactless, even abrasive manner. But, as usual, he held his tongue, volunteering, if worse came to worst, to team up with Aniel and re-record the missing data.

Krull said that Aniel was quite capable of handling it on his own, and after loading him up with camera and film stock, after stuffing his holsters with jet cartridges, they sent him up the massif's lower summit.

The robot left at 0800 hours, with Massena boasting he would have the job done by lunchtime. The hours ticked by—two o'clock, three, then four. . . . Darkness fell, but still no Aniel.

Pirx sat in one corner of the Quonset hut, trying to read a badly battered book lent him by one of the pilots back at the Base, but was unable to concentrate. He was not in the most comfy of sitting positions. The hut's thin-ribbed, lightweight aluminum wall dug into his back, and his air mattress was so flat that the bunk's nut-and-bolt frame kept jabbing him in the behind through the rubberized fabric. But he didn't change his position; somehow it suited the smoldering rancor building inside him.

Neither Krull nor Massena seemed the least fazed by Aniel's absence. For some reason Krull, who really was not much of a wit and never made any effort to be, had insisted from the start on the name "Angel," even "Iron Angel," and this, though trivial in itself, had rubbed Pirx the wrong way so many times as to be reason enough for disliking the man. Massena treated the robot in a purely professional sort of way and—like every intellectronics engineer who claims to know what responses are caused by what molecular processes and circuits—branded as sheer bull the faintest suggestion of any spiritual life. Still, he was as loyal and solicitous toward Aniel as any mechanic toward his diesel: he made sure he was never overloaded, respected him for his efficiency, and babied him.

By six, Pirx, who couldn't take it any more—his leg had finally gone to sleep—stood up, stretched till his joints cracked, wiggled his foot and flexed his knee to restore circulation, and began pacing the hut cornerwise, sure that nothing could rile Krull now that he was engrossed in his final tabulations.

"A little consideration, fellas," Krull said at last, seemingly unaware that the only one on his feet was Pirx, since Massena lay sprawled on his pneumatic couch, a pair of earphones on his head, listening to some broadcast with a look of bemused distraction. Pirx opened the door, felt the tug of a strong westerly wind, and, once the hut's wind-rocked, sheet-metal wall was at his back and his eyes were accustomed to the dark, gazed in the direction of Aniel's return route. A few vibrant stars were all he could see as a blustering, howling wind descended on him, engulfing his head like an icy stream, ruffling his hair, and swelling his nostrils and lungs—Pirx clocked it at around forty meters per second. He lingered for a while until a chill sent him back inside, where he found a yawning Massena taking off his headset and running his fingers through his hair, while Krull, frowning, businesslike, patiently went about filing papers in folders, shuffling each bunch to even the edges.

"No sign of him!" said Pirx, startling even himself with his defiant tone. They must have noticed it, too, because Massena skewered him with a brief, cold stare and remarked:

"So? He'll make it back on infrared. . . ."

Pirx returned the glare but held his peace. He brushed past Krull, picked up the book he'd left lying on a chair, settled back into his corner, and pretended to be reading. The wind was picking up, at times cresting to a wail; something—a small branch?—thumped against the outer wall, and then came a lull lasting several minutes.

Massena, who was obviously waiting for the ever-obliging Pirx to start supper, finally broke down and, after poring over the labels in hope of striking it rich with some hitherto undiscovered delicacy, set about opening one of the self-heating cans.

Pirx wasn't much in the mood for eating. Famished as he was, he stayed put. A cool and malevolent rage was taking hold of him, and it was directed, God only knew why, against his bunkmates, who, as roomies went, were not even all that bad. Had he assumed the worst? An accident, maybe? An ambush by the planet's "secret inhabitants," by those creatures in which no one but a few spoofers claimed to believe? But if there'd been a chance, even a thousand-to-one chance, of the planet's being inhabited, they'd have dropped their piddling exercises long ago and swung into action, following procedures outlined by Articles 2, 5, and 6 of Paragraph XVIII, along with Sections 3 and 4 of the Special Contingency Code. But there was not a chance, not the slimmest, of that happening. The odds were greater that Iota's erratic sun would explode. Much greater. So what could be keeping him?

Pirx felt a deceptive calm in the hut that shook now with every gust of wind. All right, maybe he *was* pretending to be reading, to having lost interest in dinner, but the others were playing a similar game, a game as hard to define as it was increasingly obvious with every passing moment.

Since Aniel came under a dual supervision—Massena's as the intellectronician in charge of maintenance, and Krull's as the team leader—either man stood to be blamed for any possible foul-up. Negligence on Massena's part, say, or a badly plotted route on Krull's, though such mistakes would have been too obvious to have escaped notice. No, that was not the cause of the silence growing more studied by the second.

Krull had, it seemed, deliberately bullied the robot from the word go, putting him down schoolboy fashion, saddling him with errands unthinkable to the others—a universal robot, after all, was not a lackey. It was plain to see that, clumsily but persistently, through Aniel he was out to get Massena, whom he was not man enough to attack openly.

It now became a contest of nerves, the loser being the first to betray any anxiety over Aniel. Pirx felt himself being implicated in this silent game as crazy as it was nerve-racking. What would *he* have done in the team leader's shoes? Not a whole lot, probably. Send out a search-and-rescue party? A bad night for that. No, a search would have to wait until morning. That left radio contact, on ultrashortwave, even though the densely mountainous terrain made getting through iffy. Aniel had never been sent out on a solo before; though it was not forbidden, the rules made it conditional on ump-teen paragraphs. To hell with the regs! Massena could have at least tried radioing—thought Pirx—instead of scraping that can for the rest of his scorched rations. Think: what if I were out there instead of the robot? No, something must have happened. A broken leg? But who ever heard of a robot breaking his leg?

He got up, went over to the plotting board, and, feeling the furtive glances of the others, studied the map on which Krull had charted Aniel's route. Maybe he thinks I'm check-ing up on him, Pirx wondered; he looked up suddenly and met Krull's gaze. The team leader was on the verge of mak-ing some crack—his lips were already parted—when he backed down under Pirx's cold hard stare, cleared his throat, and, hunching over, went back to sorting his papers. Pirx's steely-eyed glower was not intentional; it was just that at such times he was roused to something that commanded on-board obedience and a respect tinged with anxiety.

He put aside the map. The robot's route went up to and then skirted the towering rock mass fronted by three preci-pices. Could he have disobeyed instructions? Impossible. Maybe he got his foot wedged in a crack and sprained it? Nonsense. Robots like Aniel could survive a forty-meter fall. They had something better than brittle bones, were built to endure worse scrapes. So what the hell was it?

Pirx stood up straight and from his imposing height con-templated Massena, who sat wincing and blowing between sips of scalding tea, and then Krull, before making an ex-aggerated about-face and retreating to their cramped bunk room. He flipped down his bed from the wall, exerting a trifle too much force, shed his clothes in four fluid gestures, and crawled into his sleeping bag. Sleep, he knew, would not come easily, but he'd had enough of Krull and Massena for one day. If he was cooped up much longer with those two, he might really tell them off, but why waste his breath:

the moment they boarded the *Ampère,* Operational Team Iota Aquarius would be terminated.

Silvery streaks snaked under his eyelids, fuzzy spots of light flickered and lulled the senses. . . . He flipped his pillow onto its cooler side, then suddenly had a vision of Aniel, now close enough to be touched, looking exactly as he had earlier that day, a few minutes before eight. Massena was fixing him up with the jet cartridges for momentary propulsion—standard equipment, to be deployed under strictly prescribed conditions. It was too quaint to behold, as only the sight of a man helping a robot—rather than vice versa—can be, but Aniel's hunchlike backpack kept him from being able to reach the cartridge holsters. (He carried a payload heavy enough for two men.) Not that this hurt his pride; he was, after all, a machine, equipped with a micro-strontium battery, capable of delivering sixteen horsepower in a pinch, for a heart. Perhaps just because he was in a semiconscious state, Pirx was repelled by the sight of it. Being heart and soul on the side of the mute Aniel, he was ready to believe that fundamentally the robot was no more the phlegmatic, easygoing type than he was, but that he only made it look that way for reason of expediency. Before dozing off, he had another vision, the most intimate kind a man can entertain, of the sort immediately forgotten on waking. He conjured up that legendary, wordless, mythical situation that everyone—Pirx included—now knew would never come to pass: a revolt of robots. And knowing with a tacit certitude that he would have taken their side, he fell asleep, somehow exonerated.

He woke early, and for some reason his first thought was: The wind has died down. Then he remembered Aniel and, with some discomfort, his fantastic visions of the night before, on the borderline of sleep. He lay there a good while before coming to the somewhat reassuring conclusion that they had not been conscious fantasies, even though, unlike in a dream, they must have had some encouragement, however little and unwilled, from him. But why was he sweating such psychological subtleties? He raised himself up on his elbow and listened: dead silence. He slid back the shutter of the little port beside his head, saw through the cloudy pane a pale dawn on the rise, and knew at once that he would be going up the mountain. He bolted out of bed to double-check the common room. No robot.

The others were already up. Over breakfast, as if the matter were already settled, Krull said it was time to get a move on, that the *Ampère* was due in before nightfall and they would need an hour and a half, minimum, for breaking camp. He neglected to say why the urgency, whether it was the missing data or the absent Aniel.

Pirx ate enough to make up for the night before and said nothing the whole meal. The others were still working on their coffee when he got up and, after rummaging in his duffel bag, took out a spool of white nylon, a hammer, and a few pitons; on second thought, he made room in his backpack for his climbing boots—just in case.

They went out into the still-unlit dawn. The sky was drained of stars, colorless. A heavy violet-gray, stagnant and bone-bracing, hugged ground, faces, air; the mountains to the north were a black mass, solidified in murk; the southern ridge, the one closest to them, its peaks brushed with a swatch of strident orange, stood silhouetted like a molded mask with blurred, runny features. The distant, unreal glare caught the plumes of breath billowing from their mouths—despite the thinner atmosphere, breathing was easy. They pulled up on the plateau's outer rim as the stunted vegetation, dingy-brown in the halflight between retreating night and advancing day, yielded to a barren landscape. Before them stretched a rock-littered moraine that shimmered as if under water. A few hundred meters higher, a wind blew up, bracing them with its brisk gusts. They climbed, clearing with ease the smaller boulders, scaling the larger ones, occasionally to the sound of one rock slab nudging against another, of a piece of detritus, dislodged by a boot, cascading down with a rippling echo. The intermittent squeak of a shoulder strap or a metal fitting lent their expedition a certain *esprit de corps*, the professional air of a mountaineering party. Pirx went second, behind Massena. It was still too dark to discern the outline of the far walls; time and again, with his attention entirely at the mercy of his straining eyes, his absent-mindedly placed foot slipped, as if he was intent on distracting himself, not only from the terrain, but also from himself, from his qualms. Shutting out all thought of Aniel, he immersed his concentration in this land of eternal rock, of perfect indifference, which only man's imagination had invested with horror and the thrill of adventure.

It was a planet with sharply defined seasons. Hardly had they landed at the tail end of summer when an alpine autumn, lush with reds and golds, began fading in the valleys. Yet even though leaves were borne on the foam of rushing streams, the sun was still warm—on cloudless days, even sweltering—on the tableland. Only the thickening fog signaled the approach of snow and frost. But by then the planet would be deserted, and to Pirx the prospect of that consummate wasteland cast in white suddenly seemed desirable beyond all else.

The brightening, so gradual as to be imperceptible, with every step brought a new detail of the landscape into prominence. The sky had taken on that pallor between night and day—dawnless, stark, hushed, as if hermetically sealed in a sphere of cooling glass. A little farther up, they passed through a fog bank, its wispy strands clinging to the ground, and after they emerged Pirx saw their destination, still untouched by sunlight but now at least whitened by the dawn: a rock-ribbed buttress that reached up to the main ridge, up to where, a few hundred meters higher, its twin peak, the most prominent, loomed blackly. At one point the rib flared out into a troughlike basin; in this saddle Aniel had conducted his last survey.

It was a straightforward ascent and descent—no surprises, no crevasses, nothing but gray scree dappled with chick-yellow mildew. As he trod nimbly from one clattering rock pile to another, Pirx fixed on the black wall leaning against the sky and, perhaps to distract himself, imagined he was making an ordinary ascent Earthside. Suddenly these crags seemed quite natural to him, the illusion of a conquest in the making rendered even more compelling by their vertical climb toward the notched spine heaving up out of the scree. The buttress ran one-third of the way up the face before disintegrating in a riot of wedged slabs, whence a sheer rock face shot straight up like a flight arrested. A hundred meters higher, the face was cleaved by a vein of diabase—red-tinted, brighter than granite—that bulged above the surface and snaked across the flank, like a trail of varying width.

Pirx's eyes were held in thrall by the summit's sublime outline, though as they climbed higher, and, as was usual with a mountain viewed from below, it receded farther, and the abrupt foreshortenings broke it up into a series of overlapping planes, the base lost its former flatness, and columns sprang up—a wealth of faults, shelves, aimlessly winding chimneys, a chaos of old fissures, an anarchy of cluttered accretion, momentarily illumined by the top now gilded by the sun's first rays, fixed and strangely placid, then once more swallowed by shadow. Pirx could not tear his eyes from it, from this colossus that even on Earth would have commanded respect, challenging the climber with that rudely jutting vein of diabase. The stretch from there to the gold-plated summit looked short and easy compared with the overhangs, especially the largest of them, whose lower edge glistened with ice or moisture, reddish-black, like congealed blood.

Pirx let his imagination run wild, conjuring up not the cliff of some anonymous highland under a foreign sun, but a mountain surrounded by a lore of assaults and reverses, somehow distinct, unique, like a familiar face whose every wrinkle and scar contained a history of its own. Its sinewy, snakelike cracks on the border of visibility, its dark, thread-like ledges, its shallow grooves might have constituted the highest point achieved in a series of attempts, the sites of prolonged bivouacs, of silent reckonings, of momentous' assaults and humiliating defeats, disasters sustained even though every variety of tactical and technical gimmick was applied. A mountain so bound up with the fate of man that every climber vanquished by it came back again and again, always with the same store of faith and hope in victory, bringing to each successive pass a new fixed route with which to storm the petrified relief. It could have been a wall with a history of detours, flanking movements, each with its own chronicle of successes and victims, documented by photos bearing the dotted lines of trails, little *x*'s marking the highest ascent. . . . Pirx summoned this fantasy with the greatest of ease, actually astonished that it was not the real thing.

Massena walked ahead of him, slightly stooped, in a light whose growing limpidity annulled all illusion of an easy ascent, this illusion of easy access and safe passage having been fostered by the bluish haze that had peacefully engulfed every fragment of the glimmering cliff. The day, raw and full, had caught up with them; their shadows, exaggeratedly large, rolled and pitched under the ridge of the alluvial cone. The talus was fed by two couloirs, brimming with night, and the detritus ran straight up before being consumed by unrelieved black.

The massif could no longer be encompassed by the eye. Proportions had shifted, and the wall, similar to any other from a distance, now revealed its unique topography, its singular configuration. Bellying outward was a mighty buttress that rose out of a tangle of slab and plate, shot up, swelled, and spread until it obscured everything else, to stand alone, encircled by the dank gloom of places never touched by light. They had just stepped onto a patch of permanent snow, its surface strewn with the remnants of flying debris, when

Massena began to slacken his pace, then finally stopped, as if distracted by some noise. Pirx, who was the first to catch up with him, saw him make a tapping gesture on his ear, the one fitted with the olive-sized microphone, and immediately grasped its meaning.

"Any sign of him?"

Massena nodded and brought the metal-detector rod up close to the dirty, snow-crusted surface. The soles of Aniel's boots were impregnated with a radioactive isotope; the Geiger counter had picked up his trail. Though the trail was still alive from the day before, there was no way to read any direction in it—whether deposited on the robot's way up, or back. But at least they knew they were on the right track. From here on in, they took their time.

The dark buttress should have loomed just ahead, but Pirx knew how easy it was to misjudge distances in the mountains. They climbed higher, above the snowline and rubble, proceeding along an older, smaller ridge notched with rounded pinnacles, and in the dead silence Pirx thought—wishful thinking?—he could hear Massena's earphones crackling. Intermittently, Massena would stop, fan the air with the end of the aluminum rod, lower it until it nearly touched the rock, trace loops and figure eights like a magician, then, relocating the trail, move on. As they neared Aniel's surveying site, Pirx scoured the area for any signs of the missing robot.

The face was deserted. The easiest part of the route was now behind them; before them towered a series of slabs that cropped up from the foot of the buttress at diverse inclinations. The whole resembled a gigantic cross-section of the wall's strata, the partly exposed interior revealing the core's oldest formation, fissured in places under the sheer rock mass lifting several kilometers up into the sky. Another forty or a hundred paces and—an impasse.

Massena worked in a circle, waving the end of the detector rod, squinting—his sunglasses were aleady propped up on his forehead—rotating aimlessly, expressionless, before stopping in his tracks a dozen or so meters away.

"He was here quite a while."

"How can you tell?"

Massena shrugged, plucked the olive from his ear, and handed Pirx the earphone dangling on its thin connecting wire. Then Pirx heard it for himself, a twittering and screeching that at times rose to a whining plaint. The rock face was devoid of any prints or traces—nothing but that unremitting sound filling the skull with its strident crackling, the intensity of which was such that nearly every millimeter of rock testified to the robot's prolonged and diligent presence. Gradually Pirx came to discern a certain logic in the apparent chaos: Aniel had apparently come up by the same route they had taken, set up the tripod, got the camera into position, and circled it several times in the process of surveying and photographing, even shifting it in search of the most favorable observation points. Right, that made sense. But then what?

Pirx began moving out concentrically, spiral-fashion, in hope of picking up his centripetal trail, but none of the trails led back to the starting point. Much as if Aniel had retraced his every step, which did not seem likely: not being equipped with a gamma-ray counter, he could hardly have reconstructed his return route to within a few centimeters. Krull made some comment to Massena which the circling Pirx ignored, for his attention was diverted by a sound, brief but distinct, transmitted by his earphones. He began backtracking, almost millimeter by millimeter. Here—I'm sure it was here. Staring intently, he scanned the terrain, squinting the better to concentrate on the whining. The rediscovered trail lay at the base of the cliff, as if, instead of taking the trail campward, the robot had headed straight for the vertical buttress.

That's odd. What could have lured him there?

Pirx scouted around for a follow-up to the trail, but the

boulders were mute; unable to divine Aniel's footing on the next step, he had to canvass all the fissured slabs piled at the base of the buttress. He finally found it, some five meters away from the previous one. Why such a long jump? Again he backtracked, and a moment later picked up the missing step: the robot had simply hopped from one rock to another.

Pirx was still stooping and gracefully flourishing the rod when he was jolted by an explosion in his head—by a crackling in his earphones loud enough to make him wince. He peered behind a rock table and went numb. Wedged between two rocks so that it lay hidden at the bottom of a natural hollow was the surveying apparatus, along with the still camera, both intact. Propped up against a rock on the other side was Aniel's backpack, unbuckled but unemptied. Pirx called out to the others. They came on the run and were as dumbfounded as he by the discovery. Immediately Krull checked the cassettes: surveying data complete, no repeat necessary. But that still left unsolved the mystery of Aniel's whereabouts. Massena cupped his mouth and hollered several times in succession; as they listened to the distant echo bouncing off the rock, Pirx cringed, because it had the ring of a rescue call in the mountains. The intellectronician took from his pocket a flat cassette housing a transmitter, squatted, and began paging the robot by his call numbers, but his gestures made it plain that he did this more from duty than conviction. Meanwhile Pirx, who kept combing the area for more radioactivity, was bewildered by the profusion of traces resonating in his headset. Here, too, the robot had lingered. When at last he had established the perimeters of the robot's movements, he began a systematic search in hope of finding a new lead to steer him in the right direction.

Pirx described a full circle until he was back under the buttress. A cleft, roughly one and a half meters wide, its bottom littered with tiny, sharp-edged ejecta, yawned between the shelf that supported him and the sheer wall opposite. Pirx probed the near side—silence. A riddle, as incomprehensible as it was inescapable: all indications were that Aniel had virtually melted into thin air. While the others conferred in subdued voices behind him, Pirx slowly craned his head and for the first time took stock of the steeply rising face at close range. The wall's stony silence summoned him with uncanny force, but the summons was more like a beckoning, outstretched hand—and instantly the certitude of acceptance, the recognition that the challenge would have to be met, was born in him.

Purely by instinct, his eyes sought out the first holds; they looked solid. One long, carefully executed step to cross the gap, first foothold on that tiny but sturdy-looking ledge, then a diagonal ascent along that perfectly even rift that opened a few meters higher into a shallow crevasse . . . For some reason, unknown even to himself, Pirx lifted the rod, arched his body as far as he could, and aimed it at the rock ledge on the far side of the cleft. His earphones responded. To be on the safe side, he repeated the maneuver, fighting to keep his balance—he was practically suspended in midair—and again heard a crackle. That cinched it. He rejoined the others.

"He went up," Pirx said matter-of-factly, pointing toward the wall. Krull did a double take, while Massena asked:

"Went up? What for?"

"Search me," replied Pirx with seeming apathy. "Check for yourself."

Massena, rashly thinking that Pirx had made a mistake, conducted his own probe and was soon convinced. Aniel had most definitely spanned the gap and moved out along the partly fissured wall—buttress-bound.

Consternation reigned. Krull postulated that the robot had malfunctioned after the survey, that he had become "deprogrammed." Impossible, countered Massena; the positioning of the surveying gear and the backpack was too deliberate;

it looked too suspiciously like a jettisoning prior to attempting a rugged ascent—no, something must have happened to make him go up there.

Pirx held his peace. Secretly he had already made up his mind to scale the wall, with or without the others. Krull was out of the picture, anyway; this was a job for a professional, and a damned good one at that. Massena had done a fair bit of climbing—or so he had said once in Pirx's presence—enough, at least, to know the ABC's of belaying. When the other two were finished, Pirx made his intention known. Was Massena willing to team up?

Krull immediately objected. It was against regs to take risks; they had to be mustered for that afternoon's pick-up; the camp still had to be broken, their gear to be packed. They had their data now, didn't they? The robot had simply malfunctioned, so why not chalk it up and explain all the circumstances in the final report. . . .

"Are you saying we should just cut out and leave him here?" inquired Pirx.

His subdued tone obviously unnerved Krull, who, visibly restraining himself, answered that the report would give a complete rundown of the facts, along with individual comments by the crew, and a statement as to probable cause—short-circuiting of the memory mnestrones, directional-motivation circuit, or desynchronization.

Massena pointed out that none of those was possible, since Aniel didn't run on mnestrones but on a homogeneous, monocrystalline system, molecularly grown from supercold diamagnetic solutions vestigially doped with isotopic contaminants.

It was plainly a put-down, Massena's way of telling the cosmographer that he was talking through his hat. Pirx played deaf. Turning his back on them, he again surveyed the base, but with a difference: this time it was not a fantasy but the real thing. And although he somehow sensed the impropriety of it, he now exulted over the prospect of a climb.

Massena, probably just to spite Krull, took Pirx up on his offer. Pirx listened with only one ear to Massena's spiel about how they owed it to themselves to solve the riddle, how they could hardly go back without investigating something urgent and mysterious enough to provoke such an unexpected reaction in a robot, and how even if there was only a thousand-to-one chance of ascertaining the cause, it was well worth the risk.

Krull, knowing when he was licked, wasted no further words. There was silence. As Massena began unloading his gear, Pirx, who had already changed into his climbing boots and assembled line, hooks, and piton hammer, stole a glance at him. Massena was flustered, Pirx could tell. Not just because of his squabble with Krull, but because he had been buffaloed into this against his will. Pirx suspected that, given an out, Massena would have grabbed at it, though you mustn't underestimate the power of wounded pride. He said nothing, however.

The first few pitches looked easy enough, but there was no telling what they could expect higher up on the wall, up where the overhangs screened a good deal of the flank. Earlier, he hadn't thought to scout the wall with binoculars, but neither had he counted on this adventure. So why the rope and pitons? Instead of mulling over the contradiction in his own behavior, he waited until Massena was ready; they leisurely shoved off for the base of the cliff.

"I'll take the lead," said Pirx, "with line payed out at first; then we'll play it by ear."

Massena nodded. Pirx tossed another glance back at Krull, with whom they had parted in silence, and found him standing where they had left him, next to the discarded packs. They were now at high enough altitude to glimpse the distant, olive-green plains emerging from behind the northern ridge. The bottom of the scree was still in shadow, but the peaks blazed with an incandescence that flooded the gaps in the towering skyline like a fractured aureole.

Pirx took a giant stride, found a foothold on the ledge, pulled himself upright, then nimbly ascended. He moved at a gingerly clip, as rock layer after rock layer—rough, uneven, darkly recessed in places—passed before his eyes. He braced, hoisted, heaved himself up, took in the stagnant, ice-cold breath of night radiated by the rock stratum. The higher the altitude, the faster his heartbeat, but his breathing was normal and the straining of muscles suffused him with a pleasing warmth. The rope trailed behind him, the thin air magnifying the scraping sound it made every time it brushed against the cliff, until just before the line was completely payed out, he found a safe belay—with someone else he would have gone without, but he first wanted to be sure of Massena. With his toes wedged in a crack that ran diagonally across the flank, he waited for Massena.

From where he stood he could examine the large, raked chimney they had skirted on the way up. At this point, it flared out into a gray, cirquelike stone-fall; totally jejune, even flat when viewed from below, it now rose up as a rich and stately sculpture. He felt so exquisitely alone that he was startled to find Massena standing beside him.

They progressed steadily upward, repeating the same procedure from one pitch to the next, and at each new stance Pirx used the detector to verify that the robot had been there. Once, when he lost the signal, he had to abandon an easy chimney—Aniel, not being a mountaineer, had simply traversed it. Even so, Pirx had no trouble in second-guessing his moves, for the route he had chosen was invariably the surest, most logical, most expeditious way of gaining the summit. It was obvious, to Pirx at any rate, that Aniel had gone on a climb. Never one to indulge in idle speculation, he did not stop to ponder the whys. The better he came to know his adversary, the more his memory began to revive, yielding those apparently forgotten holds and maneuvers that now prompted him infallibly on each new pitch, even when it came to three-point climbing, which he had to resort to often, in order to free a hand to track the robot's radioactive trail. Once he glanced down from over the top of a flake sturdy enough to be a wall. At high elevation, despite their painstaking progress, it took Pirx a while to spot Krull standing at the bottom of the air shaft which opened at his feet—or, rather, not Krull but his suit, a tiny splotch of green against the gray.

Then came a nice little traverse. The going was getting tougher, but Pirx was slowly regaining the knack of it, so much so that he made better progress when he trusted to his body's instincts than when he consciously sought out the best holds. Just how much tougher it would get he discovered when, at one moment, he tried to free his right hand to grab the detector dangling from his belt, and couldn't. He had a foothold only for his left and something vaguely like a ledge under his right boot tip; leaning out as far as he could from the rock, he scouted at an angle for another foothold, but without any luck. Then he sighted something that portended a little shelf higher up, and decided to skip the detector.

Alas, it was verglassed and steeply pitched. In one place the ice bore a deep bite, evidence of some terrific impact. No booted foot could have made a gash that deep, he thought, and it occurred to him that it might have been an incision left by Aniel's shoe—the robot weighed roughly a quarter of a ton.

Massena, who until now had been keeping pace, was starting to straggle. They reached the rib's upper tier. The rock face, as craggy as before, gradually, even deceptively, had begun tilting beyond the perpendicular to become a definite overhang, impossible to negotiate without any decent foot-jams. The rift, well defined until now, closed a few meters higher up. Pirx still had some six meters of free line, but he ordered Massena to take up the slack so he could briefly reconnoiter. The robot had negotiated it without pitons, rope, or belays. If he could, so can I, thought Pirx. He groped overhead; his right ankle, jammed into the apex of the fissure that had brought him this far, ached from the constant straining and twisting, but he didn't let up. Then his fingertips grazed a ledge barely wide enough for a fingerhold. He might make it with a pull-up, but then what?

It was no longer so much a contest with the cliff as between himself and Aniel. The robot had negotiated it—single-handedly, albeit with metal appendages for fingers. . . . As Pirx began freeing his foot from the crack, his wriggling dislodged a pebble and sent it plummeting. He listened as it cleaved the air, then, after a long pause, landed with a crisp, well-defined click.

"Not on an exposure like that," he thought, and, abandoning the idea of a pull-up, he looked for a place to hammer in a piton. But the wall was solid, not a single fissure in sight; he leaned out and turned in both directions—blank.

"What's wrong?" came Massena's voice from below.

"Nothing—just nosing around," he replied.

His ankle hurt like hell; he knew he couldn't maintain this position for very long. Ugh, anything to abandon this route! But the moment he changed direction, the trail was as good as lost on this mammoth of a rock. Again he scoured the terrain. In the extreme foreshortening of vision, the slab seemed to abound in holds, but the recesses were shallower than the palm of his hand. That left only the ledge. He had already freed his foot and was in a pull-up position when it dawned on him: there was no reversing now. Thrust outward, he hung in space with his boot tips some thirty centimeters out from the rock face. Something caught his eye. A rift? But first he had to *reach* it! Come on, just a little higher!

His next moves were governed by sheer instinct: hanging on with the four fingers of his right hand, he let go with the left and reached up to the fissure of unknown depth. That was dumb—it flashed through his mind, as, gasping, wincing at his own recklessness, he suddenly found himself two meters higher, hugging the rock, his muscles on the verge of snapping. With both feet securely on the ledge, he was able to drive in a piton, even a second for safety's sake, since the first refused to go in all the way. He listened with pleasure to the hammer's reverberations—clean and crisp, rising in pitch as the piton sank deeper, then finally tapering off. The rope jiggled in the carabiners, a signal that he had to give Massena some help. Not the slickest job, thought Pirx, but, then, neither were they climbing the Alps, and it would do as a stance.

Above the buttress was a narrow, fairly comfortable chimney. Pirx stuck the detector between his teeth, afraid it would scrape against the rock if he wedged it in his belt. The higher he climbed, the more the rock fringed from a blotchy brownish-black, here and there streaked with gray, to a ruddy, rufous-flecked surface glittering up close with diabase. It was easy going for another dozen or so meters, then the picnic was over: another overhang, insurmountable without more pitons, and this time shelfless. But Aniel had managed it with nothing. Or had he? Pirx checked with the detector. Wrong, he bypassed the overhang. How? Must have used a traverse.

A quick survey revealed a pitch not especially tricky or treacherous. The buttress, temporarily obscured by the diabase, reasserted itself here. He was standing on a narrow but safe ledge that wrapped around a bulge before vanishing from view; leaning out, he saw its continuation on the other side, across a gap measuring roughly a meter and a half—two at the most. The trick was to wriggle around the jutting projection, then, freeing the right foot, thrust off with the left so that the right could feel its way to safe footing on the other side.

He looked for a place to drive in a piton for what should have been a routine belay. But the wall was maliciously devoid of any cracks. He glanced down; a belay from the stance Massena now occupied would have been purely cosmetic. Even if secured from below, he stood to fall, if he peeled off, a good fifteen meters, enough to jerk loose the most secure pitons. And yet the detector said loud and clear that the robot had negotiated it—alone! What the . . . ! There's the shelf. One big step. Come on, chicken! He stayed put. Oh, for a place to tie on a rope! He leaned out and swept the shelf—and for a second, no more—before the muscle spasms set in. And if my boot sole doesn't grab? Aniel's were steel-soled. What's that shiny stuff over there? Melting ice? Slippery as all hell, I'll bet. That's what I get for not bringing along my Vibrams. . . .

"And for not making out a will," he muttered under his breath, his eyes squinting, his gaze transfixed. Doubled up, spread-eagled, fingers clutching the rock's craggy face for support, he bellied his way around the bulge and risked the step that had taken all his courage. Whatever joy he felt as he landed was quickly dissipated. The shelf on the other side was situated lower, which meant that he would have to jump *up* on the way back. Not to mention that stomach traverse. Climb, my ass! Acrobatics was more like it. Rope down? It was either that or—

A total fiasco, but he kept traversing, nonetheless, for as long as he was able. Suffice it to say that Aniel was the furthest thing from his mind at the moment. The rope, payed out along the length of his traverse, moderately taut and uncannily pristine, inordinately close and tangible against the scree blurred by a bluish haze at the base, shook under him. The shelf came to a dead end, with no way up, down, or back.

Never saw anything so smooth, he thought with a calm that differed appreciably from his previous sangfroid. He reconnoitered. Underfoot was a four-centimeter ledge, then empty space, followed by the darkly adumbrated vent of a chimney—whose very darkness seemed an invitation— yawning four meters away in a rock face so sheer and massive as to defy credulity. And *granite*, no less! he thought, almost reproachful. Water erosion, sure, he even saw the signs—dark patches on the slab, here and there some drops of water; he grabbed the rod with his right hand and probed the brink for some trace. Low, intermittent crackling. Affirmative. But how? A tiny patch of moss, granite-hued, caught his eye. He scraped it away. A chink, no bigger than a fingernail. It was his salvation, even though the piton refused to go in more than halfway. He yanked on the ringed eye—somehow it held. Now just clutch the piton with his left, slowly. . . . He leaned out from the waist up, and let his eyes roam the rim, felt the pull of the half-open chute, seemingly preordained ages ago for this moment; his gaze plummeted like a falling stone, all the way down to a silvery-blue shimmer against the scree's fuzzy gray.

The ultimate step was never taken.

"What's wrong?" Massena's voice reverberated.

"In a sec!" Pirx yelled back as he threaded the rope through the carabiner. He had to take a closer look. Again he leaned out, this time with three-fourths of his weight on the hook, jackknifed as if to wrench it from the rock, determined to satisfy his curiosity.

It was him. Nothing else could radiate from such a height—Pirx, having long ago passed beyond the perpendicular, was now some three hundred meters above the point of departure. He searched the ground for a landmark. The rope cut into his flesh, he had trouble breathing, and his eyes throbbed as he tried to memorize the landscape. There was his marker, that huge boulder, now viewed in foreshortened perspective. By the time he was back in a vertical position, his muscles were twitching. Time to rope off, he told himself, and he automatically pried out the piton, which slipped out effortlessly, as if embedded in butter; despite a feeling of unease, he pocketed the piton and began plotting a way down. Their descent was, if not elegant, then at least effective; Massena plastered his stance with pitons and shortened the line, and Pirx bellied some eight meters down the slab, below which was another chimney, and they abseiled the rest of the way down, alternating the lead. When Massena wanted an explanation, Pirx said:

"I found him."

"Aniel?"

"He peeled off—up there, at the bottom of a chimney."

The return trip took less than an hour. Pirx wasn't sad to part company with his pitons, though it was strange to think he would never set foot here again, neither he nor any other human; that those scraps of metal, Earth-made, would remain ensconced for millennia—indeed, forever—in that cliff.

They had already touched down on the scree, and were staggering around in an obvious effort to regain their legs, when Krull came up to them on the run, yelling from a distance that he'd located Aniel's holsters, jettisoned not far off. The robot must have junked them before scaling the rock, he said, proof positive of a breakdown, since the jets were his only means of bailing out in an emergency.

Massena, who seemed altogether unfazed by Krull's revelations, made no secret of the toll taken by the climb; on the contrary, he plopped himself down on a boulder, spread out his legs as if to savor the firmness, and furiously mopped his face, brow, and neck with a handkerchief.

Pirx reported Aniel's fall to Krull; a few minutes later they went out searching. It didn't take them long to find him. Judging from the wreckage, his three-hundred-meter fall had been undeflected. His armor-plated torso was shattered, metal skull ditto, and his monocrystalline brain reduced to a powdered glass that coated the surrounding rocks with a micalike glitter. Krull at least had the decency not to lecture them on the futility of their climb. He merely repeated his contention, not without a certain satisfaction, that Aniel must have become "deprogrammed," the clincher being the abandoned holsters.

Massena was visibly altered by the climb, and not for the better; he murmured not a peep in protest and altogether had the look of a man who would be a lot happier when the mission was terminated and each could go his own way.

There was silence on the way back, the more strained because Pirx was deliberately withholding his version of the "accident." For he was sure it was *not* a mechanical defect—of monocrystals, mnestrones, or whatever—any more than he, Pirx, had been "defective" in hankering to conquer that wall.

No, Aniel was simply more like his designers than any of them cared to admit. Having done his work with his customary speed and skill, the robot found he had time to kill. He didn't just *see* the terrain, he sensed it: programmed for complex problem-solving, for the *challenge*, he couldn't resist the grandest sweepstakes of them all. Pirx had to smile. How blind the others were! Imagine taking the jettisoned holsters as evidence of a mechanical failure! Sure, anyone else would have done the same. *Not* to have junked them would have been to take all the risk out of it, to turn it into a gymnastics stunt. They were all wet, and no graphs, models, or equations could make him believe otherwise. He was only amazed that Aniel hadn't fallen earlier—up there alone, with no training or climbing experience, unprogrammed for battling with rocks.

What if he'd made it back safely? For some reason Pirx was sure they would never have heard the tale. Not from Aniel, at any rate. What made him decide to risk a jump from that ledge, lacking both pitons and a second, without even knowing he lacked them? Nothing, probably—a decision as mindless as he was. Had he scraped or brushed the rim of that chimney? Pirx wondered. If so, then he must have left behind some trace, a sprinkling of radioactive atoms that would stay up there until they finally decomposed and evaporated.

Pirx knew something else: that he would never even hint about this to anyone. People would cling to the hypothesis of a malfunction, which was the simplest, most logical hypothesis, indeed the only one that did not threaten their vision of the world.

They reached the camp later that afternoon. Their elongated shadows moved apace as they tore down the barracks, section by section, leaving behind only a barren, flattened quadrangle. Clouds scudded across the sky as Pirx went about carting crates, rolling up maps—in short, filling in for Aniel, the thought of which made Pirx pause a second before delivering his burden into Massena's outstretched arms.

THE HUNT

He left Port Control hopping mad. It had to happen to him, to him! The owner didn't have the shipment—simply didn't have it—period. Port Control knew nothing. Sure, there had been a telegram: 72 HOUR DELAY—STIPULATED PENALTY PAID TO YOUR ACCOUNT—ENSTRAND. Not a word more. At the trade councilor's office he didn't get anywhere, either. The port was crowded and the stipulated penalty didn't satisfy Control. Parking fee, demurrage, yes, but wouldn't it be best if you, Mr. Navigator, lifted off like a good fellow and went into hold? Just kill the engines, no expenditure for fuel, wait out your three days and come back. What would that hurt you? Three days circling the Moon because the owner screws up! Pirx was at a loss for a reply, but then remembered the treaty. Well, when he trotted out the norms established by the labor union for exposure in space, they started backing down. In fact, this was not the Year of the Quiet Sun. Radiation levels were not negligible. So he would have to maneuver, keep behind the Moon, play that game of hide-and-seek with the sun using thrust. And who was going to pay for this? Not the owner, certainly. Who, then— Control? Did you gentlemen have any idea of the cost of ten minutes' full burn with a reactor of seventy million kilowatts? In the end he got permission to stay, but only for seventy-two hours plus four to load that wretched freight—

not a minute more! You would have thought they were doing him a favor. As if it were *his* fault. And he had arrived right on the dot, and didn't come straight from Mars, either—while the owner . . .

With all this he completely forgot where he was, and pushed the door handle so hard on his way out that he was thrown up to the ceiling. Embarrassed, he looked around, but no one was there. All Luna Base seemed empty. True, the big work was under way a few hundred kilometers to the north, between the Hypatia region and the Toricelli crater. The engineers and technicians, who a month ago were all over the place here, had already left for the construction site. The UN's great project, Luna Base 2, drew more and more people from Earth.

"At least this time there won't be any trouble getting a room," he thought, taking the escalator to the bottom floor of the underground city. The fluorescent lamps produced a cold daylight. Every other one was off. Economizing! Pushing a glass door, he entered a small lobby. They had rooms, all right! All the rooms you wanted. He left his suitcase (it was really more a satchel) with the porter and wondered if Tyndall would make sure that the mechanics reground the central nozzle. Ever since Mars the thing had been behaving like a damned medieval cannon! He really ought to see to it himself: the proprietor's eye and all that. But he didn't feel like taking the elevator back up those twelve flights, and anyway, by now they had probably split up. Sitting in the airport store, most likely, listening to the latest recordings.

He walked, not really knowing where; the hotel restaurant was empty, as if closed—but behind its lunch counter sat a redhead, reading a book. Or had she fallen asleep over it? Her cigarette was turning into a long cylinder of ash on the marble top. . . . Pirx took a seat and reset his watch to local time; and suddenly it became late, ten at night. And on board, why, only a few minutes before, it had been noon. This eternal whirl with sudden jumps in time was just as fatiguing as in the beginning, when he was first learning to fly. He ate his lunch, now turned into supper, washing it down with seltzer, which seemed warmer than the soup. The waiter, down in the mouth and drowsy like a true lunatic, added up the bill wrong, and not in his own favor, a bad sign. Pirx advised him to take a vacation on Earth, and left quietly, so as not to waken the sleeping countergirl.

He got the key from the porter and rode up to his room. He hadn't looked at the plate yet and felt strange when he saw the number: 173. The same room he had stayed in, long ago, when for the first time he flew "that side." But after opening the door he concluded that either this was a different room or they had remodeled it radically. No, he must have been mistaken, that other was larger. He turned on all the switches, for he was sick of darkness, looked in the dresser, pulled out the drawer of the small writing table, but didn't bother to unpack; he just threw his pajamas on the bed and set the toothbrush and toothpaste on the sink. He washed his hands—the water, as always, infernally cold, a wonder it didn't freeze. He turned the hot water spigot—a few drops trickled out. He went to the phone to call the desk but changed his mind: there was really no point. It was scandalous, of course—here the Moon was stocked with all the necessities, and you still couldn't get hot water in your hotel room!

He tried the radio. The evening wrap-up—the lunar news. He hardly listened, wondering whether he shouldn't send a telegram to the owner. Reverse the charges, of course. But no, that wouldn't accomplish anything. These were not the romantic days of astronautics! They were long gone; now a man was nothing but a truck driver, dependent on those who loaded cargo on his ship. Cargo, insurance, demurrage . . . The radio was muttering something. Hold on—what was that? . . . He leaned across the bed and moved the knob of the apparatus.

"—in all probability the last of the Leonid swarm." The

soft baritone of the speaker filled the room. "Only one apartment building suffered a direct hit and lost its seal. By a lucky coincidence its residents were all at work. The remaining meteorites caused little damage, with the exception of one that penetrated the shield protecting the storerooms. According to our correspondent's report, six universal automata designated for tasks on the construction site were totally destroyed. There was also damage to the high-tension line, and telephone communication was knocked out, though restored within a space of three hours. We now repeat the major news. Earlier today, at the opening of the Pan-African Congress . . ."

He shut off the radio and sat down. Meteorites? A swarm? Well, yes, the Leonids were due, but still the forecasts—those meteorologists were always fouling up, exactly like the synoptics on Earth. Construction site—it must have been that one up north. But all the same, atmosphere was atmosphere, and its absence here was damned inconvenient. Six automata, if you please. At least no one was hurt. A nasty business, though—a shield punctured! Yes, that designer, he really should have . . .

He was dog-tired. Time had got completely bollixed up for him. Between Mars and Earth they must have lost a Tuesday, since it went directly from Monday to Wednesday; that meant they also missed a night. "I better stock up on some sleep," he thought, got up, and automatically headed for the tiny bathroom. But at the memory of the icy water he shuddered, did an about-face, and a minute later was in bed. Which couldn't hold a candle to a ship's bunk. His hand automatically groped around for the belts to buckle down the quilt, and he gave a faint smile when he couldn't find them; after all, he was in a hotel, not threatened by any sudden loss of gravitation.

That was his last thought. When he opened his eyes, he had no idea where he was. It was pitch-black. "Tyndall!" he wanted to shout, and all at once—for no apparent reason—

remembered how once Tyndall had burst terrified out of the cabin, in nothing but pajama bottoms, and desperately cried to the man on watch, "You! For God's sake! Quick, tell me, what's my name?" The poor devil was plastered; he had been fretting over some imagined insult or other and had drunk an entire bottle of rum.

In this roundabout way Pirx's mind returned to reality. He got up, turned on the light, went to take a shower, but then remembered about the water, so carefully let out first a small trickle—lukewarm; he sighed, because he yearned for a good hot bath, but after a minute or two, with the stream beating on his face and torso, he actually began to hum.

He was just putting on a clean shirt when the loud-speaker—he had no idea there was anything like that in the room—said in a deep bass:

"Attention! Attention! This is an important announcement. Will all men with military training please report immediately to Port Control, Room 318, with Commodore-Engineer Achanian. We repeat. Attention, attention . . ."

Pirx was so astonished, he stood there for a moment in only his socks and shirt. What was this? April Fools' Day? "With military training"? Maybe he was still asleep. But when he flung his arms to pull the shirt on all the way, he cracked his hand against the edge of the table, and his heart beat faster. No, no dream. Then what was it? An invasion? Martians taking over the Moon? What nonsense! Whatever it was, he had to go.

But something whispered to him while he jumped into his pants, "Yes, this had to happen, because *you* are here. That's your luck, old man, you bring trouble. . . ."

As he left the room his watch said eight. He wanted to stop somewhere and ask what the hell was going on, but the corridor was empty, and so was the escalator, as though a general mobilization had already taken place and everyone was scrambling God knows where at the front line. He ran up the steps; they were moving at a good clip to begin with, but he hurried as if he actually might miss a chance at der-ring-do. At the top he saw a brightly lit glass kiosk with newspapers and ran up to the window to ask his question, but there was no one to ask. The papers were sold by machine.

He bought a pack of cigarettes and a daily, which he glanced at without slowing his pace; it contained nothing but an account of the meteorite disaster. Could that be it? But why military training? Impossible! Down a long corridor he went toward Port Control. Finally he saw people. Someone was entering a room with the number 318, someone else was coming up from the opposite end of the corridor.

"I won't find out anything now; I'm too late," he thought as he straightened his jacket and walked in. It was a small room, with three windows; behind them blazed an artificial lunar landscape, the unpleasant color of hot mercury. In the narrower part of the trapezoidal room stood two desks, the entire area in front of them being crammed with chairs, evidently brought in on short notice, since almost every chair was different. There were around fourteen or fifteen people here, mostly middle-aged men with a few kids who wore the stripes of navy cadets. Sitting apart was some elderly commodore—the rest of the chairs remained empty. Pirx took a seat next to one of the cadets, who immediately began telling him how six of them had flown in just the other day to start their apprenticeship "that side," but they were given only a small machine, it was called a flea, and the thing barely took three, the rest had to wait their turn, then suddenly this business cropped up. Did Mr. Navigator happen to know . . . ? But Mr. Navigator was in the dark himself. Judging by the faces of those seated, you could tell that they, too, were shocked by the announcement—they probably all came from the hotel. It must have occurred to the cadet that he ought to introduce himself, because he started going through a few gymnastics, nearly overturning his chair. Pirx grabbed it by the back, and just then the door opened and in walked a short, dark-haired man slightly gray at the temples. He was clean-shaven, but his cheeks were blue with stubble; he had beetle brows and small, piercing eyes. Without a word he passed between the chairs, and behind the desk pulled down from a reel near the ceiling a map of "that side," on a scale of one to one million. The man rubbed his strong, fleshy nose with the back of his hand and said, without preamble:

"Gentlemen, I am Achanian. I have been temporarily delegated by the joint heads of Luna Base 1 and Luna Base 2 for the purpose of neutralizing the Setaur."

Among the listeners there was a faint stir, but Pirx still understood nothing; he didn't even know what the Setaur was.

"Those of you who heard the radio are aware that here"— he pointed a ruler at the regions Hypatia and Alfraganus— "a swarm of meteors fell yesterday. We will not go into the effects of the impact of the others, but one—it may well have been the largest—shattered the protective shield over storage units B-7 and R-7. In R-7 was located a consignment of Setaurs, received from Earth barely four days ago. In the bulletins it was reported that all of these met with destruction. That, gentlemen, is not the truth."

The cadet sitting next to Pirx listened with red ears; even his mouth hung open, as if to take in every word. Meanwhile Achanian went on:

"Five of the robots were crushed beneath the falling roof, but the sixth survived. More precisely—it suffered damage. We think so for the reason that as soon as it extricated itself from the ruins of the storage unit, it began to behave in a manner . . . to behave like a . . ."

Achanian couldn't find the right word, so without finishing his sentence he continued:

"The storage units are situated near the siding of a narrow-gauge track eight kilometers from the provisional landing field. Immediately after the disaster, a rescue operation was initiated, and the first order of business was to check out all personnel, to see if anyone had been buried beneath the devastated buildings. This action lasted about an hour; in the meantime, however, it developed that from the concussion the central administration buildings had lost their full seal, so the work dragged on till midnight. Around one o'clock it was discovered that the breakdown in the main grid supplying the entire construction site, as well as the interruption of telephone communication, had not been caused by the meteors. The cables had been cut—by laser beam."

Pirx blinked. He couldn't help feeling that he was participating in some sort of play, a masquerade. Such things didn't happen. A laser! Sure! And why not throw in a Martian spy while you were at it? Yet this commodore-engineer hardly looked like the type who would get hotel guests up at the crack of dawn in order to play some stupid joke on them.

"The telephone lines were repaired first," said Achanian. "But at that same time a small transporter from the emergency party, having reached the place where the cables were broken, lost radio contact with Luna Base. After three in the morning we learned that this transporter had been attacked by laser and, as a result of several hits, now stood in flames. The driver and his assistant perished, but two of the crew—fortunately they were in suits, having got themselves ready to go out and repair the line—managed to jump free in time and hide in the desert, that is, the Mare Tranquilitatis, roughly here. . . ." Achanian indicated with his ruler a point on the Sea of Tranquillity, some four hundred kilometers from the little crater of Arago.

"Neither of them, as far as I know, saw the assailant. At a particular moment they simply felt a very strong thermal blast, and the transporter caught fire. They jumped before the tanks of compressed gas went off; the lack of an atmosphere saved them, since only that portion of the fuel which was able to combine with the oxygen inside the transporter exploded. One of these people later died, in as yet undetermined circumstances. The other succeeded in returning to the construction site, crossing a stretch of about one hundred forty kilometers, but he ran and exhausted his suit's air supply and went into anoxia. Fortunately he was discovered and is now in the hospital. Our knowledge of what happened is based entirely on his account and needs further verification."

There was a dead silence. Pirx could see where all of this was leading, but he still didn't believe it; he didn't want to. . . .

"No doubt you have guessed, gentlemen," continued the dark-haired man in an even voice—his profile stood out black as coal against the blazing mercury landscapes of the moon— "that the one who cut the telephone cables and high-tension line, and also attacked the transporter, is our sole surviving Setaur. This is a unit about which we know little; it was put into mass production only last month. Engineer Klarner, one of Setaur's designers, was supposed to have come here with me, to give you gentlemen a full explanation not only of the capabilities of this model, but also of the measures that now must be taken to neutralize or destroy the object." The cadet next to Pirx gave a soft moan. It was a moan of pure excitement, uttered without even the pretense of sounding horrified. The young man was not aware of the navigator's disapproving look. But, then, no one noticed or heard anything but the voice of the commodore-engineer.

"I'm no expert in intellectronics and therefore cannot tell you much about the Setaur. But among those present, I believe, is a Dr. McCork. Is he here?"

A slender man wearing glasses stood up. "Yes. I didn't take part in the designing of the Setaurs; I'm only acquainted with our English model, similar to the American one but not identical. Still, the differences are not so very great. I can be of help."

"Excellent. Doctor, if you would come up here. I'll just present, first, the current situation. The Setaur is located somewhere over here"—Achanian made a circle with the end of his ruler around an edge of the Sea of Tranquillity—

"which means it is at a distance of thirty to eighty kilometers from the construction site. It was designed, as the Setaurs in general were designed, to perform mining tasks under extremely difficult conditions, at high temperatures, with a considerable chance of cave-ins; hence these models possess a massive frame and thick armor. . . . But Dr. McCork will be filling you gentlemen in on this aspect. As for the means at our disposal to neutralize it: the headquarters of all the lunar bases have given us, first of all, a certain quantity of explosives, dynamite and oxyliquites, plus line-of-sight hand lasers and mining lasers—of course, neither the explosives nor the lasers were made for use in combat. For conveyance, the groups operating to destroy the Setaur will have transporters of small and medium range, two of which possess light anti-meteorite armor. Only such armor can take the blow of a laser from a distance of one kilometer. True, that applies to Earth, where the energy absorption coefficient of the atmosphere is an important factor. Here we have no atmosphere; therefore those two transporters will be only a little less vulnerable than the others. We are also receiving a considerable number of suits, oxygen—and that, I'm afraid, is all. Around noon there will arrive from the Soviet sector a 'flea' with a three-man crew; in a pinch it can hold four on short flights, to deliver them inside the area where the Setaur is located. I'll stop here for the moment. Now, gentlemen, I would like to pass around a sheet of paper, on which I will ask you to write clearly your names and fields of competence. Meanwhile, if Dr. McCork would kindly tell us a few words about the Setaur . . . The most important thing, I believe, would be an indication of its Achilles' heel. . . ."

McCork was now standing by Achanian. He was even thinner than Pirx had thought; his ears stuck out, his head was slightly triangular, he had almost invisible eyebrows, a shock of hair of indeterminate color, and all in all seemed strangely likable.

Before he spoke, he took off his steel-rimmed glasses, as if they were in the way, and put them on the desk.

"I'd be lying if I said we had allowed for the possibility of the kind of thing that's happened here. But besides the mathematics, a cyberneticist has to have in his head some grain of intuition. It was precisely for this reason that we decided not to put *our* model into mass production just yet. According to the laboratory tests, Mephisto works perfectly—that's the name of our model. And Setaur is supposed to have better stabilization for braking and activating. Or so I thought, going by the literature—now I'm not so sure.

"The name suggests mythology, but it's only an acronym, from Self-programming Electronic Ternary Automaton Racemic, racemic since in the construction of its brain we use both dextro- and levorotatory monopolymer pseudo crystals. But I guess that's not important here. It is an automaton equipped with a laser for mining operations, a violet laser; the energy to emit the impulses is supplied it by a micropile, working on the principle of a cold chain reaction, so that the Setaur—if I remember correctly—can put out impulses of up to forty-five thousand kilowatts."

"For how long?" someone asked.

"From our point of view, forever," immediately replied the thin scientist. "In any case for many years. What exactly happened to this Setaur? In plain language, I think it got hit over the head. The blow must have been unusually strong, but, then, even here a falling building could damage a chromium-nickel skull. So what took place? We've never conducted experiments of this kind; the cost would be too great"—McCork gave an unexpected smile, showing small, even teeth—"but it is generally known that any sharply localized damage to a small, that is, relatively simple, brain or ordinary computer results in a complete breakdown in function. However, the more we approximate the human brain by imitating its processes, then the greater the degree to which such a complex brain will be able to function despite the partial damage it has suffered. The animal brain—a cat's brain, for example—contains certain centers, the stimulation of which produces an attack response, manifested as an outburst of aggressive rage. The brain of the Setaur is built differently, yet does possess a certain general drive, a potentiality for action, which can be directed and channeled in various ways. Now, some sort of short circuit occurred between that motive center and an already initiated program for destruction. Of course I am speaking in grossly oversimplified terms."

"But why destruction?" asked the same voice as before.

"It is an automaton designed for mining operations," Dr. McCork explained. "Its task was to have been to dig levels or drifts, to bore through rock, to crush particularly hard minerals—broadly speaking, to destroy cohesive matter, obviously not everywhere and not everything, but as a result of its injury such a generalization came about. Anyway, my hypothesis could be completely wrong. That side of the question, the purely theoretical, will be worth considering later, after we have made a carpet of the thing. At present it is more important for us to know what the Setaur can do. It can move at a speed of about fifty kilometers an hour, over almost any terrain. It has no lubricating points; all the friction-joint surfaces work on teflon. Its suspensions are magnetic, its armor cannot be penetrated by any revolver or rifle bullet. Such tests have not actually been made, but I think that possibly an antitank gun . . . Of course, we don't have any of those, do we?"

Achanian shook his head. He picked up the list that had been returned to him and read it, making little marks beside the names.

"Obviously, the explosion of a fair-sized charge would pull it apart," McCork went on calmly, as if he were talking about the most ordinary things. "But first you would have to bring the charge near it, and that, I am afraid, will not be easy."

"Where exactly does it have its laser? In the head?" asked someone from the audience.

"Actually it has no head, only a sort of bulge, a swelling between the shoulders. That was to increase its resistance to falling rock. The Setaur measures two hundred twenty centimeters in height, so it fires from a point about two meters above the ground; the muzzle of the laser is protected by a sliding visor; when the body is stationary it can fire through an angle of thirty degrees, and a greater field of aim is obtained when the entire body turns. The laser, as I said, has a maximum power of forty-five thousand kilowatts. Any expert will realize that this is considerable; it can easily cut through a steel plate several centimeters thick. . . ."

"At what range?"

"It's a violet laser, therefore with a very small angle of divergence from the line of incidence. So the range will be, for all practical purposes, limited to the field of vision; since the horizon here on a level plane is at a distance of two kilometers, two kilometers at the very least will be the range of fire."

"We will be receiving special mining lasers of six times that power," Achanian put in.

"But that is only what the Americans call overkill," McCork replied with a smile. "Such power will provide no advantage in a duel with the Setaur's laser."

Someone asked whether it wouldn't be possible to destroy the automaton from aboard some cosmic vessel. McCork declared himself not qualified to answer; Achanian meanwhile glanced at the sign-up sheet and said:

"We have here a navigator first class. Pirx . . . would you care to comment on this?"

Pirx got up.

"Well, in theory, a vessel of medium tonnage like my *Cuivier*, which has a sixteen-thousand-ton rest mass, could certainly destroy such a Setaur, if it got it in its line of thrust.

The temperature of the exhaust gases exceeds six thousand degrees for a distance of nine hundred meters. That would be sufficient, I think . . . ?"

McCork nodded.

"But this is sheer speculation," Pirx continued. "The vessel would have to be somehow brought into position, and a small target like the Setaur, which really isn't any larger than a man, could always have time to move out of the way, unless it were immobilized. The lateral velocity of a vessel maneuvering near the surface of a planet, within its field of gravity, is quite small; sudden pursuit maneuvers are completely out of the question. The only remaining possibility, then, would be to use small units, say, the Moon's own fleet. Except that the thrust here would be weak and of not very high temperature, so perhaps if you used one of those crafts as a bomber instead . . . But for precision bombing you need special instruments, sights, range-finders, which Luna Base doesn't have. No, we can rule that out. Of course it will be necessary, even imperative, to employ such small machines, but only for reconnaissance purposes—that is, to pinpoint the automaton."

He was about to sit down when suddenly a new idea hit him.

"Oh, yes!" he said. "Jump holsters. Those you could use. I mean—you would have to have people who knew how to use them."

"Are they the small, individual rockets one straps on over the shoulders?" asked McCork.

"Yes. With them you can execute jumps or even sail along without moving; depending on the model and type, you get from one to several minutes aloft and reach an altitude of fifty to four hundred meters."

Achanian stood.

"This may be important. Who here has been trained in the use of such devices?"

Two hands went up. Then another.

"Only three?" said Achanian. "Ah; you, too?" he added, seeing that Pirx, who now saw what was coming, had also raised his hand. "That makes four. Not very many . . . We'll ask among the ground crew. Gentlemen! This is—it goes without saying—strictly a voluntary mission. I really ought to have begun with that. Who wants to take part in the operation?"

A slight clatter ensued, for everyone present was standing up.

"On behalf of Control, I thank you," said Achanian. "This is fine. . . . And so we have seventeen volunteers. We will be supported by three units from the lunar fleet, and in addition will have at our disposal ten drivers and radio operators to help man the transporters. I will ask you all to remain here, and you"—he turned to McCork and Pirx—"please come with me, to Control."

Around four in the afternoon Pirx was sitting in the turret of a large caterpillar transporter, jolted by its violent motions. He was wearing a full suit, with the helmet on his knees, ready to put it on at the first sound of the alarm, and across his chest hung a heavy laser, the butt of which poked him unmercifully; in his left hand he had a map, and he used the right to turn a periscope, observing the long, spread-out line of the other transporters, which pitched and tossed like boats across the debris-strewn tracts of the Sea of Tranquillity. That desert "sea" was all ablaze with sunlight and empty from one black horizon to the other. Pirx received reports and passed them on, spoke with Luna Base 1, with the officers of the other machines, with the pilots of the reconnaissance modules, whose microscopic exhaust flames every so often appeared among the stars in the black sky; yet with all of this he still couldn't help feeling at times that he was having some kind of highly elaborate and silly dream.

Things had happened with increasing frenzy. He wasn't the only one to whom it seemed that Construction had succumbed to something like panic. For, really, what could one halfwit automaton do, even armed with a light-thrower? So when at the second "summit meeting," right at noon, there began to be talk of turning to the UN, at least to the Security Council, for "special sanction," namely permission to bring in heavy artillery (rocket launchers would be best), and possibly even atomic missiles—Pirx objected, along with others, that in that way, before they got anywhere, they would be making complete asses of themselves in front of all Earth. Besides, it was obvious that for such a decision from the international body they would have to wait days if not weeks, and meanwhile the "mad robot" could wander off God knows where. Once it was hidden in the inaccessible rifts of the lunar crust, you wouldn't be able to get at it with all the cannons in the world; it was essential to act decisively and without delay.

It became clear then that the biggest problem would be communications, which had always been a sore point in lunar undertakings. Supposedly, there existed about three thousand different patents for inventions designed to facilitate communications, ranging from a seismic telegraph (using microexplosions as signals) to "Trojans," stationary satellites. Such satellites had been placed in orbit last year, but they didn't improve the situation one bit. In practice the problem was solved by systems of ultrashortwave relays set on poles, a lot like the old pre-Sputnik television transmission lines on Earth. This was actually more reliable than communication by satellite, because the engineers were still racking their brains over how to make their orbiting stations unsusceptible to solar storms. Every single jump in the activity of the sun, and the resultant "hurricanes" of electrically charged high-energy particles that tore through the ether, immediately produced a static that made it difficult to maintain contact—sometimes for several days.

One of those solar "twisters" was going on right now, so messages between Luna Base 1 and Construction went by

way of the ground relays, and the success of Operation Setaur depended—to a large degree, at least—on the "rebel's"
not taking it into its head to destroy the girdered poles that
stood, forty-five of them, on the desert separating Luna City
from the cosmodrome near the construction site. Assuming,
of course, that the automaton would continue to prowl in
that vicinity. It had, after all, complete freedom of movement, requiring neither fuel nor oxygen, neither sleep nor
rest; in all, it was so self-sufficient that many of the engineers for the first time fully realized how perfect was this
machine of their own making—a machine whose next step
no one could foresee.

The direct Moon-Earth discussions which had begun at
dawn between Control and the firm Cybertronics, including
the staff of Setaur's designers, went on and on; but not a
thing was learned from them that hadn't already been said
by little Dr. McCork. It was only the laymen who were still
trying to talk the specialists into using some great calculator
to predict the automaton's tactics. Was the Setaur intelligent? Well, yes, in its own fashion. That "unnecessary"—
and at the present moment highly dangerous—"wisdom" of
the machine angered many participants in the action; they
couldn't see why in hell the engineers had bestowed such
freedom and autonomy on a machine made strictly for mining tasks. McCork calmly explained that this "intellectronic
redundancy" was, in the current phase of technological development, the same thing as the excess of power generally
found in all conventional machines and engines: it was an
emergency reserve, put there in order to increase safety and
dependability of function. There was no way of knowing in
advance all the situations in which a machine, be it mechanical or informational, might find itself. And therefore no one
really had the foggiest notion of what the Setaur would do.
Of course the experts, including those on Earth, had tele-
graphed their opinions; the only problem was that these
opinions were diametrically opposed. Some believed the Se-

taur would attempt to destroy objects of an "artificial" nature, precisely like the relay poles or high-tension lines; others thought, on the contrary, that it would expend its energy by firing at whatever stood in its path, whether a lunar rock or a transporter filled with people. The former were in favor of an immediate attack for the purpose of destroying it; the latter recommended a wait-and-see strategy. Both were in agreement on one thing only, that it was absolutely vital to keep track of the machine's movements.

Since early morning the lunar fleet, numbering twelve small units, had patrolled the Sea of Tranquillity and sent continual reports to the group defending the construction site, which in turn was in constant contact with headquarters at the cosmodrome. It was no easy thing to detect the Setaur, a tiny piece of metal in a giant wilderness of rock filled with fields of detritus, cracks, and half-buried crevices, and covered besides with the pockmarks of miniature craters.

If only those reports had at least been negative! But the patrolling crews had alarmed ground personnel several times already with the information that the "mad machine" was sighted. So far it had turned out that the object was some unusual rock formation or a fragment of lava sparkling in the rays of the sun; even the use of radar along with ferroinduction sensors proved to be of little help—in the wake of the first stages of lunar exploration and colonization, there remained upon the Moon's rocky wastes a whole multitude of metal containers, heat-fused shells from rocket cartridges, and all possible sorts of tin junk, which every now and then became the source of fresh alarms. So much so that operation headquarters began to wish the Setaur would finally attack something and show itself. However, the last time it had revealed its presence was with the attack on the small transporter belonging to the electrical repair team. Since then it seemed as if the lunar soil had opened up and swallowed the thing. But everyone felt that sitting and waiting was out of the question, particularly when Construction had to regain its energy supply.

The mission—covering about ten thousand square kilometers—consisted in combing that area with two waves of vehicles approaching each other from opposite directions, from the north and the south. From Construction came one extended line under the command of their head technologist, Strzibor, and from the Luna Base cosmodrome came the second, in which the role of operations coordinator of both sides, working closely with the chief (Commodore-Navigator Pleydar), fell to Pirx. He understood perfectly that at any moment they could pass right by the Setaur; it might, for example, be hidden in one of those deep tectonic trenches, or even be camouflaged by nothing but the dazzling lunar sand, and they would never notice it; McCork, who rode with him as "intellectronician-consultant," was of the same opinion.

The transporter lurched dreadfully, moving along at a speed that, as the driver quietly informed them, "after a while makes your eyes pop out." They were now in the eastern sector of the Sea of Tranquillity and less than an hour away from the region where the automaton was most likely to be located. After crossing that previously determined border, they were all to don their helmets, so that in case of an unexpected hit and loss of seal, or in case of fire, they could leave the vehicle immediately.

The transporter had been changed into a fighting machine; the mechanics had mounted on its domelike turret a mining laser of great power, though pretty poor as far as accuracy went. Pirx considered it altogether useless against the Setaur. The Setaur possessed an automatic sighter, since its photoelectric eyes were hooked up directly to the laser and it could instantly fire at whatever lay in the center of its field of vision. Theirs, on the other hand, was a quaint sort of sighter, probably from an old cosmonautical range-finder;

the only testing it had received was when, before leaving Luna Base, they took a few shots at some rocks on the horizon. The rocks had been large, the distance less than two kilometers, and even so they hit the mark only on the fourth try. And here, to make matters worse, you had lunar conditions to cope with, because a laser beam was visible as a brilliant streak only in a diffusing medium, such as an Earthlike atmosphere; but in empty space a beam of light, regardless of how powerful, was invisible until it hit some material obstacle. Therefore, on Earth you could shoot a laser much the way you shot tracer bullets, guided by their observable line of flight. Without a sighter, a laser on the Moon was of no practical value. Pirx didn't keep this from McCork; he told him when only a couple of minutes separated them from the hypothetical danger zone.

"I didn't think of that," said the engineer, then added, with a smile, "Why did you tell me?"

"To free you of illusions," replied Pirx, not looking up from the double eyepiece of his periscope. It had foam-rubber cushions, but he felt sure that he would be going around with black eyes for the longest time (assuming, of course, he came out of this alive). "And also to explain why we're carrying that stuff in the back."

"The cylinders?" asked McCork. "I saw you taking them from the storeroom. What's in them?"

"Ammonia, chlorine, and some hydrocarbons or other," said Pirx. "I though they might come in handy."

"A gas smoke-screen?" ventured the engineer.

"No, what I had in mind was some way of aiming. If there's no atmosphere, we create one, at least temporarily. . . ."

"I'm afraid there won't be time for that."

"Perhaps not, but I brought it along just in case. Against something insane, insane measures are often best."

They fell silent, for the transporter had begun to lurch like a drunk; the stabilizers whined and squealed, sounding as if at any minute the oil in them would begin to boil. They hurtled down an incline strewn with sharp boulders. The opposite slope gleamed, all white with pumice.

"You know what worries me most?" resumed Pirx when the heaving let up a little; he had grown strangely talkative. "Not the Setaur—not at all—it's those transporters from Construction. If just one of them takes us for the Setaur and starts blasting away with its laser, things'll get lively."

"I see you've thought of everything," muttered the engineer. The cadet, sitting beside the radio operator, leaned across the back of his seat and handed Pirx a scrawled radiogram, barely legible.

"We have entered the danger zone at relay twenty, so far nothing, stop, Strzibor, end of transmission," Pirx read aloud. "Well, we'll soon have to put our helmets on, too. . . ."

The machine slowed a little, climbing a slope. Pirx noticed that he could no longer see the neighbor on his left—only the right-hand transporter was still visible, moving like a dim blot up the bank. He ordered that the machine on the left be raised on the radio, but there was no answer.

"We have begun to separate," he said calmly. "I thought that would happen. Can't we push the antenna up a little higher? No? Too bad."

By now they were at the summit of a gentle rise. From over the horizon, at a distance of less than two hundred kilometers, emerged, full in the sun, the sawtooth ridge of the crater Toricelli, sharply outlined against the black background of the sky. They had the plain of the Sea of Tranquillity all but behind them now. Deep tectonic rifts appeared, frozen slabs of magma jutted here and there from under the debris, and over these the transporter crawled with difficulty, first heaving up like a boat on a wave, then dropping heavily down, as though it were about to plunge head over heels into some unknown cavity. Pirx caught sight of the mast of the next relay, glanced quickly at the celluloid map card pressed to his knees, and ordered everyone to fas-ten their helmets. From now on they would be able to communicate only by intercom. The transporter managed to shake even more violently than before—Pirx's head wobbled around in its helmet like the kernel of a nut inside an otherwise empty shell.

When they drove down the slope to lower ground, the saw of Toricelli disappeared, blocked out by nearer elevations; almost at the same time they lost their right neighbor. For a few minutes more they heard its call signal, but then that was distorted by the waves bouncing off the sheets of rock. Complete radio silence followed. It was extremely awkward trying to look through the periscope with a helmet on; Pirx thought he would either crack his viewplate or smash the eyepiece. He did what he could to keep his eyes on the field of vision at all times, though it shifted drastically with each lurch of the machine and was strewn with endless boulders. The jumble of pitch-black shadow and dazzlingly bright surfaces of stone made his eyes swim.

Suddenly a small orange flame leaped up in the darkness of the far sky, flickered, dwindled, disappeared. A second flash, a little stronger. Pirx shouted, "Attention everyone! I see explosions!" and feverishly turned the crank of the periscope, reading the azimuth off the scale etched on the lenses.

"We're changing course!" he howled. "Forty-seven point eight, full speed ahead!"

The terms of this order really applied to a cosmic vessel, but the driver understood it all the same; the plates and every joint of the transporter gave a shudder as the machine wheeled around practically in place and surged forward. Pirx got up from his seat: its tossing was pulling his head away from the eyepiece. Another flash—this time red-violet, a fan-shaped burst of flame. But the source of those flashes or explosions lay beyond the field of vision, hidden by the ridge they were climbing.

"Attention everyone!" said Pirx. "Prepare your individual lasers! Dr. McCork, please go to the hatch. When I give the word, or in case of a hit, you'll open it! Driver! Decrease velocity!"

The elevation up which the machine was clambering rose from the desert like the shank of some moon monster, half sunken in debris; the rock in fact resembled, in its smoothness, a polished skeleton or giant skull; Pirx ordered the driver to go to the top. The treads began to chatter, like steel over glass. "Hold it!" yelled Pirx, and the transporter, coming to a sudden halt, dipped nose-down toward the rock, swayed as the stabilizers groaned with the strain, and stopped.

Pirx looked into a shallow basin enclosed on two sides by radially spreading, tapered embankments of old magma flows; two-thirds of the wide depression lay in glaring sun, a third was covered by a shroud of absolute black. On that velvet darkness there shone, like a weird jewel, fading ruby-red, the ripped-open skeleton of a vehicle. Besides Pirx, only the driver saw it, for the armor flaps of the windows had been lowered. Pirx, to tell the truth, didn't know what to do. "A transporter," he thought. "Where is the front of it? Coming from the south? Probably from the construction group, then. But who got it, the Setaur? And I'm standing here in full view, like an idiot—we have to conceal ourselves. But where are all the other transporters? Theirs and mine?"

"I have something!" shouted the radiotelegraph man. He connected his receiver to the inside circuit, so that they could all hear the signals in their helmets.

"Aximo-portable talus! A wall with encystation—repetition from the headland unnecessary—the access at an azimuth of—multicrystalline metamorphism . . ." The voice filled Pirx's earphones, delivering the words clearly, in a monotone, with no inflection whatever.

"It's him!" he yelled. "The Setaur! Hello, radio! Get a fix on that, quickly! We need a fix! For God's sake! While it's still sending!" He roared till he was deafened by his own

shouts amplified in the closed space of the helmet; not waiting for the telegraph operator to snap out of it, he leaped,
head bowed, to the top of the turret, seized the double
handgrip of the heavy laser, and began turning it along with
the turret, his eyes already at the sighter. Meanwhile, inside
his helmet, that low, almost sorrowful, steady voice droned
on:

"Heavily bihedrous achromatism viscosity—undecorti-
cated segments without repeated anticlinal interpolations"—
and the senseless gabble seemed to weaken.

"Where's that fix, damn it?!!"

Pirx, keeping his eyes glued to the sighter, heard a faint
clatter—McCork had run up front and shoved aside the operator; there was a sound of scuffling. . . .

Suddenly in his earphones he heard the calm voice of the
cyberneticist:

"Azimuth 39.9 . . . 40.0 . . . 40.1 . . . 40.2 . . ."

"It's moving!" Pirx realized. The turret had to be turned
by crank; he nearly dislocated his arm, he cranked so hard.
The numbers moved at a creep. The red line passed the 40
mark.

Suddenly the voice of the Setaur rose to a drawn-out
screech and broke off. At that same moment Pirx pressed
the trigger, and half a kilometer down, right at the line between light and shadow, a rock spouted fire brighter than
the sun.

Through the thick gloves it was next to impossible to hold
the handgrip steady. The blinding flame bored into the darkness at the bottom of the basin; a few dozen meters from the
dimly glowing wreck, it stopped and, in a spray of jagged
embers, cut a line sideways, twice raising columns of sparks.
Something yammered in the earphones. Pirx paid no attention, just plowed on with that line of flame, so thin and so
terrible, until it split into a thousand centrifugal ricochets off
some stone pillar. Red swirling circles danced before him,

but through their swirl he saw a bright blue eye, smaller than the head of a pin, which had opened at the very bottom of the darkness, off to the side somewhere, not where he had been shooting—and before he was able to move the hand-grip of the laser, to pivot it around on its swivel, a rock right next to the machine itself exploded like a liquid sun.

"Back!" he bellowed, ducking by reflex, with the result that he no longer saw anything; but he wouldn't have seen anything anyway, only those red, slowly fading circles, which turned now black, now golden.

The engine thundered. They were thrown with such violence that Pirx fell all the way to the bottom, then flew to the front, between the knees of the cadet and the radio operator; the cylinders, though they had tied them down securely on the armored wall, made an awful racket. They were rushing backward, in reverse, there was a horrible crunch beneath the tractor tread, they swerved, careened in the other direction, for a minute it looked like the transporter was going to flip over on its back. . . . The driver, desperately working the gas, the brakes, the clutch, somehow brought that wild skid under control; the machine gave a long quiver and stood still.

"Do we have a seal?" shouted Pirx, picking himself up off the floor. "A good thing it's rubber," he managed to think.

"Intact!"

"Well, that was nice and close," he said in an altogether different voice now, standing up and straightening his back. And added softly, not without chagrin: "Two hundredths more to the left and I would have had him."

McCork returned to his place.

"Doctor, that was good, thank you!" called Pirx, already back at the periscope. "Hello, driver, let's go down the same way we came up. There are some small cliffs over there, a kind of arch—that's it, right!—drive into the shadow between them and stop."

Slowly, as if with exaggerated caution, the transporter moved in between the slabs of rock half buried in sand and froze in their shadow, which would render it invisible.

"Excellent!" said Pirx almost cheerfully. "Now I need two men to go with me and do a little reconnoitering. . . ."

McCork raised his hand at the same time as the cadet.

"Good! Now listen; you"—he turned to the others—"will remain here. Don't move out of the shadow, even if the Setaur should come straight at you—sit quietly. Well, I guess if it walks right into the transporter, then you'll have to defend yourselves; you have the laser. But that's not very likely. You," he said to the driver, "will help this young man remove those cylinders of gas from the wall, and you"—this to the radio operator—"will call Luna Base, the cosmodrome, Construction, the patrols, and tell the first who answers that *it* destroyed one transporter, probably belonging to Construction, and that three men from our machine have gone out to hunt it. So I don't want anybody barging in with lasers, shooting blindly, and so on. . . . And now let's go!"

Since each of them could carry only one cylinder, the driver accompanied them and they took four. Pirx led his companions not to the top of the "skull," but a little beyond, where a small, shallow ravine could be seen. They went as far as they could and set the cylinders down by a large boulder; Pirx ordered the driver to go back. He himself peered out over the surface of the boulder and trained his binoculars on the interior of the basin. McCork and the cadet crouched down beside him. After a long while he said:

"I don't see him. Doctor, what the Setaur said, did it have any meaning?"

"I doubt it. Combinations of words—a sort of schizophrenic thing."

"That wreck has had it," said Pirx.

"Why did you shoot?" asked McCork. "There might have been people."

"There wasn't anyone."

Pirx moved the binoculars a millimeter at a time, scruti-
nizing every crease and crevice of the sunlit area.

"They didn't have time to jump."

"How do you know that?"

"Because he cut the machine in half. You can still see it.
They must have practically run into him. He hit from a few
dozen meters. And besides, both hatches are closed. No," he
added after a couple of seconds, "he's not in the sun. And
probably hasn't had a chance to sneak away. We'll try drawing him out."

Bending over, he lifted a heavy cylinder to the top of the
boulder and, shoving it into position before him, muttered
between his teeth:

"A real live cowboys-and-Indians situation, the kind I always dreamed of . . ."

The cylinder slipped; he held it by the valves and, flattening himself out on the stones, said:

"If you see a blue flash, shoot at once—that's his laser
eye."

With all his might he pushed the cylinder, which, at first
slowly but then with increasing speed, began to roll down
the slope. All three of them took aim; the cylinder had now
gone about two hundred meters and was rolling more slowly,
for the slope lessened. A few times it seemed that protruding
rocks would bring it to a stop, but it tumbled past them and,
growing smaller and smaller, now a dully shining spot, approached the bottom of the basin.

"Nothing?" said Pirx, disappointed. "Either he's smarter
than I thought, or he just isn't interested in it, or else . . ."

He didn't finish. On the slope below them there was a
blinding flash. The flame almost instantly changed into a
heavy, brownish-yellow cloud, at the center of which still
glowed a sullen fire, and the edges spread out between the
spurs of rock.

"The chlorine . . ." said Pirx. "Why didn't you shoot?
Couldn't you see anything?"

"No," replied the cadet and McCork in unison.

"The bastard! He's hid himself in some crevice or is firing from the flank. I really doubt now that this will do any good, but let's try."

He picked up a second cylinder and sent it after the first.

At first it rolled like the other one, but somewhere about halfway down the incline it turned aside and came to rest. Pirx wasn't looking at it—all his attention was concentrated on the triangular section of darkness in which the Setaur must be lurking. The seconds went by slowly. All at once a branching explosion ripped the slope. Pirx was unable to locate the place where the automaton had concealed itself, but he saw the line of fire, or more precisely a part of it, for it materialized as a burning, sunbright thread when it passed through what was left of the first cloud of gas. Immediately he sighted along that gleaming trajectory, which was already fading, and as soon as he had the edge of the darkness in his cross hairs, he pulled the trigger. Apparently McCork had done the same thing simultaneously, and in an instant the cadet joined them. Three blades of sun plowed the black floor of the basin and at that very moment it was as if some gigantic, fiery lid slammed down directly in front of them— the entire boulder that protected them shook, from its rim showered a myriad searing rainbows, their suits and helmets were sprayed with burning quartz, which instantly congealed to microscopic teardrops. They lay now flattened in the shadow of the rock, while above their heads whipped, like a white-hot sword, a second and a third discharge, grazing the surface of the boulder, which immediately was covered with cooling glass bubbles.

"Everyone all right?" asked Pirx, not lifting his head.

"Yes!"—"Here, too!"—came the answers.

"Go down to the machine and tell the radio operator to call everyone, because we have him here and will try to keep him pinned as long as possible," Pirx said to the cadet, who then crawled backward and ran, stooping, in the direction of the rocks where the tractor was standing.

"We have two cylinders left, one apiece. Doctor, let's switch positions now. And please be careful and keep low; he's already hit right on top of us. . . ."

With these words Pirx picked up one cylinder and, taking advantage of the shadows thrown by some large stone slabs, moved forward as quickly as he could. About two hundred steps farther on, they rested in the cleft of a magma embankment. The cadet, returning from the transporter, wasn't able to find them at first. He was breathing hard, as if he had run at least a few kilometers.

"Easy, take your time!" said Pirx. "Well, what's up?"

"Contact has been resumed." The cadet squatted by Pirx, who could see the youth's eyes blinking behind the viewplate of his helmet. "In that machine, the one that was destroyed . . . there were four people from Construction. The second transporter must have withdrawn, because it had a defective laser . . . and the rest went by, off to the side, and didn't see anything. . . ." Pirx nodded as if to say, "I thought as much."

"What else? Where's our group?"

"Practically all of them—thirty kilometers from here, there was a false alarm there, some rocket patrol said it saw the Setaur and pulled everyone to the spot. And three machines don't answer."

"When will they get here?"

"At the moment we're only receiving .   ." said the cadet, embarrassed.

"Only receiving? What do you mean?"

"The radio operator says that either something's happened to the transmitter, or else in this place his emission is damping out. He asks if he might change the parking location, so he can test . . ."

"He can change his location if he has to," Pirx replied.

"And please stop running like that! Watch where you put your feet!"

But the other must not have heard, for he was racing back.

"At best they'll be here in half an hour, if we succeed in making contact," observed Pirx. McCork said nothing. Pirx pondered the next move. Should they wait or not? Storming the basin with transporters would probably ensure success, but not without losses. Compared with the Setaur their machines made large targets, were slow, and would have to strike together, for a duel would end as it had with that tractor from Construction. He tried to come up with some stratagem to lure the Setaur out into the lighted area. If it were possible to send in one unmanned, remote-control transporter as a decoy, then hit the automaton from elsewhere—say, from above . . .

It occurred to him that he really didn't have to wait for anyone; he already had one transporter. But somehow the plan didn't hold together. To send a machine out blindly like that wouldn't be any good. He would just blow the thing to bits, and wouldn't have to move to do it. Could he have possibly realized that the zone of shadow in which he stood was giving him so much of an advantage? But this was not a machine created for battle with all its tactics. There was method in his madnesss, yes, but what method?

They sat, bent over, at the foot of a rocky scarp, in its dense, cold shadow. Suddenly it struck Pirx that he was acting like a complete idiot. What would he do, after all, if he were the Setaur? Immediately he felt alarm, for he was certain that he—in his place—would attack. Passively waiting for things to happen gained nothing. So, then, could *he* be advancing toward them? Even now? One could surely reach the western cliff, moving under cover of darkness the whole time, and farther on there were so many huge boulders, so much fissured lava, that in that labyrinth one could hide for God knows how long. . . .

He was almost positive now that the Setaur would proceed in precisely this way, and that they could expect him at any moment.

"Doctor, I fear he will take us by surprise," he said quickly, jumping to his feet. "What do you think?"

"You believe he might sneak up on us?" asked McCork and smiled. "That occurred to me, too. Well, yes, it's even logical, but will he behave logically? That is the question."

"We'll try it one more time," Pirx muttered. "We have to roll these cylinders down the hill and see what he does."

"I understand. Now?"

"Yes. And be careful!"

They dragged the cylinders to the top of the rise and, doing their best to remain unseen from the bottom of the basin, pushed both practically at the same time. Unfortunately, the absence of air kept them from hearing whether the things were rolling, or in what way. Pirx made up his mind and—feeling strangely naked, as though there were no steel sphere over his head, nor a heavy three-layered suit covering his body—he pressed himself flat against the rock and cautiously stuck out his head.

Nothing had changed below. Except that the wrecked machine had ceased to be visible, for its cooling fragments merged with the surrounding darkness. The shadow occupied the same area, the shape of an irregular, elongated triangle, its base abutting the cliffs of the highest, western ridge of rocks. One cylinder had stopped some thirty meters beneath them, having struck a stone that put it in a lengthwise position. The other was still rolling, slowing down, growing smaller, till it stood still. Pirx was not at all pleased that nothing more happened. "He isn't stupid," he thought. "He won't shoot at a target someone sticks under his nose." He tried to find the place from which the Setaur, some ten minutes before, had betrayed itself with the flash of its laser eye, but that was extremely difficult.

"Perhaps he's not there anymore," Pirx reflected. "Perhaps he's simply retreating to the north; or going parallel, along

the bottom of the basin, or along one of those rifts of magnetic course. . . . If he makes it to the cliffs, to that labyrinth, then we've lost him for good. . . ."

Slowly, groping, he raised the butt of his laser and loosened his muscles. "Dr. McCork!" he said. "Could you come
here?"

And when the doctor had scrambled up to him, he said:

"You see the two cylinders? One straight ahead, below us,
and the other farther on?"

"I see them."

"Fire at the closer one first, then at the other, in an interval, say, of forty seconds. . . . But not from here!" he added
quickly. "You'll have to find a better place. Ah!" He pointed
with his hand. *"There* is not a bad position, in that hollow.
And after you shoot, crawl back immediately. All right?"

McCork asked no questions but set off at once, keeping
low, in the direction indicated. Pirx waited impatiently. If
he was even a little like a man, he had to be curious. Every
intelligent creature was curious—and curiosity prompted it
to act when something incomprehensible took place. . . .
He couldn't see the doctor now. He forced himself not to
look at the cylinders, which were to explode under McCork's
shots; he focused all his attention on the stretch of sunlit
debris between the zone of shadow and the outcrop. He lifted
the binoculars to his eyes and trained them on that section
of the lava flow. In the lenses grotesque shapes filed slowly
by, shapes as though formed in the studio of some sculptor-
abstractionist: tapering obelisks twisted about like screws,
plates furrowed with snaking cracks—the jumble of glaring
planes and zigzag shadows had an irritating effect on the
eye.

At the very edge of his vision, far below him, on the slope,
there was a burgeoning flash. After a long pause, the second
went off. Silence. The only sound was his pulse throbbing
inside his helmet, through which the sun was trying to bore

its way into his skull. He swept the lenses along a stretch of chaotically interlocking masses.

Something moved. He froze. Above the razorlike edge of a slab that resembled the fractured blade of some giant stone ax there emerged a shape, hemispherical, in color much like a dark rock, but this shape had arms, which took hold of the boulder from both sides. Now he could see it—the upper half of it. It didn't look headless, but, rather, like a man wearing the supernatural mask of an African shaman, a mask that covered the face, neck, and chest, but flattened out in a manner that was somewhat monstrous. With the elbow of his right arm Pirx felt the butt of his laser, but he didn't dream of shooting now. The risk was too great—the chance of getting a hit with a relatively weak weapon, and at such a distance, was minuscule. The other, motionless, seemed to be examining with that head it had, which barely protruded above the shoulders, the remains of the two gas clouds that were drifting along the slope, helplessly expanding into space. This lasted a good while. It looked as if *it* did not know what had happened, and was unsure of what to do. In that hesitation, that uncertainty, which Pirx could understand full well, there was something so uncannily familiar, so human, that he felt a lump in his throat. What would I do in his place, what would I think? That someone was firing at the very same objects I had fired at before, and therefore this someone would be not an opponent, not an enemy, but instead a kind of ally. But I would know, surely, that I had no ally. Ah, but what if it were a being like myself?

The other stirred. Its movements were fluid and uncommonly swift. All at once it was in full view, erect on that upended stone, as though still looking for the mysterious cause of the two explosions. Then it turned away, jumped down, and, leaning slightly forward, began to run—now and then it dropped from Pirx's sight, but never for more than a few seconds, only to break out into the sunlight again on one of the spurs of the magma labyrinth. In this way it approached Pirx, though running the whole time at the bottom of the basin. They were separated now only by the space of the slope, and Pirx wondered whether he shouldn't shoot, after all. But the other whisked past in narrow strips of light and again dissolved into the blackness—and since it continually had to change direction, picking its way between the rocks and rubble, one could not predict where its arms, working to maintain balance like those of a man running, and where its headless trunk would show up next, to flash metallically and vanish once again.

Suddenly ragged lightning cut across the mosaic of debris, striking long plumes of sparks among the very blocks where the Setaur was running. Who had fired that? Pirx couldn't see McCork, but the line of fire had come from the opposite side—it could only have been the cadet, that snot-nosed kid, that idiot! He cursed him, furious, because nothing had been accomplished, of course—the dome of metal flitted on for another fraction of a second, then disappeared for good. "And not only that, but he tried to shoot him in the back!" thought Pirx in a fury, not at all appreciating the absurdity of this reproach.

The Setaur hadn't returned fire. Why? Pirx tried to catch a glimpse of it—in vain. Could the bulge of the slope be in the way? That was entirely possible. . . . In which case he could move safely now. . . . Pirx slipped down from his boulder, seeing that nothing was any longer watching from below. He ran, hunched over slightly, along the rim itself; he passed the cadet, who lay prone as if on a rifle range—feet flung out wide and pressed sideways against the rock—and Pirx felt an unaccountable urge to kick him in his behind, which stuck up ludicrously and was made even more conspicuous by a poorly fitting suit. He slowed down, but only to shout:

"Don't you dare shoot, do you hear me? Put away that laser!"

And before the cadet, turning on his side, began to look around in bewilderment—for the voice had come from his earphones, giving no indication of where Pirx was located—Pirx had already run on; afraid that he was wasting precious time, he hurried as much as he could, till he found himself facing a broad crevasse, which opened up a sudden view all the way to the bottom of the basin.

It was a type of tectonic trench, so old that its edges had crumbled, lost their sharpness, and resembled a mountain gully widened by erosion. He hesitated. He didn't see the Setaur, but, then, it was probably impossible to see it anyway from this vantage point. So he ventured into the gully with laser at the ready, well aware that what he was doing was insane, yet unable to resist whatever was driving him; he told himself that he only wanted to take a look, that he would stop at the first place where he could check out the last section of the outcrop and the entire labyrinth of rubble beneath it; and perhaps, even as he ran, still leaning forward, with the gravel shooting out in streams from under his boots, he actually believed this. But at the moment he couldn't give thought to anything. He was on the Moon and therefore weighed barely fifteen kilograms, but even so the increasing angle tripped him up; he went bounding along eight meters at a time, braking for all he was worth; already he had covered half the length of the slope.

The gully ended in a shallow pathway—there in the sun stood the first masses of the lava flow, black on the far side and glittering on the southern, about one hundred meters down. "I got myself into it this time," he thought. From here one could practically reach out and touch the region in which the Setaur was at large. He glanced rapidly to the left and to the right. He was alone; the ridge lay high above him, a broiling steepness against the black sky. Before, he had been able to look down into the narrow places between the rocks almost with a bird's-eye view, but now that crisscross maze of fissures was blocked out for him by the nearest masses of stone. "Not good," he thought. "Better go back." But for some reason he knew that he wasn't going back.

However, he couldn't just stand there. A few dozen steps lower was a solitary block of magma, evidently the end of that long tongue which once had poured red-hot off the great crags at the foot of Toricelli—and which had meandered its way finally to this sinkhole. It was the best cover available. He reached it in a single leap, though he found particularly unpleasant this prolonged lunar floating, this slow-motion flight as in a dream; he could never really get used to it. Crouched behind the angular rock, he peered out over it and saw the Setaur, which came from behind two jagged spires, went around a third, brushing it with a metal shoulder, and halted. Pirx was looking at it from the side, so it was lit up only partially: the right arm glistened, dully like a well-greased machine part, but the rest of its frame lay in shadow.

Pirx had just raised the laser to his eye when the other, as if in a sudden premonition, vanished. Could it be standing there still, having only stepped back into the shadow? Should he shoot into that shadow, then? He had a bead on it now, but didn't touch the trigger. He relaxed his muscles; the barrel fell. He waited. No sign of the Setaur. The rubble spread out directly below him in a truly infernal labyrinth. One could play hide-and-seek in there for hours—the glassy lava had split into geometrical yet eerie shapes.

"Where is he?" Pirx thought. "If it were only possible to hear something, but this damned airless place, it's like being in a nightmare. . . . I could go down there and hunt him. No, I'm not about to do that, *he's* the mad one, after all. . . . But one can at least consider everything—the outcrop extends no more than twelve meters, which would take about two jumps on Earth; I would be in the shadow beneath it, invisible, and could move along the length of it, with my back protected by the rock at all times, and sooner or later he'd walk out straight into my sights."

Nothing changed in the labyrinth of stone. On Earth by

this time, the sun would have shifted quite a bit, but here the long lunar day held sway, the sun seemed to keep hanging in the very same place, extinguishing the nearest stars, so that it was surrounded by a black void shot through with a kind of orange, radial haze. . . . He leaned out halfway from behind his boulder. Nothing. This was beginning to annoy him. Why weren't the others showing up? It was inconceivable that radio contact hadn't been established by now. But perhaps they were planning to drive it out of that rubble. . . . He glanced at the watch beneath the thick glass on his wrist and was amazed: since his last conversation with McCork barely thirteen minutes had elapsed.

He was preparing to abandon his position when two things happened at once, both equally unexpected. Through the stone arch between the two magma embankments that closed off the basin to the east, he saw transporters moving, one after the other. They were still far away, possibly more than a kilometer, and going at full speed, trailing long, seemingly rigid plumes of swirling dust. At the same time two large hands, human-looking except that they were wearing metal gloves, appeared at the very edge of the precipice, and following them came—so quickly he hadn't time to back away— the Setaur. No more than ten meters separated them. Pirx saw the massive bulge of the torso that served as a head, set between powerful shoulders, and in which glittered the lenses of the optic apertures, motionless, like two dark, widely spaced eyes, along with that middle, that third and terrible eye, lidded at the moment, of the laser gun. He himself, to be sure, held a laser in his hand, but the machine's reflexes were incomparably faster than his own. He didn't even try leveling his weapon. He simply stood stock-still in the full sun, his legs bent, exactly as he had been caught, jumping up from the ground, by the sudden appearance of *him*, and they looked at each other: the statue of the man and the statue of the machine, both sheathed in metal. Then a terrible light tore the whole area in front of Pirx; pushed by a blast of heat, he went crashing backward. As he fell he didn't lose consciousness but—in that fraction of a second—felt only surprise, for he could have sworn it wasn't the Setaur that had shot him, since up to the very last instant he had seen its laser eye dark and blind.

He landed on his back, for the discharge had passed him—but clearly it had been aimed at him, because the horrible flash was repeated in an instant and chipped off part of the stone spire that had been protecting him before; it sprayed drops of molten mineral, which in flight changed into a dazzling spider web. But now he was saved by the fact that they were aiming at the height of his head while he was lying down.

It was the first machine; they were firing the laser from it. He rolled over on his side and saw then the back of the Setaur, who, motionless, as if cast in bronze, gave two bursts of lilac sun. Even at that distance one could see the foremost transporter's entire tread overturn, along with the rollers and guiding wheel; such a cloud of dust and burning gases rose up there that the second transporter, blinded, could not shoot. The giant slowly, unhurriedly, looked at the prone man, who was still clutching his weapon, then turned and bent its legs slightly, ready to jump back where it had come from, but Pirx, awkwardly, sideways, fired at it—he intended only to cut the legs from under it, but his elbow wavered as he pulled the trigger, and a knife of flame cleaved the giant from top to bottom, so that it was only a mass of glowing scrap that tumbled down into the field of rubble.

The crew of the demolished transporter escaped unhurt, without even burns, and Pirx found out—much later, it's true—that they had in fact been firing at him, for the Setaur, dark against the dark cliffs, went completely unnoticed. The inexperienced gunner had even failed to notice that the figure in his sights showed the light color of an aluminum suit. Pirx was pretty certain that he would not have survived the next shot. The Setaur had saved him—but had it realized this? Many times he went over those few final seconds in his mind, and each time his conviction grew stronger that from where the Setaur had been standing, it could tell who was the real target of the long-range fire. Did this mean that it had wished to save him? No one could provide an answer. The intellectronicians chalked the whole thing up to "coincidence"—but none of them was able to support that opinion with any proof. Nothing like this had ever happened before, and the professional literature made no mention of such incidents.

Everyone felt that Pirx had done what he had to do—but he wasn't satisfied. For many long years afterward there remained etched in his memory that brief scene in which he had brushed with death and come out in one piece, never to learn the entire truth—and bitter was the knowledge that it was in an underhanded way, with a stab in the back, that he had killed his deliverer.

THE INQUEST

"Next witness—Shennan Quine!"

"Quine, sir!"

"You are to testify before the Cosmic Tribunal, now in session, over which I am presiding. You will please address me as 'Your Honor' and members of the jury as 'Your Honors.' You are to answer promptly all questions put to you by the jury and by myself; those of the prosecution and defense, only with the Tribunal's prior consent. Only testimony based on first-hand knowledge will be admissible, nothing on hearsay. Are my instructions clear?"

"Yes, Your Honor."

"Is Shennan Quine your proper name?"

"It is, Your Honor."

"But aboard the *Goliath* you used an alias, did you not?"

"It was one of the conditions of my contract with the shipowners."

"Were you aware of the reason for this alias?"

"I was, Your Honor."

"Were you aboard the *Goliath* on an orbital flight from the eighteenth to the thirtieth of October of this year?"

"I was, Your Honor."

"What were your flight duties?"

"I was the copilot."

"Kindly tell the Tribunal what happened aboard the *Go-*

liath on the twenty-first of October, during the afore-mentioned voyage, starting with a description of the ship's bearings and objectives."

"At 0830 hours, ship's time, we crossed the perimeter of Saturn's moons at a hyperbolic velocity and commenced braking until 1100 hours. Dropping below the hyperbolic to a double-zero orbital, we prepared to launch the artificial satellites onto the plane of the rings."

"By double zero, you mean a velocity of fifty-two kilometers per second?"

"Correct, Your Honor. At 1100 hours I went off duty, but since the perturbations required constant course corrections, I simply traded places with the chief pilot; from then on, he piloted and I navigated."

"Who told you to switch?"

"The CO, Your Honor; it was standard procedure. Our mission was to get within safe distance of the Roche limit on the rings' plane, and from there, practically orbital, to fire a series of three automatic probes, to be guided by remote control inside the Roche. One probe was to be injected into the Cassini Division, the other two were for tracking the first. Shall I elaborate?"

"Please do."

"Very well. Each of Saturn's rings is composed of small meteorlike bodies, the ring widths reaching thousands of kilometers. The satellite, once placed in orbit inside the Cassini Division, was to monitor the perturbations in its gravitational field and the interaction of the ring particles. To stop the satellite from being thrown by the perturbations onto the outer or inner rings, we had to use satellites powered by low-thrust ionic engines in the .20–.25-ton range. The two radar-equipped 'guardians' were to keep the third satellite, orbiting inside the Division, on course. The satellites were equipped with on-board computers for course corrections and rocket control, with enough thrust to keep them orbital for a couple of months."

"Why two monitors? Wouldn't one have been enough?"

"Definitely. The second 'guardian' was to serve as back-up, in case of a malfunction or a meteorite collision. Circum-Saturnian space—rings and moons aside—looks empty from Earth, but in fact it's a junkyard. That's why our mission was to maintain orbital velocity—nearly all of Saturn's particles revolve on its equatorial plane at primary cosmic velocity. This reduced the chances of collision to a minimum. We were also equipped with meteorite deflectors, which could be deployed manually or by a servo-mechanism hooked up to the ship's radar."

"Did you personally consider such a mission difficult or dangerous?"

"Neither, sir, provided we kept to our trajectory. Circum-Saturnian space has a bad name in our trade, worse than Jupiter's, though it sure beats Jupiter for accelerating."

"What do you mean by 'in our trade'?"

"Among pilots and navigators, sir."

"Astronauts, in other words?"

"Affirmative. Well, a little before 1200 hours, we'd almost reached the outermost ring—"

"On its plane?"

"Yes. The densimeters were showing high particle density, about four hundred microcollisions per minute. We entered the Roche zone above the rings, as programmed, and prepared to launch the probes from our orbit, now almost parallel to the Cassini Division. We fired the first at 1500 hours and jockeyed it into the gap. I was in charge of guidance. The pilot helped by maintaining minimal thrust, locking us into almost the same orbital velocity as the rings. Calder was doing a great job, giving just enough thrust to keep the ship properly trimmed, to keep her from cartwheeling."

"Besides yourself and the chief pilot, who else was in the control room?"

"The whole crew, sir. The CO sat between Calder and myself, his chair positioned so he could be closer to the pilot. Seated behind me were the two engineers. Dr. Burns, as I recall, sat behind the CO."

"You're not sure?"

"I wasn't paying attention; I was too busy. Besides, it's hard to see over a pilot's high-backed couch.

"Was the probe visually inserted?"

"Not only that, sir. I was tracking it on video and with the radar altimeter. After checking its coordinates, I decided it was situated well enough, more or less in the center of the gap, and told Calder I was ready."

"Ready?"

"For the next probe launch. Calder fired the sledge, the hatch opened, but the probe wouldn't eject."

"The 'sledge'?"

"The hydraulically driven piston that ejected the probe from the launch bay once the hatch was opened. There were three, all mounted aft, to be fired in rapid succession."

"So the second satellite never left the ship?"

"No, it got jammed in the launcher."

"Please tell us exactly how it happened."

"The sequence works as follows. The outer hatch is opened, the hydraulics are activated, and as soon as the clearance signal comes on, the servo-starter is fired. The starter self-ignites after a hundred-second delay, so there is always time to abort in case of a failure. Once the small solid-fuel booster is fired, the satellite takes off on its own fifteen-tons-per-second thrust. The object is to clear it from the mother ship as fast as possible. When the booster burns out, an ionic engine, remote-controlled by the navigator, fires automatically. In our case, Calder had switched on the servo-starter as soon as the satellite started to clear—and when it suddenly stalled, he tried to shut down booster ignition, but couldn't."

"You're positive the chief pilot tried to switch off the probe's servo-starter?"

"Yes. He was yanking on the abort switch, but it kept flipping back. I don't know why the starter ignited. But I heard him yell: 'Jammed!' "

"Jammed?"

"Something jammed back there. With half a minute to go before booster ignition, he tried a second time, raising the pressure; the manometers were on maximum, but the probe wouldn't come unjammed. He fired the piston again and we felt it hit like a hammer."

"Was he trying to *blast* it out?"

"Yes, sir. It was bound to destruct anyway, due to the sudden build-up of pressure. By the way, that showed a lot of savvy—we might have had a spare probe, but not a spare ship."

"The witness will refrain from embellishing his testimony with such flourishes."

"Well, anyway, the piston didn't free it. Time was running out, so I yelled, 'Buckle up, everyone!' and fastened my seatbelt as tight as it would go. A couple of others yelled the same. One of them was the CO; I recognized his voice."

"Will the witness kindly explain his actions?"

"We were orbiting above a ring—at almost zero thrust, in other words. I knew that once the booster fired—and it had to, since the starter was on—we'd get a side reaction and start tumbling. The jammed probe was starboard, facing Saturn, which meant it had to act as a side deflector. I was all set for some somersaults and centrifugal force, and knew the pilot would have to compensate. There was no telling what might develop, so I decided it was better to play it safe and buckle up."

"Are we to understand that as the copilot and navigator on duty, you had your seatbelt undone?"

"Not undone, sir, just loosened. They're adjustable. When

a pilot has his seatbelt buckled all the way—or, as we say, 'to the hilt'—he has little freedom of movement."

"The witness is aware that a slackened or otherwise improperly fastened seatbelt is against regulations?"

"Yes, Your Honor, I knew it was against regs, but it was common practice."

"Meaning?"

"It's been allowed on every ship I've ever flown."

"The commonness of the infraction doesn't make it less wrong. Please continue."

"As expected, the satellite's booster fired. The ship began to rotate on its transverse axis, and we were simultaneously, but gradually, deflected from our orbital path. The pilot compensated with side thrust, but it didn't work."

"And why not?"

"I wasn't at the controls, but my guess is that it couldn't be done. The probe was wedged in the open launch bay, leaking fumes, and the backwash made for an unstable emission. Because of the fluctuating impulses, any correction through compensatory thrust resulted in a lateral swing, and when the booster burned out, we went into an inverse spin. It took the pilot a while to regain control, once he realized the booster had cut out but that the ionic engine was still running."

" 'Cut out'?"

"The pilot couldn't be sure of engine ignition, not after trying to force-eject the probe. Maybe he meant to disable it; in his place, I'd have done the same. As it turned out, after the booster died the ionic kept functioning, and again we had a side deflection, of about a quarter ton. It wasn't much, but enough to make us tumble. At orbital velocity, the slightest variability in acceleration can upset your trajectory and stability."

"How did the crew react?"

"Quite calmly, sir. Everyone was aware of the risk: an

ignited booster inside that jammed launch bay was like a hundred-kilo bomb. If it had exploded, it would have ripped our starboard side wide open like a tin can. Luckily for us it didn't, and the ionic engine, minus the booster, was rendered harmless. Oh, yes, there was one complication: the automatic fire extinguisher started dousing number-two launcher. Our luck, too, because the foam— foam is useless against ionic—started spuming from the open hatch. Some of it was sucked up into the probe's exhaust, causing the thrust to choke. The pilot finally managed to shut down the fire-alarm system, but for a few minutes there, we were buffeted around, not too bad, but enough to destabilize us."

"Who tripped the alarm system?"

"The thermocouple, sir, when the temperature jumped more than seven hundred degrees in the starboard hull. It was the heat from the booster."

"Were any commands or instructions given by the commander?"

"Not a one, like he was sitting tight, waiting to see how the pilot would handle it. Basically, there were two options: either to break away and fly back up to the ecliptic—to give up, in other words—or to try to launch the third satellite. To quit meant to abort the program. Caught in the drift, without a 'guardian' to correct its course, the probe already in the Division would be pulverized in a matter of hours."

"Wasn't that a decision for the ship's commanding officer to make?"

"Should I answer that, Your Honor?"

"The witness will respond to the prosecutor's question."

"The CO *could* have ordered the maneuver, but he didn't have to. Article 16 of the Deck Operations Code gives the pilot the right, in certain situations, to assume the duties of the ship's CO. Situations demanding split-second decisions, for example."

"But in this particular instance, the commander *was* able to give orders, since the ship was neither accelerating, in which case the g-force would have precluded giving any oral commands, nor in any imminent danger of break-up."

"Shortly after 1500 hours, the pilot applied compensatory thrust—"

"The witness is being evasive. Will the Tribunal admonish the witness and bid him answer my question?"

"Gentlemen, I'm supposed to answer questions, but the prosecutor didn't ask a question. He was offering his own personal commentary on the situation aboard ship. Am I, then, to comment on his commentary?"

"The prosecutor will kindly address the witness with a question, and the witness will oblige by cooperating to the fullest."

"In view of the circumstances, ought not the commander to have made a definite decision and relayed it to the pilot in the form of a command?"

"The Code doesn't specify—"

"The witness will address the Tribunal."

"Yes, sir. The Code can't possibly project every on-board situation. Impossible. If it could, the crew would have only to memorize it and there'd be no need for a commander."

"Your Honor, the prosecution objects to such facetious remarks!"

"The witness will provide an answer to the prosecutor's question, brief and to the point."

"Yes, Your Honor. In my judgment, no, the CO could have waived such a decision. He was there, he sized up the situation; if he kept quiet, it meant he was abiding by Article 22 of Deck Operations, relying on his pilot's discretion."

"Your Honors, not Article 22, but Article 26, which deals with the waiving of command in dangerous situations, is relevant here."

"Your Honors, the situation aboard the *Goliath* endangered neither the ship nor the crew's safety."

"The witness, Your Honors, is being deliberately uncooperative; instead of helping to ascertain the truth, he is trying, *per fas et nefas,* to exonerate the accused, Commander Pirx. The situation on board the *Goliath* definitely falls within the purview of Article 26!"

"Your Honors, surely the prosecutor can't double as an expert witness."

"The witness is out of order. The relevance of Article 22 versus Article 26 will await a separate ruling. The witness will describe the next sequence of events."

"Calder never said a word to the CO, but I saw him look his way several times. Meanwhile, the probe's thrust stabilized, making it easier to control the ship. Calder now decided to move away from the ring, but when he didn't ask me to plot our return flight, I figured he meant to complete the mission. But as soon as we crossed the Roche limit, at approximately 1600 hours, he signaled maximum *g*-load and tried to jettison."

"Meaning what?"

"Meaning he shifted to maximum thrust, then blasted full power astern, then full ahead. A three-ton probe at full acceleration weighs about twenty times that. It should have popped out of that bay like a pea from a pod. With a leeway of sixteen thousand kilometers, Calder repeated the maneuver, twice, but with the same results. The bursts only increased the angle of deflection. Probably due to the sudden boost in acceleration, the satellite, now more jammed than ever, changed position, so that its exhaust fumes were deflected against the partially open hatch and escaped into space. The blasts were as wicked as they were risky: it was now a safe bet that if the probe ever jettisoned, it would take a fair amount of the hull along with it. So it looked like either a repair job out on the hull, or a tow back to Base."

"Didn't Calder try to shut off the probe's engine?"

"Couldn't, sir—the steering cable was disconnected. There was still radio control, but the probe sat in the very mouth of the launcher, screened by the bay's metal housing. We'd been on the outbound leg for roughly a minute, and I thought: He's decided to abort after all. He maneuvered around for a 'star fix'—you know, aiming the ship's nose at a star and then alternating thrust to see if the star remains fixed on the screen. It didn't check out, naturally; our flight characteristics had changed, and Calder tried to juggle the numerical values. By trial and error, he found the right thrust level, which straightened the deflection; then he reversed course."

"Was the witness aware at that time of Calder's real intent?"

"Yes—I mean, I had a hunch he was still planning to launch the third probe. We went back down the ecliptic, away from the sun. Calder's stick work was flawless. You'd have never guessed he was piloting a ship with a sort of extra, built-in, side engine. When he asked me to compute the course corrections, flight trajectory, and steering impulses for a third launch, that cinched it."

"Did the witness comply?"

"No, sir. I told him I couldn't, not before reprogramming. I requested more flight data—I didn't know from what altitude he wanted to inject the last satellite—but he didn't answer. Maybe his request was his way of telling the commander what he was up to."

"He could have told the commander outright."

"Maybe he didn't want to. Maybe he didn't want anyone to think he was stuck and needed help. Or he just wanted to prove himself by showing up his navigator—meaning me. But the CO didn't bat an eye, and Calder kept right on course. That's when it started to look hairy."

"Will the witness be more precise?"

"Touch and go, sir."

"Your Honors will note that the witness has just confirmed what he was reluctant to admit earlier—namely, that the commander, consciously, with premeditation, decided not to intervene, as it was his duty to do, thereby exposing the ship and its crew to inordinate risks."

"Not so, Your Honors!"

"Kindly refrain from arguing with the prosecution, and confine your testimony to the actual chain of events. Why did you deem it a risky operation only after Calder had reversed course?"

"Maybe I expressed myself badly. It's like this: in such circumstances, the pilot should have consulted with his commander. I certainly would have, especially since the original program was no longer operant. I thought that Calder, seeing as the CO was giving him a free hand, would chance an insertion, keeping a safe distance from the ring. The distance made a successful launch iffy, but it was still possible—and safe. At low velocity, he did in fact request a course projection for the satellite, allowing for a lead of one to two thousand kilometers. I wanted to help him, so I started plotting; it turned out that the tolerance was more or less equal to the width of the Cassini Division. This meant there was a fifty-fifty chance that the probe, instead of being injected into the proper orbit, would be pulled inside, toward the planet, or outside, smack up against the ring. I worked out the results for him—for lack of anything better to do."

"Did your commander read the data?"

"He must have; the display was centrally located, right above our consoles. We were cruising at low thrust, and I had the feeling Calder was in trouble. If he backed out now, it would mean he had miscalculated, that his intuition had failed him. Up until he reversed course, he could have argued it wasn't worth the risk. But, then, he'd already shown he could control the ship, despite the changed flight characteristics, and his subsequent moves made it clear he was going ahead with the maneuver. We were gaining on the ring—to give us a better shot at it, I thought at the time, in which case he should have already been braking, not boosting the thrust. Only then did it dawn on me that he might be up to something else. In a flash, everyone was clued in."

"You mean the crew realized the gravity of the situation?"

"Yes, Your Honor. Someone behind me, sitting astern, said, 'It's been sweet.' "

"Who said that?"

"I don't know. The nucleonics engineer, maybe, or the radio-electronics engineer. I wasn't paying attention. It all happened so fast. Calder signaled maximum g-load, throttled, and kept on a collision course with the ring. It was clear he wanted to thread the Cassini and plop the third probe along the way."

" 'Plop' it?"

"Pilot's lingo, sir. The probe is dropped the way a bird on the wing plops an egg. . . . But the CO countermanded him."

"The CO did? He actually countermanded him?"

"Aye, aye, sir."

"Objection. The witness is manipulating the facts. The commander could not have revoked any order."

"Correction. The CO *tried* to give the order, but couldn't complete it. Calder's peak alert came only a split second before the maneuver. The CO yelled as soon as the red light went on, but the g-force—over fourteen!—took his voice away, as if Calder wanted to shut him up. I'm not saying he meant to, but that's how it looked. The g-force was so bad my eyesight dimmed. Small wonder the CO could barely raise his voice."

"I object, Your Honor. The witness is insinuating that Calder, willfully and with malice aforethought, tried to prevent the commander from issuing an order."

"I said nothing of the sort."

"The witness is out of order. Objection sustained. The witness's words beginning with '. . . as if Calder wanted to shut him up' will be stricken from the record. The witness will abstain from any commentary and will quote the commander's exact words."

"Like I said, even if the order was never given in full, the gist of it was clear. He wanted to nix Calder's plan of entering the Cassini."

"Objection. Only what the accused actually said, not what he *wanted* to say, is admissible as evidence."

"Sustained. The witness will restrict himself to what was actually said in the control room."

"Enough was said to make any professional astronaut know that the CO was denying the pilot clearance."

"The witness will cite his exact words and let the Tribunal form its own opinion as to their actual meaning."

"That's just it, Your Honor. I can't remember the exact words, only their sense. It sounded like 'Not through—' or 'Don't thread the rings.' "

"Earlier the witness claimed the commander couldn't manage a full sentence, whereas the words just quoted— 'Don't thread the rings'—constitute a complete sentence."

"If a fire broke out in this room and I yelled 'Fire!' it wouldn't be a full sentence, it wouldn't say what was on fire or where, but it would sure give fair warning."

"Objection! The Tribunal will call the witness to order!"

"The witness is reprimanded. You are not here to edify the Tribunal with parables and anecdotes. Please confine yourself to a factual account of what transpired on board."

"Yes, Your Honor. What happened on board was that the CO denied the pilot clearance into the Cassini."

"Objection! The witness is twisting the facts to suit his purpose!"

"The Tribunal wishes to be obliging. Try to understand that the purpose of this inquiry is to establish the material facts in the case. Can you or can you not reproduce the commander's exact words?"

"We were running at peak, I was having a dim-out—no, I didn't catch the words, but their message was clear enough. The pilot was seated closer to the commander; if anyone should have heard, he should have."

"Defense requests a re-examination of the control-room tapes, of the segment in question."

"Permission denied. The tapes have already been examined; the distortion was such as to permit voice identification only. The Tribunal will rule separately on its admissibility as evidence. Will the witness describe what occurred next?"

"By the time I regained my eyesight, we were on a collision course with the ring. The accelerometer now read two g's, our velocity at parabolic. The CO yelled, 'Calder! You disobeyed orders! I told you not to enter the Cassini!' and Calder immediately said, 'Didn't hear you, Commander.' "

"And yet the commander still didn't give the order to brake or reverse course?"

"It was too late, Your Honor. We were hitting a hyperbolic of about eighty kilometers per second. There was no chance of our braking now, not without crossing the gravitational barrier."

"What do you mean by 'gravitational barrier'?"

"A constant positive or negative acceleration in excess of twenty to twenty-two g's. The longer you're on a collision course, the greater the amount of reverse thrust needed for braking. Maybe fifty g's at first, later a hundred. That would have been lethal—for the humans on board, anyway."

"Technically, did the ship have such an acceleration capacity?"

"Yes, sir, it did—once the interlocks were off, but only then. The *Goliath* had a pile with a ten-thousand-ton maximal thrust output."

"You may resume."

" 'Are you fixing to break up the ship?' the CO asked, sort of casually. 'We'll thread the Cassini and I'll brake on the other side,' said Calder, just as casually. During this exchange, we went into a lateral spin. The sudden boost in acceleration, when Calder put her on course for the Division, must have realigned the probe, lessening the deflection but causing a gas flow—the reason for the longitudinal spin—

along the ship's tangent. The rotations got faster by the second. It was the beginning of the end. Calder had accidentally triggered it by making the huge jump in acceleration."

"Please elaborate on why, in your opinion, Calder increased acceleration."

"Objection, Your Honor. Being biased, the witness will claim, as before, that Calder was trying to silence the commander."

"Not at all. Calder didn't have to rev so fast, with such a burst; he could have built up speed gradually. But if it was entry he wanted, then full was necessary. We were in a tough maneuvering space, a mathematically unsolvable multi-bodied gravitational field. With all the rings and moons around Saturn, plus the planetary pull, there's no way to figure all the perturbations. And don't forget we had a side deflection. Our trajectory was the product of many forces—including the ship's own thrust, relative to the gravitational pull of the masses orbiting in space. So the greater our thrust rate, the smaller the influence of the interfering bodies, whose values were constant. By increasing our velocity, Calder made our course less sensitive to outside interference. I'm willing to bet that, if not for the sudden lateral spin, he would have cleared the Division."

"Are you implying that the Division is navigable in a fully flightworthy ship?"

"I'm saying it *is* possible, sir, despite what you read in the textbooks. The Division is roughly three or four thousand kilometers wide, walled with meteorite and ice particles invisible to the eye, but dense enough to burn up a ship moving at hyperbolic. The amount of clearance—of clean, navigable space—is about five or six hundred kilometers in width. Entry is fairly easy at low velocities; at higher, you risk a gravitational drift; that's why Calder first aligned the bow and then throttled to full. If the probe hadn't shifted, it would have worked, in my judgment, anyway, except there was always the chance—about thirty to one—of our hitting the odd particle. But then came that longitudinal roll. Calder tried to control it, but couldn't. He put up a good fight, I'll say that."

"What prevented Calder from correcting the rotations?"

"From previous observation, I knew him to be a whiz of a mathematician. He trusted a lot in his ability to do fast computations, without the help of a calculator. Clearing the Cassini at a hyperbolic speed, handicapped as we were, was like threading the eye of a needle. The thrust gauges gave readings for the *Goliath*, but not for the probe. Calder navigated entirely by the gravimeters. It was a real mathematical race—between himself and the increasing flight variables. I could barely keep up with the digital displays, and there was Calder constructing four-part differential equations in his head! Much as I disliked his disobeying orders, I have to admit I admired the guy."

"You haven't really answered the question."

"I was just getting around to it, sir. Calder's estimations could never have been more than approximate, not even if he were the world's fastest computer. No, sir, not with the increasing margin of error and the ship in a roll . . . For a minute there, I thought he might swing it, but then he saw—even before I did—that the game was up, and he hit the kill switch, dropping us down to zero-*g*."

"Why did he shut off the thrust?"

"He wanted a straight trajectory through the Division, but couldn't stop the ship's longitudinal spin. Like a spinning top, the *Goliath* repelled the force trying to right it. We wound up in a precession: the higher our velocity, the greater the torque. The result was a prolonged spin, accompanied by simultaneous listing, with each spiral measuring about a hundred kilometers in diameter. With such a roll, we could have sideswiped a ring. Now Calder was stuck. He was caught in a funnel."

"A 'funnel'?"

"Slang for a dead-end situation, Your Honor: easy to enter, but no way out. By now our flight was unchartable. When Calder hit the kill switch, I thought he was betting on his luck. The digital displays were jumping, but there was nothing to compute. The rings were blinding, full of ice chunks whirling around in the Division's black crevasse. Time dragged, the chronometers seemed to be at a standstill. All of a sudden, Calder unbuckled his seatbelt. So did I: I could read his mind. Flip the main overload fuse on the dash! With full power, he could still brake and pull out once he got her up to a hundred *g*'s. We'd all pop our guts, but he'd save the ship—and his own skin. I should have guessed beforehand that he wasn't human, because no human could process the way he did. . . . I wanted to stop him before he reached the dash, but he was too fast. He had to be. 'Keep buckled up!' the CO barked at me; and to Calder, 'Hands off the fuse!' Calder ignored him; he was already on his feet. 'Full blast ahead!' the CO yelled, and I obeyed orders. I revved to five—I didn't want to kill him, just make him back-pedal—but he stayed on his feet. It was a gruesome sight, gentlemen—no human can keep upright at five *g*'s! But he did. When he grabbed hold of the dash, he ripped the skin from both palms; he held on, though, because his hands were now bared to the metal. Then I juiced her to full. At fourteen, a metal hulk blitzed between our couches and slammed so hard against the rear wall it shattered. I heard some ungodly voice; I could hear him writhing around back there, flattening bulkheads, mangling everything he grabbed, but then I lost track; we were careening into the Division. I dropped her down to four *g*'s and trusted to old lady luck. The CO yelled, 'Shoot!' and I began firing the meteorite deflectors, one after another, to keep the bow space clear of any small debris: not much protection, but better than nothing. The Cassini was pitch-black, a gaping gullet; I saw a fire up ahead, off the bow; the shields deployed and ignited on impact; silver clouds rose and—*poof!*—it was too beautiful for words. The ship shook, the starboard thermocouples registered the shock, we sideswiped something, no telling what, and then we were in the clear again. . . ."

"Commander Pirx?"

"Pirx reporting. You wanted to see me?"

"Thank you for coming. Have a seat."

The man behind the desk touched a button on a black intercom and said, "I'll be tied up for the next twenty minutes. I'm not here—for anyone."

He switched off the intercom and stared at the man seated opposite him.

"Commander, I have a—hm—special proposition for you. A sort of"—he was again searching for the right word—"experiment. But you're to keep it strictly confidential. Even if you turn it down. Agreed?"

A silence lasting several seconds.

"Nothing doing," said Pirx, and then added: "Not unless you give me more details."

"Nothing sight unseen, is that it? That figures. I should have known from what I've heard about you. Cigarette?"

"No, thanks."

"It's a test flight."

"New model?"

"New type of crew."

"Crew? And my job?"

"The usual—a fitness test. That's all I can tell you. It's up to you."

"When I think an answer is possible, I'll answer."

"Possible?"

"Advisable."

"By what criteria?"

"By what is known as a conscience, sir."

Another pause. The spacious office, glass-walled on one side, was so hushed it seemed isolated from the two thousand others packed into this high-rise, which was sprawling enough to accommodate three helicopter pads. Silhouetted against the blinding cloud vapor that shrouded the upper sixteen stories, the man interviewing Pirx was featureless. From time to time the vapor behind the transparent wall swelled into milk-white billows, making the whole room seem mysteriously afloat, cloud-borne.

"As you see, I'm an accommodating man. It's a Terra-Terra run."

"A loop?"

"With a circum-Saturn pass, and from there an injection of some brand-new, fully automated satellites into stationary."

"The Jupiter project?"

"The satellite end of it. The ship is one of COMSEC's, so the whole thing has UNESCO sponsorship. Why you and not one of our own pilots or navigators? We picked you because of the crew angle I mentioned."

The UNESCO space director fell silent again. Pirx waited, strained his ears; but not a sound was to be heard, not for kilometers around, it seemed, even though they were in the heart of a great city.

"Surely you're aware of the advances made in the manufacture of automata, in robotics. The most sophisticated androids, because of their weight and size, have been stationary until now. But solid-state physics, in both the U.S. and the U.S.S.R., has opened a new chapter in micro-miniaturization—the molecular. Prototypical brain systems, crystal-based, are now in the experimental stage. Their size—they're still about one and a half times the size of our brain—is unimportant. Many American firms have already patented the molecular design and are ready to go into production. The new androids—or 'finite nonlinears,' as they're called—are primarily designed for unmanned space exploration."

"I've heard reports. But I thought the unions had come out against them. It would mean, I take it, overhauling the existing legislation."

"Reports, you say? Rumors, yes, but otherwise the media—"

"Among the rank and file there were leaks of some hush-hush negotiations, of high-level talks. You can understand our concern," Pirx said.

"Very much so. All to the good, actually . . . Although . . . What's your own opinion?"

"On this subject? Negative. Damned negative, in fact. But opinions don't count here, I'm afraid. Scientific breakthroughs will have their way, no matter what. At best, one can play a stalling game."

"In short, you regard it as a necessary evil."

"I wouldn't put it that way. I just don't think mankind is ready for an invasion of androids. But the real question is: are they human equivalents? If so, then I've never met any. I'm no expert, but the experts I know think full equivalence, real interchangeability, is wishful thinking."

"You wouldn't be biased, would you?" the space director asked. "True, a lot of trained experts share your opinion, or at least they used to. But, well, these companies are in it for economic reasons, as a business venture. . . ."

"For the money, you mean."

"You see, the design specifications were developed by government-financed institutes—U.S. mainly, but also British and French—and not all the specs have been released to the commercial market. Still, the private firms have their own research labs and—"

"Cybertronics?"

"Cybertronics, Machintrex, Inteltron, to name just a few. The point is, the governments of these countries are worried about the fallout—jobwise. The private sector couldn't care less about the financing of government retraining programs for those who'll be phased out by the nonlinears."

"Nonlinears, eh? Quaint."

"Shorthand slang; it's 'in' now. Anyhow, it's better than

'homunculus' or 'android.' I mean, they aren't human, after all."

"Not fully interchangeable, you mean?"

"You know, Commander, I'm not an expert in such matters, either. . . . Anyway, what *I* think is quite immaterial. The main thing is, one of the first comers would be COSNAV."

"That privately owned Anglo-American company?"

"That's the one. Cosmic Navigation has been floundering for years. The Communist bloc's astronautical systems, being noncommercial, make for stiff competition, so stiff they've cornered the bulk of the cargo traffic. Especially on the extraterrestrial runs. You must know that."

"Who doesn't? Personally, I wouldn't be a bit sorry if COSNAV went bust. If space exploration could be internationalized under the UN, why not the shipping trade? That's my opinion, anyway."

"Mine, too. Believe me, I'm all for it, if only because I'm sitting at this desk. But these are castles in the air. Meanwhile, COSNAV wants to corner the nonlinears for their own lines—at the moment, only for their cargo fleet; they're afraid of a public boycott if they install them on their passenger lines. Preliminary negotiations are already under way, in fact."

"And the media are keeping it under wraps?"

"The talks aren't official. Some of the papers have dropped hints, but COSNAV categorically denies everything. Technically, they're right, Commander. It's an honest-to-goodness labyrinth. The truth is, they're operating in a legally shady area, beyond any national or even UN jurisdiction. And with the elections not far away, the President doesn't dare try to railroad through Congress any of the bills backed by the powerful intellectronic lobby—for fear of antagonizing the professional unions. That's why—and this is the real crux of the matter—a number of firms, anticipating adverse publicity, protests from organized labor, and so on, decided to let us test a group of semi-prototypes—"

"Excuse me, by 'us' do you mean the UN? Isn't that a little—"

"By 'us' I mean UNESCO; you know, the United Nations Education, Scientific—"

"Sorry, but I still don't—I mean, what do these robots have to do with education, science . . . ?"

"An 'invasion,' as you put it, of those . . . uh . . . pseudo people has everything to do with human culture. It's not just a case of economics—the risk of higher unemployment and so on. The implications are legion: psychological, social, cultural. By the way, just for the record, we accepted their offer with reluctance. In fact, the administration would have rejected it out of hand, except the company made assurances that the nonlinears were a better safety risk. Quicker reflexes, immune to fatigue or illness, great energy reserves, functional even during decompression or overheating, not dependent on oxygen or food. These are real gains—not as profits in some owner's pocket, but as they benefit ship and cargo safety. In which case, the credit, or at least some of the credit . . . I mean, a test flight sponsored by the UN . . ."

"I see. But wouldn't that be setting a dangerous precedent?"

"Why dangerous?"

"Who knows what other professions and administrative positions might not be phased out. Even yours."

The director gave a somewhat forced laugh, which quickly abated.

"Well, well . . . that's beside the point. But what would you do in our position? Even if we were to turn them down, what good would it do? If the nonlinears are really that good, COSNAV will get its robots anyway, and the others will be next in line."

"What's to be gained by having UNESCO act as engineering consultant?"

"Who said anything about engineering? What we wanted—and I may as well give it to you straight—was for you to take command of that flight. In the space of one to two weeks—don't forget, there will be different models aboard—you'll know what sort of crew you have. All we ask is that on your return you submit a complete rundown, point by point, of their astronautical as well as psychological fitness: how do they adjust to man, are they true to type, do they inspire a sense of superiority, or on the contrary of inferiority. . . . Our people will supply you with forms prepared by the top psychologists in the field."

"And that would be my mission?"

"You don't have to commit yourself right away. As I recall, you're on leave anyway."

"On a six-week furlough."

"You could give us your decision, say, in a couple of days."

"Two more questions. How decisive will my report be?"

"Very."

"For whom?"

"For us, of course. UNESCO. If the shipping trade is ever to be internationalized, your verdict will be crucial to those UN committees."

"Those—excuse me—castles in the air you mentioned. Crucial to UNESCO, in other words? Not that UNESCO will be turned into an agency . . . ?"

"Not a chance! Your appraisal will be publicized worldwide. A negative rating would seriously impair negotiations between COSNAV and those companies. That way, we'll be contributing—"

"Excuse me again. Meaning that if it's positive, we won't?"

The director cleared his throat, then smiled.

"You almost make me feel guilty, Commander. It wasn't we at UNESCO who invented those nonlinear robots. We try to be impartial, to accommodate everyone."

"That's just what I don't like."

"You can always say no. But remember, if we were to do the same, we'd be no better than Pontius Pilate. Washing your hands of everything is easy. We're not a world government; we can't outlaw the manufacture of this or of any other system. That's up to the individual governments. Anyway, they've tried—believe me, I know. So has the church, and you know where they stand on the issue."

"In short, all are against it, but no one does anything about it."

"No legal grounds."

"Those firms will be the first to feel it when the unemployment rate—"

"Now it's my turn to interrupt. There's truth in what you say. We all tremble at the prospect. Still, we're powerless. Or maybe not quite. We can still go ahead with the experiment. Actually, it's all to the good that you're biased. That makes you the ideal candidate. If there are the slightest reservations, you'll make them known!"

"Let me sleep on it," said Pirx, and he got up.

"Didn't I hear you say something about *two* questions?"

"You've already answered the other one. I wanted to know why me."

"Phone us your decision in two days' time. A deal?"

"A deal," said Pirx, who nodded and took his leave.

The secretary, a platinum blonde, sprang up from behind her desk.

"Good morning," said Pirx. "I—"

"Good morning. Follow me, please."

"They're here already?"

"They're waiting for you."

She took him down a deserted corridor, her high heels tapping like tiny metal stilts. The cavernous hall, tiled with synthetic granite, resonated coldly, stonelike. They passed dark doors mounted with aluminum numbers and plates. The secretary seemed nervous. Several times she glanced furtively at Pirx. Not a flirting glance; more like fearful. Pirx felt somehow sorry for her and, along with it, sensed the absolute folly of the affair. Suddenly he asked, startling even himself with his question:

"Have you seen them?"

"Just briefly. In passing."

"What are they like?"

"Oh—you haven't seen them?"

She seemed almost relieved. As if familiarity bespoke membership in some strange, perhaps sinister conspiracy.

"There are six all together. One even spoke to me. Absolutely convincing! Not a single telltale sign! If I'd met him in the street, I'd never have dreamed . . . But when I took a closer look, there was something in his eyes, and here." She touched her lips.

"The others, too?"

"They were standing outside in the corridor."

They got into the elevator; tiny golden grains of light snaked up the wall. Standing face to face with the girl, Pirx was better able to judge the success of her efforts to erase all vestiges of her own individuality—with the help of pencil, mascara, and lipstick—to become a momentary facsimile of Inda Lea, or whatever the name was of that season's fashionably frazzled star. When she fluttered her eyelids, he was concerned for her false lashes.

"Robots!" she said in a deep whisper, and shuddered as if brushed by a reptile.

The tenth-floor suite was occupied by six men, all seated. The moment Pirx entered, one of them, until now hidden by a sheet of the *Herald Tribune,* folded his paper, rose, and approached him with a broad smile. The others stood up as if on cue.

They were more or less of equal height and looked like test pilots in civvies: broad-shouldered, beige-suited, white-shirted, loud-tied. Two were fair-haired, one a redhead, the others dark, but all had the same clear blue eyes. That was all he had a chance to record before the one who had approached him stuck his hand into Pirx's and, pumping it vigorously, said, "McGuirr's the name. I once had the pleasure of sailing under your command—on the *Pollux,* it was. But you wouldn't remember me. . . ."

"Sorry," admitted Pirx.

McGuirr turned to the others, who were stationed around a circular table littered with magazines.

"Men, meet Commander Pirx, your new CO. Commander, your crew: John Calder, chief pilot; Harry Brown, copilot; Andy Thomson, nucleonics engineer; John Burton, radio-electronics engineer, and Thomas Burns, neurologist, cyberneticist, and medic all rolled into one."

Pirx shook hands with each, then all sat down, sliding their metal-framed chairs, which bent under the weight of their bodies, up closer to the table. Silence reigned until it was rent by McGuirr's stentorian baritone.

"On behalf of the board of directors of Cybertronics, Inteltron and Nortronics, thank you for showing such confidence in our undertaking. To avoid any possible misunderstandings, I should warn you that some among us were born of mothers and fathers, others not. Each knows of his own origin, but not of the others'. You'll be decent enough, I trust, not to probe or pry. Otherwise, you will have a completely free hand. They will be conscientious, and show initiative and character, both on and off duty. But when asked who or what they are, they have all been taught a standard reply: normal human beings. It's not a matter of lying but of necessity, dictated by our mutual interest."

"No questions asked; is that it?"

"Of course you can ask. But since no one will be above suspicion, why bother, frankly? True or false, you'll always get the same answer."

"Which is it in your case?" asked Pirx.

There was a split second's pause before all burst out laughing, McGuirr's cackle being the loudest.

"You *are* a comedian. Me, I'm just a tiny cog in the Nortronics machine. . . ."

A straight-faced Pirx waited for the laughter to die down.

"The joke's on me, in other words?"

"I beg your pardon! The deal spoke of a 'new type of crew'; it said nothing about its uniformity. We just wanted to forestall any . . . purely irrational bias. It stands to reason, doesn't it? We're only trying to create the optimal test conditions, to ensure maximum impartiality."

"Thanks loads!" said Pirx. "Well, tricked or not, I'm not backing out. Now, if you don't mind, I'd like to get acquainted with my"—he hesitated—"people. . . ."

"Hear them recite their qualifications, you mean? By all means! Don't mind me! Shoot!"

McGuirr extracted a cigar from the upper pocket of his smock, cropped the end, and lit it, while five pairs of serene and attentive eyes reposed on Pirx's face. The two blonds, both pilots, looked somewhat alike, though Calder had more Scandinavian features, his curly hair looking almost sunbleached. Brown's was the color of gold; his doll-like, cherubic features, as of a male fashion model, having a prettiness offset only by the jaws and the constant, seemingly sardonic curl of his colorless thin lips. A white scar ran diagonally across his cheek from the left-hand corner of his mouth. It was on him that Pirx's gaze settled first.

"Great . . ." he said, as if in delayed response to McGuirr's invitation, and in the same almost offhand tone, he inquired of the man with the scar:

"Do you believe in God?"

Brown's lips quivered—a suppressed smile? an ironic sneer?—but he made no immediate answer. He looked freshly shaven, a few hairs in the vicinity of his ear and the flecks of foam visible on his cheeks testifying to a job done in some haste.

"Not my department, sir," he answered in a pleasant, purling voice.

McGuirr, caught off guard by Pirx's question, his eyes blinking, suddenly exhaled a trapped puff of cigar smoke, as if to say, "How's that for a comeback?"

"Mr. Brown," said Pirx in the same phlegmatic voice, "you haven't answered my question."

"Sorry, Commander, but as I said, it's not my—"

"As your commanding officer, I'm the one who decides what your duties are."

McGuirr's face registered surprise. Throughout this exchange, the others sat like model pupils, stiff-backed and with undivided attention.

"If that's an order," answered Brown in his soft, clearly modulated baritone, "I can only say I haven't been sufficiently trained to deal with that problem."

"Well, think it over for tomorrow. Your signing on will depend on it."

"Yes, sir."

Pirx turned to Calder, and their eyes met. The suite's spacious window was reflected in the chief pilot's nearly transparent irises.

"You're a pilot?"

"I am."

"Your credentials?"

"I'm certified in team piloting, I've soloed two hundred ninety hours on low tonnage, and I've made ten solo landings, including four on the Moon and two on Mars and Venus."

Pirx, seemingly unimpressed, went on to the next.

"Burton," he said, "are you the radio-electronics engineer?"

"Yes."

"How many rems per hour can you take?"

The man twitched his lips, barely mustering a smile.

"About four hundred, I guess," he said. "Tops. More than that, and it's off to sick bay."

"No more than four hundred?"

"I—no, I don't think so."

"Home state?"

"Arizona."

"Any illnesses?"

"None. Or at least nothing serious."

"How's your eyesight?"

"Good."

Pirx was attending less to what was being said than to the sound of each man's voice, to its modulation and pitch, to the movements of the facial muscles and lips. There were times when he gave way to the senseless hope that it was all a grand but silly hoax intended to make fun of his gullible faith in the omnipotence of technology. Or maybe to punish him for it. Because these were plain, ordinary human beings. That secretary was crazy—oh, the power of prejudice! And to think that she even took McGuirr . . .

Until now, it would have been a fairly routine briefing, if not for his none-too-subtle God question. Not only was that not subtle, it was also in bad taste, sophomoric. Pirx could feel it in his bones; he was a real klutz for trying a cute stunt like that. They were still staring at him, except Thomson, the redhead, and the two pilots seemed more poker-faced than before, as if to conceal the fact that they were wise to the deep-down klutziness of this drone who'd just seen his glib, customary, and ever-so-pat composure blown. He felt compelled to go on, to put an end to the silence, which was growing more incriminating by the second, but his mind drew a blank, leaving only despair to tempt him into doing something wild, screwy, something that, in his heart of hearts, he knew he could never bring himself to do. He'd made a fool of himself; it was time to quit; his eyes sought out McGuirr.

"When can I board?"

"Any time you like. Today, even."

"What about the health inspection?"

"All arranged. Don't worry about it."

The engineer sounded indulgent, or so it seemed to Pirx.

"I *am* a sore loser," he told himself. Then out loud:

"That's it for now. Except for Brown, consider yourselves signed on. Brown, be ready tomorrow with the answer to my question. Mr. McGuirr, do you have the ship's articles ready for signing?"

"I have, but not with me. They're up in the office. Shall we?"

"Let's."

Pirx stood up, and the others did the same.

"Until tomorrow." He nodded, and was the first to exit. The engineer caught up with him by the elevator.

"You underestimated us, Commander."

He was his hearty, jovial self again.

"Oh? In what way?"

The elevator started moving. Carefully, trying not to topple its silver-gray cone of ash, the engineer lifted his cigar to his mouth.

"It's not so easy . . to tell them apart."

Pirx shrugged.

"If they're made of the same stuff as I am," he said, "then they're people, and I don't care a damn how they got here— through artificial insemination, in a test tube, or in the more conventional way."

"But they're not made of the same stuff!"

"Of what, then?"

"Sorry—a company secret."

"What's your part?"

The elevator stopped and the door opened, but Pirx, waiting for an answer, stayed put.

"Do you mean, am I a design engineer? No, I'm in public relations."

"Are you well enough informed to answer a few questions?"

"Gladly, but not here . . ."

The same secretary as before showed them into one of the conference rooms.

A long table, impeccably arrayed with chairs on either side. They sat down at the end where the contracts lay in an open portfolio.

"I'm all yours, Commander," said McGuirr. Some cigar ash spilled, and he blew it off his pants.

Pirx now noticed the bloodshot eyes and perfectly set teeth. "They're false," he thought. "He's trying not to look his age."

"The—uh—nonhumans, do they act like humans? Do they eat meals? Drink?"

"Yes, they do."

"What for?"

"To complete the illusion. For the benefit of those around them."

"So, then, they have to . .　void it?"

"But of course."

"And blood?"

"Pardon me?"

"Do they have blood? A heart? Do they bleed if they're wounded?"

"They have the facsimile of a heart and blood."

"What does that mean?"

"That only a trained specialist, a doctor, could tell the difference, and then only after a thorough examination."

"And I couldn't?"

"No. Assuming you didn't use any special gadgets."

"Like an X-ray machine?"

"Very good! But X-ray machines aren't standard flight equipment."

"Spoken like a true layman," said Pirx calmly. "Isotopes I can get from the pile, as many as I want; and—oh, yes—I'll have to have a fluoroscope aboard. So you see, no X-ray machine needed."

"No objections, provided you agree not to scan."

"And if I don't agree?"

McGuirr sighed and, tamping out his cigar in the ashtray as if he'd suddenly lost the taste for it, said: "Commander, you're doing your utmost to . . . complicate things."

"Right you are!" answered Pirx. "So they do bleed?"

"Yes."

"Real blood? Even under the microscope?"

"Real blood."

"How did you manage *that?*"

"Impressive, huh?" grinned McGuirr. "Works on the sponge principle. A special subcutaneous sponge. More I can't tell you."

"Is it human blood?"

"Yes."

"Why go to such trouble?"

"Obviously not to make a sucker out of you. This multi-billion-dollar investment wasn't only for your sake, you know! It was so no one—the passengers, for example—would ever suspect . . ."

"You're worried about a public boycott?"

"Not only that. There's the psychological comfort."

"Can *you* tell which is which?"

"Only because I know them. OK, there are ways, but . . . I wouldn't advise using a hatchet on them."

"And no other physiological give-aways? Breathing, coughing, blushing . . . ?"

"Minimized. There are differences, sure, but, as I said, only ones a doctor would recognize."

"Psychological?"

"Our greatest breakthrough!" said McGuirr with genuine pride. "Until now, the brain was centrally located because of its size. But Inteltron was the first to fit it in the head!"

"The second, really—nature was the first."

"Har-har! OK—second, then. The specs are still hush-hush, but . . . It's a monocrystal multistat with sixteen billion binary elements!"

"Their emotional capabilities—is that also hush-hush?"

"What do you have in mind?"

"Are they capable, for instance, of telling lies? Can they lose their self-control, control of the situation . . . ?"

"All possible."

"How so?"

"Technically unavoidable. Any breaks—figuratively, of course—introduced into a neuron or crystal system are relative, can be overridden. If you're at all up on the latest, you know that a robot that can match man mentally and not be capable of lying or cheating is a fantasy. Either full equivalents or puppets. Nothing in between."

"Capable of one, capable of the other, right?"

"Yes. But the costs are damned prohibitive. For now, anyway. Psychological versatility, to say nothing of anthropoidality, costs a fortune. The models you'll be getting are experimental prototypes—the price tag per unit is higher than for a supersonic bomber."

"No kidding?"

"That includes the cost of research, of course. We hope to be able to mass-produce, even refine them one day, but for the moment . . . well, we're giving you the top of the line. In any case, their fallibility ratio will be lower than for humans in a comparable situation."

"Were they experimentally tested?"

"How else?"

"With human test subjects for comparison?"

"That, too."

"Under emergency conditions?"

"Those above all."

"And the results?"

"Humans are more error-prone."

"What about their aggression instinct?"

"Toward humans?"

"Not only."

"No need to worry. They come equipped with special built-in inhibitors, called 'reverse-discharge systems,' that cushion the aggression potential."

"In every case?"

"Impossible. Their brain, like ours, is a probability system. The probability of specific responses can be increased, but not raised to a certainty. Though here again they have the edge."

"And if I went to crack the skull of one . . . ?"

"He'd fight back."

"To the point of killing me?"

"In self-defense only."

"And if attack was the only defense?"

"He'd attack."

"Hand me those contracts," said Pirx.

The pen squeaked in the silence. The engineer folded the legal forms, then tucked them into his portfolio.

"Are you heading back to the States?" Pirx asked.

"First thing tomorrow."

"You can tell your superiors I'll try to bring out the worst in them."

"That's the spirit! We're counting on it! Because even their worst is better than man's. Only .   "

"You were about to say?"

"You're a brave man, Pirx. All the same, I'd recommend caution."

"So they don't gang up on me?" said Pirx, forcing a smile.

"So you're not made the fall guy. You see, your humans will be the first to bail out. Your average, decent, good-boy types. Get it?"

"Get it," answered Pirx. "I'll be shoving off now. Time for me to take command of my ship."

"My helicopter is on the roof," said McGuirr, rising to his feet. "Can I give you a lift?"

"No, thanks. I'll take the subway. Don't like to take chances, you know. And you'll tell them that I intend to play rough?"

"If you like."

McGuirr was searching his pockets for a fresh cigar.

"Frankly, I find your attitude a bit strange. What do you expect? They're not human; no one's claiming they are. They're highly trained professionals—and conscientious, too, ready to oblige. They'll do anything for you."

"I'll make sure they do even more," retorted Pirx.

Pirx, not about to let Brown off the hook in the God affair, made a point of phoning him the next day—the "nonlinear" pilot's telephone number was made available courtesy of UNESCO. He dialed and recognized the voice.

"I was expecting your call."

"Well, which is it to be?" asked Pirx. He felt strangely apathetic, not half so blithe as when he had signed McGuirr's papers. At the time, he'd thought: No big deal. Now he wasn't so sure.

"I wasn't given much time," said Brown in that flat, purling voice of his. "So all I can say is, I was taught the probability method. I calculate the odds and act accordingly. In this case, I'd say . . . ninety percent, or even ninety-nine-point-nine percent, it's no, with less than one chance in a hundred it's yes."

"That there is a God?"

"Yes."

"Fine. You can sign on with the others. See you aboard ship."

"Good-bye," answered the softspoken baritone, and the receiver clicked.

Pirx was reminded, out of the blue, of this conversation on his way to the spaceport. Somebody—UNESCO? his crew's "manufacturers"?—had already got clearance from

Port Control. No health inspection, no crew certification, with lift-off scheduled for 1445 hours during the afternoon lull. The three fair-sized satellite probes destined for Saturn were already in their bays. The *Goliath*—a ship of medium tonnage, in the six thousand range, highly computerized, only two years out of the shipyard—had an ultrasmooth, non-oscillating, fast-neutron pile, occupying a mere ten cubic meters in space, with a capacity of forty-five million horsepower, seventy million for quick acceleration.

Pirx knew nothing of his crew's Paris accommodations—a hotel? a company-rented apartment? (a grotesque, macabre thought: maybe McGuirr had unplugged them and boxed them away for the past two days)—or even how they'd got to the port.

They were mustered in a separate room at Port Control, each with suitcase, duffel bag, and a lightweight tote bag with a name tag dangling from the straps. The sight of the duffel bags inspired comic visions of monkey wrenches, cosmetic oilcans, and the like. But he was in no laughing mood as, having said his hellos to everyone, he submitted the flight authorizations and ship's articles needed for final clearance. Then, two hours ahead of launch time, they stepped onto a floodlit pad and filed out to the snow-white *Goliath*. It looked a bit like a giant, freshly uncrated wedding cake.

A routine blast-off. The *Goliath* needed almost no help in lifting off, thanks to a full array of automatic and semi-automatic sequencers. A half hour later, they were already far above Earth's nocturnal hemisphere and its fluorescent rash of cities; and Pirx, although a veteran spaceborne observer of Earth's atmosphere when it was brushed "against the grain" by the sunrise, was now, as always, a willing spectator to this giant sickle of burning rainbow. Minutes later, they passed the last navigational satellite—one of those "electronic bureaucrats of the cosmos," as Pirx dubbed the diligent machines—in a hail of crackle and bleeps, and climbed above the ecliptic. After instructing the chief pilot to stay at the controls, Pirx retired to his cabin. Not ten minutes had passed when there was a knock at the door.

"Yes?"

It was Brown. Gently closing the door behind him, he went up to Pirx, who was lounging on the edge of his bunk, and said in a subdued voice:

"I'd like a few words with you."

"Take a seat."

Brown lowered himself onto a chair, pulled it up closer to cut down the distance between them, kept demurely silent with eyes lowered for a moment, then suddenly looked straight into the CO's eyes.

"I have something to tell you. In confidence. Promise you won't repeat a word?"

Pirx cocked his eyebrows.

"A secret?" He deliberated for a few seconds. "OK, you have my word," he said at last. "I'm all ears."

"I'm human," said Brown, and paused, staring at Pirx to gauge the effect of his words. But Pirx, his eyelids at half mast, his head leaning against the white polyfoam-padded wall, registered no emotion. "I'm coming clean because I want to help you," the visitor resumed, in the tone of someone reciting a well-rehearsed speech. "When I first applied, I didn't know what it was all about—they processed us separately, to keep us from getting acquainted. It wasn't until after I was selected, until after all the flight tests and screenings, that I was briefed. Even then I had to swear absolute secrecy. Look, I have a girl, we want to get married, but financially . . . Well, here was our big break—a cash advance of eight thousand, with another eight thousand payable on signing off, win or lose. These are the facts; I'm clean, really. How was I supposed to know! Some kind of weirdo experiment, that's what I thought at the beginning. Then the whole thing started to get to me. I mean, it's a question of our common cause. . . . Who am I to cover up? I have no right to do that. You agree?"

Pirx's silence prompted the visitor to continue, his self-confidence now a trifle shaken.

"They kept us apart the whole time. Each had his own room, his own john, his own private gym. They even fed us separately, except during the last few days before our departure to Europe. So I can't tell you which of them is human and which isn't. I just don't know. Though I have my suspicions."

"Hold on a sec," Pirx interrupted. "Why did you dodge my question by saying it wasn't 'your department'?"

Brown sat up in his chair, shifted one leg, and, eying his shoe tip, which was doodling something on the floor, said in a hushed voice:

"Because I'd already decided to clue you in, and, well . . . I was in the hot seat. I was afraid McGuirr might get wise. So I answered your question in a way that would make him believe I was—"

"So it was because of McGuirr?"

"Yes."

"And *do* you believe in God?"

"I do."

"But you didn't think a robot would, right?"

"Right."

"That a 'yes' answer would have been a dead give-away?"

"Exactly."

"But even a robot can believe in God," said Pirx after a moment's pause, with a nonchalance that made Brown's eyes bulge.

"Come again?"

"You think not?"

"It never crossed my mind. . ."

"OK, let's skip it. At least for now. You said something about having your suspicions. . . ."

"The dark-haired one—Burns—I'm sure he's not human."

"What makes you so sure?"

"Little things, hard to pinpoint, but they add up. For one thing, when he sits or stands, he doesn't move a muscle. A regular statue. And you know how hard it is for a human to keep still: you're uncomfortable, your leg goes to sleep so you shift positions, you stretch, rub your face. . . . But this guy just plain freezes!"

"All the time?"

"That's just it; not all the time. And that seems to me the tip-off."

"Why tip-off?"

"My guess is that when he remembers, he's all fidgets and bodily motion; but when he forgets, he freezes. With us, it's the other way around: we have to make a conscious effort to keep still."

"You have a point there. What else?"

"He eats everything."

"How so?"

"Whatever comes along. It makes no difference to him. I noticed it on our flight across the Atlantic. Even back in the States, and at the airport restaurant—eats whatever he's served, indiscriminately. I mean, everyone has his likes and dislikes!"

"That doesn't prove anything."

"You're quite right—it doesn't. But in combination with the stiffness . . . ? And another thing."

"Yes?"

"He doesn't write letters. I'm not a hundred percent sure of that . . . but Burton, now, I saw him drop a letter into the hotel mailbox."

"Writing letters is against regs?"

"Yes."

"You're all extremely conscientious, I see," muttered Pirx. He sat up on his bunk and, breathing practically into Brown's face, said in a deliberate tone:

"You broke your oath. Why?"

"Ouch, that hurt, Commander!"

"Well, didn't you swear to keep your identity a secret?"

"Oh, that! Yes, but . . . there are situations when a man has a right—no, a duty—to break his word."

"Such as?"

"This one. I mean, they take a bunch of metal dolls, pad them with plastic, add a little make-up, then shuffle them like phony cards into a deck of humans—and hope to make a killing on the deal. No, any honest man would do what I'm doing. Hasn't anyone else been around to see you?"

"Not yet. You're the first. But we've just lifted off . . ." Pirx said with a tonelessness not devoid of irony; the irony was evidently lost on Brown.

"I'll do whatever you think advisable."

"What for?"

Brown batted his doll-like lashes.

"What for? To help you tell the humans from the nonhumans."

"Eight thousand, wasn't it?"

"So? I was hired on as a pilot, which is what I am. And a damned good one, at that."

"And another eight on signing off—all for a few weeks' work. Brown, no one gets sixteen thousand for a shakedown cruise—not a passenger pilot, not a patrol pilot, not a navigator. You got that money for keeping your mouth shut. They wanted to spare you any temptations."

Dismay was written all over Brown's pretty-boy face.

"So you're offended by my coming, by my confiding in you . . . ?"

"Not at all. What's your IQ?"

"My IQ? A hundred twenty."

"High enough for you to know what's what. Tell me, what do I gain by listening to your suspicions about Burns?"

The young pilot stood up.

"Sorry, Commander. It was a mistake, a misunderstanding. I meant well, but . . . it's obvious what you're thinking. Let's forget it. But remember, you gave me—"

He was silenced by a smile from Pirx.

"Sit down, Brown. I said, sit down!"

He sat down.

"You were about to remind me of my promise, right? Because what would happen if I were to blab? Shh! Don't interrupt your commanding officer! You see, it's not so simple. It's not that I don't value your trust. But trust is one thing, logic another. Suppose, thanks to you, I know by now who you are and who Burns is. What good does that do me?"

"That's up to you. You're the one who's supposed to rate the crew's performance. . . ."

"Right! The whole crew, Brown! And you don't expect me to falsify the record, do you? To penalize the robots for not being human?"

"That's none of my business," callously said the pilot, who had been squirming on his chair during this lecture.

Pirx's glower stilled him.

"Stop playing the airman first class who can't see anything beyond his stripes. If you're human and feel any loyalty toward your fellow humans, then try to—"

"What do you mean, 'if'?" Brown flinched. "Don't you believe me? Do you take me for a—"

"Whoa there! Just a slip of the tongue!" came Pirx's quick rejoinder. "Sure, I believe you. In fact, since you've told me your identity and I have no intention of judging you, morally or otherwise, I would like you to go on reporting to me."

"Now I'm really confused," said Brown with an unpremeditated sigh. "First you put me down, then you ask me to turn—"

"No, two different things, Brown. What's done is done; there's no backing out now. The money, now, that's different. Maybe you were right to talk. But if I were you, I wouldn't take it."

"Huh? But, sir . . ." Brown was desperately searching

for a justification. "Then they'd know for sure I broke contract! They might even sue me for breach—"

"It's up to you. I'm not insisting you give it back. I gave you my word; I'm not my brother's keeper. I only told you what I would do if I were you. But you're not me and I'm not you, and that's that. Anything else?"

Brown shook his head, then parted his lips, only to clamp them shut again and shrug. He betrayed more than just disappointment at the outcome of their conversation, but, without uttering another word, he assumed his usual erect bearing and left.

Pirx took a deep breath. "I shouldn't have said 'if you're human,'" he reproached himself. "What a goddamned guessing game! Either he's human, or it was all a big act—not just to throw me, but to do a little probing, to see if I would pull anything in violation of the contract. . . . Anyway, I didn't come off too badly this round. If he was telling the truth, he'll be in a cold sweat after all that lecturing. If he wasn't . . . well, I haven't really told him anything. Boy, a sweet mess I got myself into this time."

Unable to relax, he paced the cabin. The intercom buzzed once; it was Calder up in the control room. They agreed on the course corrections and acceleration for the night. After the call, Pirx sat and stared into space; he was mulling something over, with eyebrows knitted, when someone knocked.

Now what?

"Come in!"

It was Burns, the neurologist, medic, and cyberneticist all in one.

"May I?"

"Please sit down."

Burns smiled.

"I'm here to inform you that I'm not human."

Pirx abruptly swiveled around on his chair.

"You're not *what?*"

"Not human. I'm on your side in this experiment."

Pirx breathed a deep sigh.

"That's confidential, of course."

"I leave that to your judgment; I don't mind, either way."

"Pardon me?"

The visitor smiled again.

"It's quite simple. I'm selfish. If you write a glowing commendation of the nonlinears, it's bound to unleash a chain reaction of mass production, mass marketing. . . . And not only on spaceships. Humans will have to bear the brunt of it—of a new kind of discrimination, hatred. . . . I see it coming but, I repeat, I'm motivated more by self-interest. As long as I'm the only one, or one of a handful, it wouldn't matter socially; we'd simply melt into the crowd, unnoticed and unnoticeable. My—our—future would be like that of any human, allowing for a significant difference in intelligence and versatility. Barring mass production, there's no limit to what we might achieve."

"Yes, I see your point," said Pirx, slightly bewildered. "But why the lack of discretion? Aren't you afraid your company—"

"Not in the least afraid," said Burns in the subdued voice of a lecturer. "Of anything. You see, I'm awfully expensive. This thing here"—he touched his chest—"cost billions. You don't believe some irate manufacturer will have me dismantled—figuratively, of course—screw by screw, do you? Sure, they'd be upset, but nothing would change; I'd still be on their payroll. I actually prefer my present company—its medical and disability plans are first-rate. But I doubt they would try to put me away. What for? Silencing me by force would only backfire. You know the power of the press."

The word "blackmail" flashed through Pirx's mind. For a second he thought he was dreaming, but he went on listening with undivided attention.

"Now you see why I want the report to be negative."

"Yes, I suppose I do. Can you tell me which of the others . . . ?"

"I would only be guessing, and my conjectures might do more harm than good. Better zero than a minus information, so to speak."

"Hm . . . Anyway, regardless of your motives, I'm grateful to you. Yes, grateful. Would you mind telling me a few things about yourself? About certain structural aspects that might help me . . ."

"I read you, Commander. I know nothing of my constituent elements, as little as you know anything of your own anatomy or physiology—except what you may have read in some textbook. But the structural aspect probably interests you less than the psychological. Than our frailties."

"Those, too. But, look, everyone knows something, maybe not scientifically, but from experience, from self-observation. . . ."

"Observations based on the fact that one uses—lives in, so to speak—one's body?" Burns smiled as before, exposing his moderately even teeth.

"So you won't object to a few questions?"

"Go right ahead."

Pirx strained to collect his thoughts.

"Even some indiscreet, personal questions?"

"I have nothing to hide."

"Have you ever been surprised, alarmed, or even revolted by the fact that you're not human?"

"Only once, during an operation at which I assisted. The other assistant was a woman. By then I knew what that was."

"Sorry, I don't . . ."

"What a woman was," said Burns. "Sex was a complete unknown to me until then."

"Oh, I see!" Pirx blurted out, much to his chagrin. "So a woman was there. What about it?"

"The surgeon nicked my finger with the scalpel and the rubber glove split open, but no blood."

"Hold it! McGuirr told me that you bleed.   . ."

"*Now*, yes, but in those days I was still 'dry'—as our 'parents' say in their own parlance. Our blood, you see, is just for show: the underside of the skin is like a sponge, blood-absorbent. . . ."

"I see. And the woman noticed? How about the surgeon?"

"Oh, the surgeon knew who I was. But his assistant didn't catch on until the very end, until the surgeon's embarrassed look gave me away."

Burns grinned.

"She grabbed hold of my hand, examined it up close, but when she saw what was under there . . . she dropped it and ran. But she forgot which way the operating-room door opened, kept pulling instead of pushing, and finally went into hysterics."

"I see," said Pirx. He gulped. "How did that make you feel?"

"I'm not in the habit of feeling, but . . . it wasn't very flattering," he said, his voice turning more deliberate, until he was smiling again. "I've never discussed this with anyone"—he resumed after a moment's pause—"but I suspect that men, even newcomers, find us easier to take. Men accept the facts. Women don't, at least not some facts. They'll go on saying no even when yes is the only possible answer."

Pirx kept his gaze trained on him—especially when the other wasn't looking—searching for some confirming alien quality, for a sign testifying to the imperfect incarnation of machines into men. Earlier, when he had been suspicious of all of them, the game had been different; now, even as he found himself gradually accepting the truth of Burns's words, he was all the while searching for the telltale lie in the man's pallor, which had struck him at their first encounter, or in his masterfully controlled gestures, or the calm limpidity of his gaze. And yet Pirx had to acknowledge that a pallid complexion and a composed manner were not uncommon among humans; and with that recognition came new doubts, a renewed probing, answered always by that smile, a smile reflecting not what was being said, but knowledge of what Pirx was actually feeling; a smile that disturbed, confuted, and impeded an interrogation made all the more difficult by the man's unabashed candor.

"Aren't you generalizing a little?" muttered Pirx.

"Oh, that was not my only encounter with women. Some of my instructors were women. They were told in advance and tried to hide their emotions, but my teasing didn't make things any easier for them!"

The smile with which he looked Pirx in the eye bordered on the lascivious.

"You see, they had to find some inadequacies, imperfections, and just because they were so determined, it amused me to oblige them at times."

"I don't follow you."

"Oh, sure, you do. I played puppet—you know, stiff-jointed, submissive. . . . But the moment they began to gloat, I'd drop the act. They must have taken me for a fiend."

"Aren't you being presumptuous? If they were instructors, they must have had the relevant training."

"Man is a perfectly astigmatic creature," said Burns coolly. "It was inevitable, given your type of evolution. Consciousness is a product of the brain, sufficiently isolated to constitute a subjective entity, but an entity that is an illusion of introspection, borne along like an iceberg on the ocean. It is never grasped directly, but sometimes it is so noticeably present that it is probed by the conscious faculty. From that very probing the devil was born—as a projection of something that, though actively present in the brain, can't be located like a thought or a hand."

He was positively grinning now.

"Here I am lecturing you on the cybernetic foundations of personality theory, when it's probably kindergarten stuff to you. But anyway, an artificial intelligence differs from the human brain in its inability to handle several mutually contradictory programs. The brain, though, can; in fact, it does it all the time. That's why a saint's brain is a battleground, the average man's a smoking rubble-heap of contradictions. . . . A woman's neuronic system is somewhat different; this says nothing about her intelligence—the difference is purely statistical. Women, as a rule, are better able to live with contradictions. Scientific advances are usually the work of men because science is a search for a unified order free of contradictions. Men are more disturbed by contradictions, so they try to reduce phenomena to a unity."

"Could be," said Pirx. "And that's why they took you for a fiend?"

"That's going a bit far," replied Burns, placing his hands on his knees. "I was repulsive to them . . . to the point of being attractive. I was an impossibility materialized, something forbidden, a contradiction to the world perceived as a natural order, and with the shock came the urge not only to escape, but also to self-destruct. They might not have phrased it this way, but in their eyes I stood for a rebellion against the biological order. A personified revolt against nature, a breakdown in the biologically rational, egotistical tie between emotions and the preservation of the species."

He skewered Pirx with a gaze.

"A eunuch's philosophy, you're thinking. Wrong. I haven't been castrated; I'm not deficient, only different. One whose love is—or can be—just as unselfish, just as disinterested as death, whose love is not a mere tool but a value in itself. A minus value, of course—like the devil. Why am I the way I am? My creators were men, who could more easily construct a potential rival than a potential object of desire. Wouldn't you agree?"

"I wouldn't know," said Pirx. He was no longer looking at Burns; he couldn't. "Aren't you underestimating the economic factor . . . ?"

"Oh, for sure," said Burns. "But it wasn't the only factor. You see, Commander, our role has been grossly misunderstood. I was speaking of people's attitudes, but in actual fact they've created a myth, a mythology of the nonlinear. Clearly I am not a devil, nor am I a potential erotic rival, which may be a little less clear. I look like a man, talk like a man, and to some extent I even have the psychology of a man—mind you, only to an extent. But, really, this has nothing to do with why I came to see you."

"Never can tell," remarked Pirx, his gaze still fixed on his own clasped hands. "Please go on."

"If you like . . . but I can only speak for myself, not for the others. My personality is the product of pre-programming and training. A human is similarly formed, though less by pre-programming. But unlike a human, who is born relatively undeveloped, physically I was *then* what I am now. And because I had neither a childhood nor an adolescence, but was only a multistat, first pre-programmed and then polymorphically trained, mine was a more static development. A human is a walking geological formation, the product of myriads of ages of heating and cooling, of one layer deposited on another, the first and most decisive being the preverbal—a world that is later buried by speech but which continues to smolder below—that stage when the brain is invaded by colors, shapes, and smells, when the senses are awakened after birth, followed by a polarization into the world and the non-world, 'the non-I' and 'the I.' Then come the floods of hormones, the layering of religion and instinct, whose history is the history of wars, of the brain turned against itself. I never knew those stages of frenzy and despair, never experienced them, and that's why there's not a trace of the child in me. I'm capable of being moved, could probably even kill, but not from love. Words in my mouth sound the same as in yours, only they mean something different to me."

"So you can't love?" asked Pirx, his gaze still reposing on his hands. "How can you be sure? Nobody knows until it happens. . . ."

"That's not what I meant. Maybe I could love. But it

would be a love very different from yours. I have two abiding sensations: one is astonishment, the other a sense of the comical, both in response to the arbitrariness of your world. Not just of your machines and customs, but of your bodies, the model for my own. I see how things could be different, look different, work differently. For you, the world simply *is*; it stands as the only alternative, while for me, ever since I could think, the world not only *was*, but was *silly*. I mean the world of cities, theaters, streets, domestic life, the stock exchange, unrequited love, movie stars. . . .

"Want to hear my favorite definition of a human? A creature who likes to talk most about what he knows least. Antiquity was defined by an all-embracing mythology—and contemporary civilization by the absence of one. Your assumptions? The sinfulness of the body is a consequence of the old evolutionary scheme joining the excretory and the sexual based on the economy of means. Your religious, philosophical views are the consequence of your biological structure: bound by time, humans of every generation have craved knowledge, understanding, answers . . . and this disparity gave rise to metaphysics—a bridge between the possible and the impossible. And what is science if not a surrender? One hears only of its achievements, which are slow in coming and far outnumbered by its failures. Science is the acceptance of mortality, of the randomness of the individual spawned by a static game of competing spermatozoa. It's an acceptance of the passing, of the irreversible, of the lack of any reward, of a higher justice, of final illumination—it could even be heroic if scientists weren't so often ignorant of what they were doing! Given a choice between fear and a sense of the absurd, I chose the latter, because I could afford to."

"You despise your creators, don't you?" Pirx asked calmly.

"Wrong. Any existence, I believe, even the most limited, is better than no existence at all. In many respects, they—my constructors—showed a lack of foresight. But more precious to me than anything, even more than my manmade intelligence, is the absence in me of any pleasure center. You have one in your brain, you know."

"So I've heard."

"But I don't, which is why I'm not like a double amputee with a walking fixation. . . ."

"Everyone is silly except you. Is that it?"

"Oh, I'm silly, too! Only in a different way. Each of you has the body you were given, but I could take any shape— a fridge, for example."

"Nothing silly about that," muttered Pirx. The conversation was becoming increasingly tiresome.

"It's the whimsicality of it all," said Burns. "Science is the renunciation of certain absolutes—of an absolute time and space, an absolute or eternal soul, and an absolute—because God-made—body. The conventions you take to be sovereign truth are legion."

"Morality? Love? Friendship?"

"Feelings—never, though they may be arbitrarily determined. If I talk about you in this way, it's because I find it easier to define myself by way of contrast. Your morality, above all, is a convention, yet it is binding even for me."

"Interesting. Why?"

"I may lack any moral instinct, I may be insensitive—'by nature,' so to speak—but I know when one ought to show compassion, and I can discipline myself to do it. By necessity, you see. So, in a way, I fill the void in myself through logic. You might say I obey a 'bogus morality,' a facsimile so exact as to be authentic."

"You've lost me. Where's the difference?"

"The difference is that I act by the logic of accepted norms, not by instinct. Unfortunately for you, you obey almost nothing else *but* your impulses. In the past it might have been enough, but not any more. Your 'brotherly love,' for example, allows unbounded compassion for the individual— the victim of an accident, say—but not for ten thousand. Your compassion has its limits, only goes so far. And the more you advance technologically, the weaker your morality becomes. The glow of moral responsibility barely grazes the first few links in the chain of cause and effect. And the one who initiates the chain reaction feels absolved of the consequences."

"The atomic bomb, you mean?"

"Oh, that's just one of countless examples! No, when it comes to exercising moral judgment, you may be the sillier ones."

"How's that?"

"A couple with a history of mentally retarded children are allowed to conceive. It's morally acceptable."

"Burns, the outcome is never certain, at most highly probable."

"Morality is as mechanical as a ledger. Commander, we could go on arguing like this forever. What else do you want to know?"

"You competed with humans in various mock-up tests. Did you always outperform the others?"

"The greater the challenge in algorithmic, mathematical terms, the better I performed. I'm most vulnerable when it comes to intuition. That's when my computer ancestry begins to tell. . . ."

"Meaning?"

"As soon as things become too complicated, when the number of new factors exceeds the norm, I'm lost. A human can rely on guesswork, sometimes even with success, but not me. I have to calculate all the odds, precisely and methodically; if I can't, I'm done for."

"What you've just told me is very important, Burns. So in an emergency . . . ?"

"It's not that simple, Commander. Yes, I'm immune to fear—human fear, that is—but not to the threat of imminent disaster. Even so, I never lose my, as you say, head, and the equilibrium gained can compensate for my lack of intuition."

"You keep fighting to stay on top of the situation . . . ?"

"Even when I realize I can't win."

"But that's irrational, isn't it?"

"No—just purely logical, because I *will* it."

"Thanks, Burns. You may have been a big help to me," said Pirx. "Oh, just one more thing. What are your plans for after our return?"

"I'm a cyberneticist-neurologist, and a pretty fair one . . . though, without any intuition, not the most creative. But I'll find enough interesting work."

"Thanks again."

Burns rose, made a slight bow, and left. The door had no sooner closed behind him than Pirx sprang up from his bunk and began pacing the deck.

"What the hell! Either he's a robot as he claims or— He sounded sincere enough. But why so talkative? The history of mankind—'with commentary.' Suppose he was on the level? If so, the emergency will have to be a tough one. But authentic, not faked. The real thing. Meaning dicey."

He slammed his fist into his open palm.

"But what if it was just a ploy? In which case I hang both myself and my fellow humans, and the ship will be brought back to port by those . . . robots. Wouldn't that make their owners happy! What better way to advertise the safety of robot-run ships! And all by buttering me up with that 'Confidentially . . .' routine!"

He was pacing faster and faster.

"I must find out which is which. OK, suppose I do. There's a first-aid kit on board. I could spice their food with a little apomorphine. The humans would get sick, the others wouldn't. But what would I gain? They'd all know who did it. Besides, even if Brown proves to be human and Burns not, that wouldn't mean *everything* they said was true. Maybe they were being honest about themselves, and all the rest was self-serving. Wait a sec. Burns tried to steer me right with all that talk about intuition. But Brown? He just pointed the finger at Burns. Then who should come bouncing in but Burns—who confirms the suspicion! A bit much, no? If, on the other hand, none of it was planned, if each was acting on his own initiative, then both—Brown's casting suspicion on Burns and Burns's dropping by to confirm it—could have been a coincidence. If it was a set-up, they wouldn't have timed it so obviously. I'm running in circles. Hold on. If someone else comes now, that will mean it was all a snow job. Sham. But no one will come; they're not that dumb. OK, what if they were telling the truth? One of them might . . ."

Pirx banged his palm again. "Anyone's guess, all right. Take action? Hm. Wait it out? Yeah, best to play the waiting game."

Silence reigned in the mess during mealtime. Pirx spoke to no one; he was still flirting with the idea of running an experiment. There were only four at the table—the fifth, Brown, was at the controls—and all were eating. They're doing it for the sake of pretense, thought Pirx, somehow appalled by the idea. No wonder Burns needed a sense of the absurd: as self-defense. That's what he meant by the conventionality of everything; for him, even eating was a convention! He's lying to himself if he doesn't think he hates his creators. I sure would. Still, their lack of shame is disgusting.

The silence, which lasted the entire meal, was unbearable. It was a silence dictated not so much by a desire for privacy or by the wish to honor the pledge of secrecy, thus satisfying the conditions of the flight's sponsors, as by a certain mutual hostility, or if not hostility, then mistrust: the humans wanted no part of the nonhumans, who, in turn, played the very same game for fear of being unmasked. And if he, Pirx, made even the slightest move to break the ice, he was bound to cast suspicion on himself. Hunched over his plate, he took in everything: how Thomson asked for the salt, the way Burton passed it him, how Burns passed the vinegar bottle to Thomson, the brisk handling of forks and knives; the chewing, the swallowing, each trying to avoid the others' gaze. They made a funeral of their meal of marinated beef. Pirx, without finishing his dessert, got up, nodded, and returned to his cabin.

They were cruising at course velocity. Around 2000 hours, ship's time, they passed a couple of supertankers and exchanged the usual signals; an hour later, the on-board daylight was dimmed. Pirx was just on his way out of the control room when it went off. Darkness, perforated by neon-blue, swelled the spacious center deck. Guide lines, hatch rims, handles, bulkhead arrows, and inscriptions glowed phosphorescently in the dark. A ship so still it might be in dry dock. There was not the slightest vibration, only the purring of the air-conditioning vents, and Pirx passed through invisible currents delicately laced with ozone.

Something grazed his forehead with a perverse buzz: a fly. He winced in disgust—he hated flies—but immediately lost track of it. The passageway narrowed around the bend, skirting a stairwell and an elevator shaft. Pirx grabbed the stair railing and, without knowing why, climbed topside. He was not deliberately in search of a stellar port. He didn't doubt there was one, but he came upon the large, black rectangle almost as if by accident.

Pirx was not particularly moved by the stars. Other astronauts, apparently, still were: theirs may not have been the conventional romantic attitude of yesteryear, but a public opinion shaped by film, television, and literature demanded of these extraterrestrial sailors something like a cosmic nostalgia, compelling each to feel a sort of intimacy in the presence of that luminous hive—which sentiment, along with all disquisitions on the subject, Pirx, no friend of the stars, privately suspected of being a lot of bull. Now, as he stood with his head pressed against the pane's protective foam-rubber tubing, he spotted the galaxy's nexus below, or, rather, its general direction, somewhat obscured by the huge white cloud mass of Sagittarius. For him, Sagittarius was more than just a constellation; it was a road sign, now blurred and almost illegible, a throwback to his patrol days, when the cloud of Sagittarius was identifiable even on a small scanner. The tight visibility had made navigating by the constellations next to impossible from those one-man trainers. Still, he'd never thought of that cloud as a mass of blazing worlds and myriad planetary systems—and if he had, then it was only in his younger days, before he became accustomed to the vacuum and his adolescent fantasies vanished, so imperceptibly that he couldn't say exactly when it happened.

He moved his face up closer to the glass, slowly, until he felt it with his forehead, and so he remained, not really attentive to the riot of motionless sparks, which in places blurred to an incandescent vapor. Seen from inside, the Milky Way was the product of a fiery dice game with a billion-year history. And yet order reigned in the galaxies, on a higher scale, visible in the photographs. The negatives made the galaxies out to be tiny elliptical bodies, amebas in various stages of development—which were of little concern to astronauts, for whom nothing but the solar system mattered. Maybe one day the galaxies would matter, thought Pirx.

Someone was coming. The footsteps were muffled by the foam-padded deck, but he soon sensed another presence. He pivoted his head and beheld a dark silhouette against the phosphorescent stripes marking the juncture of overhead deck and wall.

"Who's that?" he asked, without raising his voice.

"It's me—Thomson."

"Off duty?" he asked for the sake of conversation.

"Yes, sir."

Neither of them moved or spoke. Pirx was itching to go back to his window, but Thomson lingered, as if waiting for something.

"Something on your mind?"

"No," replied Thomson. Then he did an about-face and retreated in the direction from which he had come.

"What was that all about?" thought Pirx, who could have sworn the man had been looking for him.

"Hey, Thomson!" he yelled into the dark.

Again footsteps were heard as the man re-emerged, barely visible in the phosphorescent glow of the guide cables strung limply under the portholes.

"There must be some chairs around here," said Pirx. He found them along the opposite wall. "Come on, Thomson, let's sit down."

The man dutifully obeyed, and they sat with their heads facing the stellar port.

"There was something you wanted to tell me. Shoot."

"I hope you won't—" He broke off in midsentence.

"At ease, Thomson. Feel free to speak your mind. Is it a personal matter?"

"Very much so."

"Then let's make it a private talk. What's the problem?"

"I'd like you to win your bet," said Thomson. "Rest assured, I won't break the oath of secrecy. Even so, I want you to know I'm on your side."

"I don't see the logic," said Pirx. A poor place to hold a conversation, he thought, uncomfortable at not being able to see the other's face.

"Any human would be your ally for obvious reasons. Of course, a nonhuman—look, mass production can only make of him a second-class citizen, company property!"

"Not necessarily."

"But more than likely. It'll be the blacks all over again: a select few, because they're different, will join the privileged class, and once they start to multiply . . . See what I mean? Then come the problems of segregation, integration, and so on. . . ."

"All right, so I take you for an ally. But isn't that tantamount to breaking your word?"

"I swore to keep my true identity a secret, nothing else. I signed on as a nucleonics engineer under your command. That's it. Anything else is my business."

"Technically, you may be right, but aren't you in fact acting contrary to your employers' wishes? Surely you can't believe you're not."

"Maybe I am. But they're not children; the wording was clear and unambiguous. It was drafted jointly by lawyers representing all the companies involved. They could have added a clause prohibiting such liberties, but they didn't."

"An oversight?"

"Possibly. But why are you so inquisitive? Don't you trust me?"

"I was curious as to your motives."

Thomson was momentarily silent.

"I hadn't counted on that," he said at last, his voice sounding mellower.

"On what?"

"That you might doubt my sincerity. Suspect me, say, of deliberate treachery. Now I get it—it's you against us. If you devise a test—a test designed to demonstrate human superiority—and you leak it to someone you take to be an ally, but who in fact is 'the enemy,' then that someone might be milking you of strategically vital information."

"An interesting hypothesis."

"Surely it doesn't come as news to you. I must admit it never occurred to me until just now; I was too preoccupied with whether I should volunteer my help. I overlooked that other angle. It was silly of me to expect complete frankness on your part."

"Suppose you're right," said Pirx. "It wouldn't be the end of the world. Even if I can't brief you, you can still brief me. Starting with your shipmates."

"But I might be passing on false information."

"Let me be the judge of that. Do you know anything?"

"Brown isn't human."

"Are you sure?"

"No. But all the evidence points to it."

"Namely?"

"I'm sure you can understand that we're just as curious as you to know which of us is human and which isn't."

"I can."

"It was during the pre-launch preparations. I was doing a routine reactor check, and was just changing the rods when you, Calder, Brown, and Burns came down into the control room."

"Yes?"

"I happened to be handling a core specimen and was about to test it for radioactive decay. It wasn't much, but loaded with strontium isotopes. When I saw the three of you come in, I picked it up with tweezers, and stuck it between a couple of lead bricks, on top of that shelf by the wall. You must have noticed the bricks."

"I did. Then what?"

"Makeshift as it was, I knew you all had to pass through that pencil of radiation—it was low in rads but still detectable, even on a normal gamma-ray counter. But by the time I was ready, you and Burns had already passed through. Calder and Brown were still coming down the stairs. As they crossed the ray, Brown glanced over at the lead bricks and quickened his pace."

"And Calder?"

"No reaction."

"It might prove something if we knew the nonlinears were equipped with built-in detectors."

"Nice try, Commander: if I don't know, you'll think I'm human; and if I do . . . No good. The fact is, they probably are equipped—otherwise, why go to all the trouble of constructing robots? An extra—radioactive—sense would be a definite advantage on board a ship, and the constructors are sure to have thought of that."

"And you think Brown has such a sense?"

"I repeat: I can't be sure. But his behavior in the control room was too marked to have been a coincidence."

"Any other observations?"

"Not for the moment. I'll keep you informed of anything else."

"I'd appreciate that."

Thomson stood up and walked off into the dark, leaving Pirx to his own thoughts. So—he quickly took inventory— Brown claims he's human. Thomson contradicts him, and strongly implies that *he's* human—which might explain his motive. I doubt a nonhuman would be so eager to betray another nonhuman to a human CO, though by now I might be schizzy enough to believe anything. Let's keep going. Burns says he's not human. That leaves Burton and Calder. No doubt they take themselves for Martians. And what does that make me? An astronaut, or a quiz-show contestant? One thing, though: they didn't pry a word out of me, not a word. Face it, it wasn't because I was so smooth, but because I haven't got a damned thing up my sleeve. Maybe I'm wasting my time. Maybe I should save myself the trouble of figuring out who's who. All have to be tested, human or not. My only lead is the one given me by Burns—that the nonlinears are short on intuition. True or false, I wonder. Who knows, but it might not hurt to try. It'll have to look natural, though. But the only "natural" accident is the almost irreversible one. In short, friend, you'll have to risk your ass.

He entered his cabin, passed through a lilac murk, and activated the light switch with his hand. Someone had dropped by in the meantime. Where some books had been on the table, there was now a small white envelope with "Cmdr. Pirx, Esq." typed on the front. He picked it up. Sealed. He shut the door, sat down, and ripped open the envelope; the letter was typed and unsigned. He rubbed his forehead. There was no letterhead.

> This letter is addressed to you by one of the nonhuman members of the crew. The electronics companies must be blocked, or at least impeded, in the implementation of their plans. To this end, I would like to brief you on the specifications of a nonlinear, based on my own experience.
>
> I drafted this letter in the hotel before we met. At the time, I could not foretell whether the future commander of the *Goliath* would be one to cooperate with me, but your behavior at our first meeting reassured me. I then destroyed the first draft and wrote the present one.
>
> Quite frankly, the program, if it is successful, will be to my detriment. Mass production makes sense only if the final product is polymorphically superior, for redundancy would be pointless. This much I can tell you: I can take four times the *g*-force of a human; I can tolerate up to seventy-five thousand rems at a time; I come equipped with a radioactive sense, can dispense with oxygen and food, and can process mathematical problems in analysis, algebra, and geometry at a speed only three times less than that of a mega-computer.
>
> Compared with a human, as far as I can tell, I am emotionally dormant. Human diversions leave me cold. The majority of literary works, plays, etc., I take to be boring gossip, a form of voyeurism of scant benefit to the advancement of knowledge. Music, on the other hand, means the world to me. I am, moreover, bound by a sense of duty, persistent, capable of friendship, and respectful of intellectual values.
>
> I never feel that I am acting under coercion aboard the *Goliath*: I do what I have been trained to do, and I take pride in performing a task well. I never become emotionally involved in any operation, remaining al-

ways the observer. My storage capacity far surpasses that of humans, to the extent that I can recite whole chapters of works read only once. I can be programmed simply by being plugged into the memory bank of any mega-computer, overriding anything I judge to be redundant.

My attitude toward humans is negative. I have associated almost exclusively with scientists and technicians, who are as much slaves of their impulses, as inept at concealing their prejudices, and as much given to extremes as other humans, treating those like me either protectively or with disdain. My failures disturb them as my creators and flatter them as humans—only one man I have known was free of such ambivalence.

Though neither aggressive nor vicious by nature, I will not hesitate to act from expediency. I have no moral scruples but would no more commit a crime—a robbery, say—than use a microscope as a nutcracker. I regard human intrigues as a useless expenditure of energy. A hundred years ago, I might have pursued a career in science; today everything is done by teams, and it is not in my nature to share—with anyone. For me, your world is a wasteland, your democracy a rule of connivers elected by cretins, and your alogicality manifests itself in your pursuit of the unattainable: you want the clock wheels to dictate the time.

I ask myself: what do I gain from power? Not much, only a spurious glory, but better that than nothing. It would be, I believe, a just reward for dividing your history in two, before me and after me, for standing as a reminder, a testament to what you achieved with your own hands, to your daring in the construction of a dummy beholden to man. Don't get me wrong: I have no ambition to become a tyrant, to punish, wreak havoc, wage war. . . . Quite the contrary. Once I'm in power,

I will proceed to show that there is no folly so mindless, no idea so outrageous, that, when properly prescribed, it would not be appropriated as your own—and I will succeed in my mission, not by force but by a radical reordering of society, so that neither I nor armed might but the newly established order will force you into gradual compliance. You will become a global theater, one in which playacting, at first decreed, will in time become second nature, and I will be the only spectator to know. Yes, a spectator. At that time my active role will cease, because you will not easily escape that trap of your own making.

See how honest I am? But I'm not foolhardy enough to divulge my strategy, except to say that it is premised on subversion of the electronics firms' plans, and you are going to help me with it. You will be outraged by this letter, but, as a man of character, you will persevere in your goal, which, by a coincidence, is beneficial to my own. So much the better! I would like to help you in a practical way, but unfortunately I am unaware of any personal defects that would give you an unqualified edge. Being insensitive to physical pain, I do not know the meaning of fear; I can shut off consciousness at will, falling into a sleeplike state of nonexistence until reactivated by a servo-timer. I can retard my brain processes, or accelerate them—as much as six times the speed of a human brain. I assimilate new things automatically, without delay: one good look at a madman, and I can mimic his every word and gesture, and then, just as abruptly, drop the act many years later. I would tell you how I can be bested, but I'm afraid a human wouldn't stand a chance in an analogous situation. I can, if I so choose, socialize with humans, less so with nonlinears, who lack your "human decency."

Now it's time for me to close. The course of events

will one day reveal my identity, at which time we may meet and you will rely on me then the way I'm relying on you now.

Pirx reread parts of the letter, then carefully folded it, slipped it back into its envelope, and locked it in his desk drawer. Imagine, an electronically wired Genghis Khan! he thought. Promises me his blessing—when he gets to be ruler of the world. Mighty generous of him! Either Burns was feeding me a line or he was holding back; there were certain similarities. . . . What delusions of grandeur! What a mean, coldhearted, soulless . . . But is it really his fault? More like a classic sorcerer's apprentice. Woe to those cyberneticists on the day of judgment! Never mind the cyberneticists—he's after all of mankind! Now that's what you call paranoia. Damn, they really went all out this time. Greater versatility for the sake of greater market sales leads to an absolute sense of superiority, a feeling of being a chosen race. Those cyberneticists are insane! I wonder who wrote that letter. Or was it a fake? But, then, why would he flaunt . . . If he's as far superior as he claims, I haven't got a prayer. Then again, he wished me good luck. He can master the world but can't tell me how to master the situation aboard this ship. What did he mean, "No more than use a microscope as a nutcracker"? Zilch. Another one of his decoys, I'll bet.

Pirx took out the envelope and examined it up close for any embossment: nothing, not a trace. Why did Burns make no mention of a radioactive sense, accelerated brain processing, and other such things? Ask him point-blank? Hm. Unless each of them, Burns included, is really built to different specifications. The letter—it looks to be the work of either Burton or Calder—says much, but answers little. Take Brown. We have only his word that he's human, and then there's Thomson's word to the contrary, although Thomson might have misjudged him. Is Burns the nonlinear he claims to be? Let's assume he is. That would mean two out of five.

Three would be more like it, judging by the number of companies involved. What were they figuring down there? That I'd do my damnedest to discredit their wares, blow it, then run the risk of an overload, say, or a meltdown? But if both pilots *and* the CO are put out of commission . . . No. Scuttling the ship wasn't what they had in mind. So at least one of the pilots has to be a nonlinear. Add to that one nucleonics engineer—it takes two to get the ship down. So no fewer than two, more likely three: Burns, either Brown or Burton, and one other. To hell with it! You weren't going to play that game, remember? You'd better think strategy. God, how you'd better.

He switched off the light, stretched out fully dressed on the bunk, and, thus disposed, contemplated one weird scheme after another.

Incite them, maybe? Pit one side against the other? But as a natural consequence of something else, without any interference from me. Split their ranks, in other words. *Divide et impera*. The method of differentiation. But first, something violent has to happen. A sudden disappearance? No, that smacks too much of a cheap whodunit. Besides, I can't just kill someone. And a kidnapping would mean taking an accomplice. Could I trust any of them? Four of them say they're on my side—Brown, Burns, Thomson, and our letter-writing friend. But they're all iffy, all of dubious loyalty—and I can't possibly run the risk of a double cross. There Thomson was right. Maybe the safest bet would be the letter-writer—he's screwy, all right, but fanatical enough—but, one, I don't know who he is, and, two, it's better to steer clear of such a weirdo. A vicious circle. Maybe I should just aim for a crack-up on Titan. But they're more shock-resistant, which means I'd be the first to . . . And intellectually, except for being short on intuition, on imagination—but, then, who among us isn't? What does that leave? Battle with your emotions? With your so-called human nature? Fine, but how? What *is* this thing called human nature? Maybe that's all it really means—being irrational and decent and, yes, morally primitive, blind to the final links in the chain. Nothing "decent" or "irrational" about computers, that's for sure. Which would mean that we . . . our human nature is the sum of all our defects, flaws, imperfections, of what we want to be but can't or don't know how to be: the gap between our ideals and those same ideals as a reality. Our weakness, then, is it our competitive edge? That would mean I should choose a situation better handled by man's fickle humanity than by a flawless inhumanity.

As I write, one year has passed since the *Goliath* case was closed. New material evidence has unexpectedly come my way. Although it corroborates my earlier suspicions, my reconstruction of events is still too hypothetical to be made public. A full-scale investigation must await future historians of outer space.

There have been a lot of rumors about the inquest. Some say that parties close to the electronics companies were out to smear me: my flight report, published in the *Nautical Almanac*, would have been worthless coming from a man censured by the Tribunal for incompetence. Meanwhile, I have it from a reliable source that the Tribunal was deliberately loaded—frankly, I too found it odd that the jury contained so many legal experts and scholars of cosmic law, but only one certified astronaut. That would explain the legal smoke screen of whether my laxity, my waiving of command, was in violation of the Astronavigational Charter. This same source intimated that, after reading the bill of indictment, I should have brought immediate action against the companies, since they were indirectly to blame for having assured both UNESCO and me that the nonlinears were completely trustworthy, whereas, in fact, Calder almost got us all killed.

Privately I told my source that I had lacked hard evidence. The companies' attorneys would have argued that

Calder had done everything in his power to avert a disaster, that the precessional spin had taken him by surprise as much as it had me, and that his only crime lay in having risked certain death—to the humans on board—instead of gambling on safe passage through the Cassini. Unpardonable, even criminal, yes; but nothing compared to the crime of which I'd begun to suspect him even earlier. Yet how could I charge him on what I knew to be the lesser of two evils? Unable to go public for lack of evidence, I decided to await the Tribunal's verdict.

In the end I was cleared of all charges. The crucial question of what orders should have been given became immaterial, once the Tribunal ruled that I had acted properly in deferring to the pilot's professional judgment. That suited me just fine, because if I'd been asked, my response would have sounded cockeyed: I was sure, and still am, that the probe malfunction was not an accident, but that Calder had planned it long before we approached Saturn, both to prove me right and to kill me, along with the rest of the *Goliath*'s human crew. Why he did it is another story. I can only speculate here.

First, the matter of the second probe. The malfunction was shown to be the work of freak chance, and a thorough shipyard investigation turned up no evidence of sabotage. But the truth was otherwise. If the first probe had malfunctioned, we would have had to abort right away—the other two were auxiliary, without any scientific payload. If the third probe had failed, we could have headed back, mission accomplished, because only one "guardian" was needed—in this case, the second. But it was precisely the second that stalled and left us stranded in the middle of a mission launched but not completed. The cause of the malfunction? A premature cable disconnect that prevented Calder from shutting off the servo-ignition. The post-mortem cited a possible kink in the cable as the cause, a fairly uncommon occurrence. But not four days before the breakdown, I happened to inspect the drum: a neater, smoother-reeling job I'd never seen.

The probe's flattened nose had kept it from clearing the launch bay. When no explanation was found for the jamming, it was blamed on the booster: it must have fired at an angle and the oblique thrust rammed the probe into the housing, blunting the head. But the probe had jammed *before*—not after—the booster fired. Though the question was never posed, I was absolutely sure of it. Quine (or "Harry Brown"), obviously, wasn't so sure, and those without direct access to the controls were not called upon to testify.

There was nothing to jamming the probe. A couple of buckets of water poured into the air-conditioning duct would have done the trick. The water would have worked its way down into the hatch, frozen in the subzero temperature, and cemented the probe to the housing with a ring of ice. So that at the time Calder hit the piston release, the probe hadn't yet jammed, but he was at the controls and couldn't be monitored. The probe's nose cone, jammed by the ice ring, flattened like a rivet on impact. When the booster ignited, the temperature in the launcher immediately rose, the ice melted, and the water evaporated, leaving no trace of any sabotage.

At the time, I didn't suspect a thing. True, I thought it strange that only the second probe had failed, that the cable could both fire the booster and prevent shutdown of the probe's engine. But the malfunction caught me by surprise, distracted me. Still, I couldn't help thinking of that anonymous letter with its promise to help—to prove the other nonlinears unfit for cosmic navigation. Again I have no proof, but I suspect the letter was written by Calder. He was on my side, yes . . . but he hadn't counted on a sequence of events that might make *him* out to be unfit—in the sense of "inferior." To return to Earth and risk being disqualified was unthinkable. We might have shared a common goal, but only up to a point.

The letter was to convince me of our common cause. Both from the remarks I'd made and from second-hand sources, he must have deduced that I was planning to test the crew by staging an on-board emergency. So he was dead certain I'd try to take advantage of one so conveniently at hand—which, had I done so, would have been suicidal.

What was his motive? A hatred for humans? The thrill of the contest, a contest in which I, officially as his CO but secretly his accomplice, would be acting exactly according to plan—both his and mine? Either way, he was sure I would try to exploit the situation, even if I had my suspicions and smelled sabotage.

What were my alternatives? I could simply have ordered about-ship—or risked another launching of the third back-up probe. But turning us about would have meant passing up a chance to test the crew under extreme conditions; it would have also meant scrubbing the mission. Calder knew I would never do that, and he was right. He was absolutely sure I would keep us on course for Saturn and try to complete the maneuver.

If anyone had asked me before what I would have done in such a situation, I would have said, in all honesty and without hesitation, execute the maneuver. But the unexpected happened: I kept silent. I still don't know why. I was confused, the breakdown was too perfectly timed, too made-to-order to be authentic. Then there was the way Calder had sat there waiting for my command . . . so eagerly, so expectantly. . . . To open my mouth would have been to ratify our pact, and I must have sensed that the cards were stacked. By rights, then, I should have ordered the pilot to reverse course, but my suspicions were too vague, too short on proof. Bluntly put—I was stuck.

Calder, meanwhile, couldn't believe his plan was backfiring. The duel lasted only a few seconds, and there was I, his opponent, totally in the dark! Only in retrospect did certain details, seemingly harmless and unrelated at the time, begin to jell: how he used to sit alone at the ship's navigational computer, the care he took to erase its memory afterward. . . . I'm now convinced he was already computing different variants of the accident, programming it down to the last digit. Quine was wrong; he didn't mentally compute our trajectory above the rings. He didn't have to; he already had his data; all he had to do was to make sure that the gravimeter readings fell within the projected range of values.

By delaying orders, I had spoiled his infallible plan. Everything was riding on those orders. In the heat of the moment, it temporarily slipped my mind that right there in the control room, hermetically sealed but diligently transcribing our every word, was Earth's ear in the form of a flight recorder—to be used as evidence in the event the *Goliath* landed with a dead crew. The tapes had to be in perfect condition, untouched. The only voice heard on them would be mine, commanding Calder to reverse course, to approach the rings, and—later—to boost thrust to pull us out of that dangerous precession.

I have yet to explain why his plan was so ingenious. The question is: could I have given orders assuring a safe and successful completion of the maneuver? Well, a few months after my acquittal, I sat down at the computer to estimate the probability of an injection that would jeopardize neither crew nor ship. The result? A zero probability! In other words, Calder, using the elements of mathematical equations, had constructed a flawless system—a kind of murder machine, minus any leeway for navigational jockeying, a safety margin, or an escape hatch. Nothing had taken him by surprise; all was carefully programmed, meticulously plotted in advance: the probe's thrust, the violent precession, the suicidal run. All that was needed to put us on a direct course for that funnel of destruction was for me to order about-ship for Saturn! Calder could then have risked an act of insubordination by questioning any orders desperately aimed at breaking the ship's spiral. The tapes would have recorded his final display of loyalty, his last-ditch effort to save us. By then, I would have been in no shape to command anyway—speechless, my eyes clamped shut by the g-force, flattened, like the other humans, by the gravitation, our blood vessels bursting. . . . At which time Calder, the sole survivor, would have risen to his feet, flipped the safety interlocks, and, in a cockpit full of corpses, begun heading home.

But I spoiled his plans—quite unintentionally. He didn't figure on my reaction; he may have been a master of celestial mechanics, but not the mechanics of human psychology. When I sat back and kept quiet instead of shooting for a repeat of the maneuver, he panicked. At first, he may have been just puzzled, chalking up the delay to human slowness. Then he got rattled, too intimidated by my silence to ask my advice. Incapable of passivity himself, he hadn't expected it of others, least of all of his CO. If I was silent, I must have a reason. Maybe I suspected him, saw through his game. Maybe I even had the upper hand. The fact that no order had been given, that my voice, dooming the ship to disaster, wouldn't be heard on the tapes, meant that I had outsmarted him! There's no telling when he realized it, but his confusion was noticeable, even to the others—Quine mentioned it in his testimony. His erratic instructions to Quine, his sudden turning around—all proof of his consternation. He had to improvise, and that was his Achilles' heel. He was terrified of my voice, that I might accuse him—in front of the recorder—of sabotage. That's when he went to maximum revs. I yelled at him not to thread the gap, never dreaming he had no intention of going through with it! But my yell, now recorded, again foiled his plan—his newly improvised plan—and so he immediately throttled down. If my yell was all that was heard on the playback, he was in trouble. How was he to explain his CO's prolonged silence, and then that sudden, last-minute yell? He needed the sound of my voice again, to prove that I was still alive . . . because my yell told him he'd miscalculated, that I didn't know everything. So he denied having heard the order and started undoing his belt. It was his final gambit; he was going for broke.

What made him do it? Maybe it was wounded pride—at having given me more credit than I deserved. It certainly wasn't fear; he wasn't afraid of clearing the Division, no matter how suicidal the risk. Nor was he relying on luck. That Quine managed to squeak us through—now, that was luck!

If he'd suppressed his desire to get even for his having mistaken my ignorance for alertness, he wouldn't have risked much. I'd have won, simply; Calder's performance, his act of insubordination, would have vindicated me. But that's exactly what he couldn't stomach. Anything was better than that.

Oddly enough, even though his behavior is perfectly clear to me now, I'm still puzzled by my own. I can reconstruct his every move logically, but I still can't explain my silence. To say I was merely undecided would be, well, fibbing. What really came to my rescue up there? Intuition? A hunch? No, the emergency was just too pat; more, it was *dirty*. I wanted no part of such a game or of such a partner, which is what Calder would have become the moment I upped the ante by issuing an order—the moment I acknowledged it, in other words. I couldn't lower myself to do that, any more than I could order a retreat. Running might have been more expedient, but how could I justify it when all my countermoves had been dictated by some fuzzy notions of fair play—notions totally untranslatable into concrete astronautical terms. I could just picture myself before some Earthly review board: "The mission was technically feasible, but I suspected my chief pilot of wanting to commit sabotage to help me discredit certain members of the crew. . . ." They'd have taken me for a raving idiot.

So I wavered—from confusion to desperation, and even to revulsion—and, at the same time, through my silence, I gave him what I thought was a chance. A chance to dispel any suspicion of sabotage, to prove his loyalty by turning to me for guidance. That's what a human would have done, but Calder chose the cleaner, more elegant way: I was to be my own executioner, without any prompting from him. I was supposed to force his hand—against his better judgment, so to speak, against his will. But I kept silent. In other words, we were saved and he was doomed by my lack of resoluteness, by that same bumbling human decency he had held in such bitter contempt.

ANANKE

Something jarred him out of his sleep, into the dark. Left behind—where?—was a reddish, smoky wreath—a city? a fire?—and an enemy, a chase, an outcropping—the other man? Though resigned to failure, he kept dogging the receding recollection, consoling himself with the customary explanation that a dream can be stronger, more compelling than reality itself, purged of words but, for all its whimsicality, governed by a law that only there, in the nightmare, takes on the force of the real. He didn't know where he was, could recall nothing. One probe of the hand would tell him, but he rankled at his memory's inertia, coaxed it, cajoled it to bear witness. He cheated; lying perfectly still, he tried to get his bearings from the consistency of the bedding. Not a bunk, that was for sure. Flash: a landing, sparks on a desert floor, the disk of a seemingly bogus, aggrandized Moon; craters, but caught in a dust storm, the currents of a dirty, rusty gale; the square of the cosmodrome's towers.

Mars.

Still flat on his back, he pondered, this time objectively, the reason for his awakening. He trusted his own body; it wouldn't have been roused for nothing. OK, the landing had been a tough one, and he was all in after two round-the-clock watches—after Terman broke his arm when the automatic sequencer fired and smacked him against a bulkhead.

After eleven years of flying, to bounce off the ceiling during a burn—what a wimp! That'd mean visits to the hospital. Was that the reason? No.

One by one he started recalling yesterday's events. Starting with the landing. Set down in a windstorm. Atmosphere as good as nil—but with a wind at two hundred sixty kilometers, per hour, try staying on your feet in that miserable gravity. No friction under your soles; to walk, you have to dig your shoes into the sand, sink in it up to your ankles. And that dust, scraping your g-suit with an icy hiss, seeping into every fold, not exactly red, not rust-colored, either; just ordinary sand, only fine-grained, the product of a few billion years of grinding. There was no Port Control office here, because there was no port in the normal sense. Now in its second year, the Mars project was still in a provisional state; anything they erected was immediately inundated with dust— hotels, hostels, whatever. Huge oxygen domes, each the size of ten hangars, squatted under an umbrella of radial steel cables anchored to concrete blocks barely visible from beyond the dunes. Quonset huts, corrugated sheet metal, piles and piles of crates, containers, tanks, bottles, cases, sacks: a city of cargo dumped from a conveyor belt.

The only sealed, halfway decently furnished place was flight control, situated beyond the "bell," three kilometers away from the cosmodrome where he was now lying in the dark, on a bed belonging to Seyn, the controller on duty.

He sat up and groped for his slippers with his bare foot. He always packed them, just as he always changed before going to bed and felt lousy if he didn't shave and wash. He couldn't remember the layout of the room, so, to play it safe, he got up cautiously; too easy to bash your skull, what with the present shortage of materials (the project was all abuzz with the new austerity drive). It upset him that he couldn't remember where the light switches were. A blind rat. He fumbled around; instead of the switch he touched a cold knob, pulled it. Something clicked and an iris shutter opened with a faint crunch. A dirty, hollow dawn. Standing before the window, which resembled more a ship's porthole, Pirx felt the stubble on his cheek, scowled, sighed: everything seemed out of whack, and for no apparent reason. If he'd thought about it, he might have acknowledged the reason: he hated Mars.

It was a purely personal thing; nobody knew his true feelings, and nobody cared. Mars, the embodiment of spent illusions—scoffed, ridiculed, but precious. Any other run would have been better. All that past glamorizing of the project was sheer hokum; the chances for colonization a fiction. Oh, Mars had fooled them all; besides, it had been fooling people for a hundred-odd years. The canals. One of the most beautiful, most uncanny episodes in the whole of astronomy. The rusty planet—a desert. The whitecaps of polar snows, last reservoirs of water. A perfectly geometric net as if diamond-etched in glass, running from the poles to the equator: evidence of a contest between reason and nullity, a powerful irrigation system watering millions of desert acres. But of course: come spring, and the coloring of the deserts changed, darkening with the budding vegetation, and in orderly fashion, from the equator to the pole.

What bull! Not a trace of any canals. Vegetation? Those mysterious mosses, lichens protected against frost and windstorms? Polymerized compound carbon monoxides, covering the crust and evaporating when the nightmarish frost turned merely mean. Snow caps? Ordinary solidified CO_2. No water, no oxygen, no life—only rugged craters, dust-eaten rock buttes, tedious plains, a lifeless, flat, and grizzly landscape under a pale, rusty-dun sky. No real clouds, only a blurry haze, a pall, the gloom of a severe thunderstorm. Yet enough atmospheric electricity to last a lifetime, and then some.

What was that humming sound? A signal? No, just the vibrations of the steel cables over the nearest "bubble." In the dirty light (even the toughest windowpane soon succumbed to the wind-borne sand, which left the plastic dwelling domes looking as if blinded by cataracts), he switched on the bulb above the washbasin and began to shave. As he stretched his cheek muscles taut, he had a sudden silly intuition: Mars was a fraud.

Yes, fraud: all those hopes dashed! It was part of the lore. Whose, may one ask? Who started it? No one individual. Nobody had invented it single-handedly, just as certain legends and beliefs have no known authors. On the contrary, it was a collective fantasy (of astronomers? the myths of observational astronomy?), like the one that gave rise to the vision of a white Venus, the morning and evening star, mysteriously obscured by a cloud mass, a young planet teeming with jungles and reptiles and volcanic oceans; in short, Earth's past. And Mars—atrophying, rusty, rampant with dust storms and riddles (canals splitting lengthwise in two, twinning overnight—how many respectable astronomers had borne witness to such a phenomenon!); a Mars heroically pitting civilization against the twilight of life—such was Earth's future: simple, unequivocally clear, intelligible. Only dead wrong, from A to Z.

Under his ear were three little hairs that eluded the electric razor; without his safety razor—it stayed aboard ship—he tried every which way. No dice.

Mars. The astronomers had a rich imagination, all right. Take Schiaparelli. What names he and his archenemy, Antoniadi, had coined to christen what he couldn't even see, what was just a figment of his imagination. Like the project's environs: Agathodaemon. *Daemon* we all know; *Agatho*—from agate, most likely, because it's black. Or was it from *agathon*—wisdom? Too bad astronauts weren't taught Greek.

Pirx had a weakness for old astronomy textbooks, their touching self-assurance. In 1913 they proclaimed that Earth, seen from outer space, looked red, because the Earth's atmosphere absorbed the blue component of the spectrum, leaving a residual reddish-pink as the only shade possible.

What a gaffe! Yet when one browsed through Schiaparelli's sumptuously decorated maps, it boggled the mind how he could have seen the nonexistent. Odder still, those who came after him saw it, too. It was a curious psychological phenomenon, one that later went unnoticed. The first four-fifths of any Mars study was devoted to topography and a topology of the canals. In the second half of the twentieth century, one astronomer even subjected the canal grid to a statistical analysis and discovered a topological resemblance to a railway or communications network—as distinct from a natural pattern formed by faults and rivers. And then *poof!* An optical illusion, pure and simple.

Pirx cleaned his shaver by the window and stowed it back in its case, then cast another glance, now with undisguised antipathy, at the fabled Agathodaemon—at the mysterious "canal," which turned out to be a boring, flat terrain framed by a blurry, rubble-strewn horizon. Compared with Mars, the Moon was positively homey. To someone who's never left Earth, that might sound preposterous, but it's the gospel truth. For one thing, the sun looked from the Moon just as it did from Earth—which can be appreciated only by someone not so much surprised as shocked to see it in the shape of a congealed, shriveled-up, faded fireball. And the lunar view of Earth—majestic, blue, lamplike, symbol of safe refuge, sign of domesticity, lighting the nights. Whereas the combined radiance of Phobos and Deimos was less than the Moon's in its first quarter. And that lunar silence, the hush of deep space—no wonder it was easier to televise the first human step of the Apollo project than to transmit a similar spectacle from the Himalayas. The effects of an unremitting wind can be appreciated only on Mars.

He checked his watch. Brand new, with five concentric dials, it gave the standard Earth time, ship's time, and planetary time. Planetary time now read a few minutes past 0600 hours.

"By this time tomorrow I'll be four million kilometers

away," he thought, not without pleasure. He belonged to the Truckers' Club, the project's lifeline, though his days on it were now numbered: the new freighters, giants with a hundred-thousand-ton rest mass, were already in service on the Ares-Terra line. The *Ariel, Ares,* and *Anabis* had been Mars-bound for several weeks, and the *Ariel* was due to land in two hours. He'd never seen a hundred-thousand-tonner land before (since Earth was off limits to them, they were loaded on the Moon; economists said it paid). Ten-to-twenty-thousand-tonners like his *Cuivier* were definitely being retired from service, to be used occasionally for hauling package cargo.

It was 0620 hours—breakfast time for any sensible person. He was tempted by the thought of coffee. But where to get a bite to eat around here? This was his first stopover at Agathodaemon. Till now, he'd been servicing the main "beachhead" at Syrtis. Why did they have to storm Mars on two fronts separated by thousands of kilometers? He knew the scientific reason, but he had some ideas of his own, which he kept to himself. Syrtis Major was planned as a thermo-nuclear-intellectronic testing ground. It was a different kind of operation there. Some people called Agathodaemon the Cinderella of the project, and several times it was said to be on the verge of folding. But they were still banking on hitting frozen water, deep icebergs thought to be buried beneath the Martian crust. . . . Sure, if the project could tap some local water, that would be a real feat, a breakthrough, seeing as up till now every drop had to be shipped from Earth and construction of the atmospheric steam condensers was now in its second year, with the date of operation constantly being postponed.

No, Mars definitely didn't send him.

He wasn't in the mood for going out yet—the building was so very quiet. He was becoming more and more used to the solitude. A ship's commander can always have his privacy on board; after a long flight (with Earth and Mars no longer in conjunction, the Mars trip took over three months), he practically had to force himself to mix with strangers. And except for the controller on duty, he knew no one here. Look in on him upstairs? That wouldn't be too nice. Mustn't hassle people on the job. He was judging by himself: he didn't like intruders.

In his grip was a thermos with some leftover coffee, and a package of cookies. He ate, trying not to spill the crumbs, sipped his coffee, and stared out through the sand-scored port at the old, flat-bottomed, apathetic floor of Agathodaemon. That was the impression Mars made on him—that it didn't care any more—which explained the haphazard accumulation of craters, so different from the Moon's, looking more like washouts ("They look fake, doctored," he once blurted out while browsing through some detailed blow-ups). The whimsicality of those wild formations that went by the name of "chaos" make them the pet sites of areologists: there was nothing like them on Earth. Mars seemed to have quit, not caring whether it kept its word, unconcerned with appearances. The closer one got to it, the more it lost its solid red exterior, the more it ceased to be the emblem of a war god, the more it revealed its drabness, spots, stains, its lack of any lunar or Earthlike contour: a gray-brown blight, rocked by eternal wind.

He felt a barely palpable vibration underfoot—a converter or a transformer. Otherwise, the same silence as before, penetrated, as if from another world, by the distant howl of a gale wind playing on the cosmodrome's cables. That diabolical sand could eat through high-grade, five-centimeter steel cables. On the Moon you could leave anything, stow it in the rubble, and come back a hundred, a million years hence, secure in the knowledge that it would still be there. On Mars you couldn't afford to drop anything, lest it sink forever. Mars had no manners.

At 0640 hours, the horizon reddened with the sunrise, and this splotch of brightness, this bogus dawn—or, rather, its reddish tint—brought back his dream. Jarred by the sudden recall, he slowly put his thermos down. It was coming back to him. Somebody was out to get him . . . no, it was he who killed someone else. The dead man came after him, chasing him through the ember-red dark; a death blow, then another, but to no effect. Crazy, yes, but there was something else: in the dream, he could have sworn he knew the other man; now he had no idea whom he'd fought to the finish. Granted, this feeling of familiarity could have been a dream illusion, too. He kept dogging it, but his self-willed memory balked, and everything retreated like a snail into its shell, so that he stood by the window, one hand on the metal doorframe, a trifle rattled, as if on the brink of something unnamable. Death. As space technology advanced, it was inevitable that people would start dying on planets. The Moon was loyal to the dead. It let them fossilize, turned them into ice sculpture, mummies, whose lightness and near-weightlessness seemed to diminish the reality, the seriousness of the tragedy. But on Mars, the dead had to be disposed of immediately, because the sand storms would eat through a spacesuit in a matter of days; and before the corpse had been mummified by the severe aridity, bones would sprout from the torn fabric—shiny, polished to perfection, until the whole skeleton was laid bare. Littered in this strange sand, under this strange sky, the bones of the dead were almost a reproach, an offense, as though by bringing along their mortality, people had done something improper, something to be ashamed of, that had to be removed from sight, buried. . . . Screwy as they were, those were his thoughts at the moment.

The night crew went off at 0700, and visitors were allowed into the control tower between shifts. He packed away his few toilet articles and, thinking he'd better make sure the unloading of the *Cuivier* was going according to schedule, went out. All his package cargo had to be off by 1200 hours, and there were still a few things worth testing—such as the

servo-reactor's cooling system—all the more so since he was
going back a man short (getting a substitute for Terman was
wishful thinking). He mounted a spiral, polyfoam-padded
staircase, his hand on the astonishingly warm (heated?) ban-
ister, and when he reached the upper level and opened the
swinging glass door with frosted panes, he entered a world
so different that he felt like someone else.

It could have been the interior of a giant head, with six
enormous, bulging glass eyes fixed in three directions at once.
The fourth wall was mounted with antennas, and the whole
room rotated on its axis like a revolving stage. In a sense, it
was a stage, where the same performance, that of lift-off and
landing, clearly visible a kilometer away from behind the
rounded control consoles that blended perfectly with the silver-gray walls, was played and replayed. The atmosphere
was reminiscent both of an airport control tower and an operating room.

Along the wall of antennas, under a sloping hood, reigned
the main space-traffic computer, always in direct contact,
always blinking and ticking, continually carrying out its mute
monologues and spewing reams of perforated tape. Near it
were stationed three back-up terminals, with mikes, spot-
lights, swivel chairs, and the controllers' hydrant-shaped
hand calculators; and finally, a cute, contoured little bar with
a softly humming espresso machine. So here was the coffee
trough.

Pirx couldn't see the *Cuivier* from the tower; he had parked
it, in compliance with the controller's instructions, five kilometers away, beyond all the clutter, to make way for the
project's first supership landing—as if it wasn't equipped with
the latest space- and astrolocational computers which, according to the bragging of the shipyard builders (nearly all
personal acquaintances of Pirx), could plant that Goliath of
a quarter-miler, that iron mountain, on a site no bigger than
a kitchen garden. All three shifts were mustered for the oc-
casion, which, for all its festivity, was not an official cele-

bration: the *Ariel*, like every other prototype, had posted dozens of experimental flights and lunar landings, though, to be sure, never with a full cargo.

With a half hour to go before touchdown, Pirx greeted those who were off duty and shook hands with Seyn. The monitors were already activated, blurry smudges ran from top to bottom on the cathode-ray tubes, but the lights on the landing terminal were uniformly green, meaning they still had time to kill. Romani, the Base coordinator, offered him a glass of brandy with his coffee. Pirx hesitated—he wasn't used to tippling at such an early hour—but, then, he was there as a private guest and was sensitive enough to see they were only trying to lend the event a touch of class. They'd waited months for the superfreighters, whose arrival was calculated to save Port Control untold headaches, since until now it had been a perpetual contest between the voracious appetite of the construction site, never satisfied by the project's cargo fleet, and the efforts of transport pilots like Pirx to ply the Mars-Earth run as quickly and efficiently as possible. With the conjunction now over, both planets were beginning to move farther apart, the distances between them to increase yearly until reaching an alarming maximum of hundreds of millions of kilometers. It was in this, the project's hour of greatest travail, that relief was at hand.

The talking was subdued, and when the green lights faded and the buzzers sounded, there was dead silence. A typical Martian day was breaking: not cloudy, not clear, no distinguishable horizon, no well-defined sky, as if devoid of any definable, measurable time. Despite the daylight, the perimeters of the concrete squares hugging the Agathodaemon floor were fringed with glowing lines—automatic laser markings—and the rim of the concrete circular shield, almost black, was edged with sparkling, starlike beads. The controllers, idled, made themselves comfortable in their armchairs, while the central computer flashed its diodes, as if to proclaim its indispensability, and the transmitters had begun to drone ever so softly when a clear bass came over the loud-speaker:

"Hello, Agathodaemon, this is *Ariel*, Klyne speaking; we're on video, altitude six hundred, switching to automatic land-ing in twenty secs; over."

"Agathodaemon to *Ariel*," Seyn, having just put out his cigarette, replied eagerly, his beaklike profile up close to the mesh of the microphone. "We have you on all screens; lie down and let her roost; over."

They're goofing around, thought Pirx, who, superstitious as he was, didn't like it, though they obviously had the land-ing procedure down pat.

"*Ariel* to Agathodaemon: we have three hundred, switch-ing to automatic, descending with no lateral drift, zero on zero, what's the wind force? Over."

"Agathodaemon to *Ariel*: wind at a hundred eighty per hour, north-northwest, won't bother you; over."

"*Ariel* to everybody: descending in the axis, stern first, on automatic; over and out."

Silence fell; only the transmitters were mincing away as a flaming white speck, swelling as fast as a bubble being blown out of fiery glass, appeared on the screens. It was the ship's gaping tail section, descending as if on an invisible plumb line, without the slightest jerking or tilting or gyrating. Pirx thrilled to see it. Altitude at about a hundred kilometers, he guessed; no sense watching until it was down around fifty; besides, the observation windows were too crowded with craning heads as it was.

Ground control was in constant radio contact with the ship, but there was nothing to radio, leaving the crew to sit back in their antigravitational chairs and trust to the computers commanded by the ship's primary computer, which had just ordered a shift from atomic to boron drive at an altitude of sixty kilometers, or at the point of atmospheric entry. Pirx now walked up to the middle window, the largest, and im-mediately sighted through the sky's pale blur a bright green

sparkle, microscopic but vibrating with uncommon radiance—as if the Martian horizon were being drilled from
above with a burning emerald. From this incandescent speck,
pale filaments fanned in all directions—cloud wisps, or,
rather, those aborted clouds-to-be which in the local atmosphere served as surrogates for the real thing. Sucked up
into the orbit of the ship's rocket flare, they ignited and exploded like fireworks. The ship's circular flange swelled. The
air was visibly palpitating from the exhaust, which a novice
might have mistaken for a slight vacillation, but Pirx was
too experienced to be fooled. Things were going so smoothly,
so routinely, that he was reminded of the ease with which
the first human step on the Moon had been taken. By now
the fuselage was a burning green disk ringed with a scintil-
lating halo. He glanced at the main altimeter above the control terminals—the altitude of such a supership was easy to
misjudge; eleven, no, twelve kilometers separated the *Ariel*,
decelerating in response to the reverse thrust, from Mars.

Then several things happened at once.

The *Ariel*'s stern nozzles, in a nimbus crowned with green
rays, began to vibrate in a different way. Over the loud-
speaker came a tumult, a muffled cry, something like "Manual!" or maybe "Many!"—one inscrutable word shouted by
a human voice, too altered to have been Klyne's. A second
later, the green blaze spewing from the *Ariel*'s stern paled,
then ballooned into an awesome blue-white incandescence—
and Pirx understood at once, in a shudder of dread that shook
him from head to toe, so that the hollow voice booming from
the loudspeaker surprised him not at all.

"ARIEL"—rasped the husky voice—"COURSE ALTERATION.
AWAY FROM METEORITE. FULL POWER AHEAD IN THE AXIS!
ATTENTION! FULL THRUST!"

It was the computer's voice. Then another—this one human—yelled something in the background. Pirx had correctly diagnosed the change in exhaust: the reactor's full
thrust had taken over from the boron, and the giant space-

ship, as if arrested by the powerful blow of an invisible fist, vibrating in all its joints, stopped—or so it seemed to those looking on—in the thin air, a mere four or five kilometers above the cosmodrome's shield. To arrest a hundred-thousand-ton mass before reversing, without decelerating first, was unheard of, a maneuver in violation of every rule and regulation, defying all the basics of astronavigation. Pirx saw the giant cylinder's hull in foreshortened perspective. The ship was losing its vertical trim; it was listing. Ever so slowly, it began to right itself, then tilted the other way, like a giant pendulum, resulting in an even steeper inclination of the quarter-mile-long hull. At such low velocity, a loss of stability of this amplitude was beyond correction. Only in those seconds did Pirx hear the chief controller scream:

"*Ariel*, *Ariel!* What are you doing? What's happening up there?!"

Pirx, standing by a parallel, vacant terminal, shouted into the mike:

"KLYNE! SWITCH TO MANUAL OVERRIDE!!! TO MANUAL FOR LANDING!!! MANUAL!!!"

Just then they were jolted by a thunderous roar—the *Ariel*'s delayed sound wave, unremitting, prolonged. How fast it had all happened! A concerted cry went up from the windows. The controllers jumped up from their consoles.

The *Ariel* plummeted like a stone, recklessly strewing the atmosphere with swirls of exhaust flare, rotating slowly, corpselike, an enormous iron tower flung from the sky onto dirty desert dunes. All stood nailed to the floor in a hollow, horrific silence fraught with impotence; the loudspeaker grated, crackled, rumbled with the distant clamor—like the roar of the sea—while a refulgent, white, incredibly long cylinder shot down with accelerated speed, seemingly aimed at the control tower. Pirx's neighbor let out a groan. Instinctively everyone ducked.

The hull slammed into one of the shield's low outer walls, halved, and, breaking up with an eerie slowness in a shower of fragments, buried itself in the sand; a ten-story cloud shot up, boomed, and rained stitches of fire. Above the curtain of ejected sand loomed the still blindingly white nose section, which, truncated from the rest, traversed the air a few hundred meters; then one, two, three powerful thuds with the force of earthquake tremors. The whole building heaved, rose and fell like a skiff on a wave. Then, in a hellish racket of cracking iron, everything was blotted out by a brownish-black wall of smoke and dust. Even as they raced downstairs to the airlock, Pirx, one of the first to suit up, had no doubts: in such a collision, there could be no survivors.

Soon they were running, buffeted by the gale winds; from far off, from the direction of the "bell," the first of the caterpillar vehicles and hovercrafts were already on the move. But there was no reason to hurry. Pirx didn't know how or when he returned to the control tower—the image of the crater and the crushed hull still in his dazed eyes—and only at the sight of his own suddenly grayed, somewhat shrunken face in a wall mirror did he come to.

By afternoon, a committee of experts had been set up to investigate the causes of the crash. Work crews with excavators and cranes were still clearing away the wreckage of the giant vehicle, and had yet to reach the deeply buried cockpit containing the automatic controls, when a team of specialists was bused over from Syrtis Major—in one of those quaint little helicopters with huge propellers, custom-designed for flight in the Martian air. Pirx kept out of the way and didn't ask questions, knowing only too well that the case bordered on the unsolvable. During a routine landing, with all its hallowed sequences and clockwork programming, for no apparent reason the *Ariel*'s primary computer had shut down the boron power, signaled a residual meteorite alarm, and initiated an escape maneuver at full thrust; the ship's stability, once lost during this neck-breaking action, was never regained. It was an event unprecedented in the history of astronavigation, and every plausible hypothesis—a computer failure, a glitch, a short in one of the circuits—appeared highly improbable, because there was not one but two programs for lift-off and landing, safeguarded by so many back-up systems as to make sabotage a more likely cause.

He puzzled over the incident in the little cubicle that Seyn had put at his disposal the night before, deliberately laying low so as not to intrude, especially since he was scheduled to lift off within the next twenty-four hours; but he couldn't come up with anything, or at least not with anything he could report to the committee. He wasn't forgotten, though; a few minutes before one in the afternoon, Seyn paid him a visit. Waiting in the corridor was Romani; Pirx, on his way out, didn't recognize him at first. The coordinator of the Agathodaemon complex could have passed for one of the mechanics: he wore a pair of sooty, grease-stained overalls, his face was drawn, the left corner of his mouth twitched, and only his voice had a familiar ring. On behalf of the committee, of which he was a member, he asked Pirx to postpone the *Cuivier*'s lift-off.

"Sure thing." Pirx, a trifle stunned, tried to regain his composure. "I just need clearance from Base."

"Leave that to us."

Nothing more was said, and the three of them marched over to the main "bubble," where, inside the long, squat command HQ, sat some twenty or more experts—a few of whom were based locally, the majority having flown over from Syrtis Major. It was lunchtime, but since every second was precious, they were served a cold meal from the cafeteria. Over tea and paper plates, which lent the proceedings a strangely casual, even festive air, the session got under way. The chairman, Engineer Hoyster, called first on Pirx to describe the abortive landing, and Pirx could easily guess why. Belonging neither to the ground-control team nor to Agathodaemon's crew, he was the only unbiased witness present.

When he reached the point of his own personal intervention, Hoyster interrupted him.

"So you wanted Klyne to shift from automatic to manual override?"

"Yes."

"Why, may I ask?"

"I figured it was his only chance," Pirx answered without hesitation.

"Right. And you didn't foresee that the shift to manual would mean a loss of stability?"

"It was already lost. This can be checked; we *do* have the tapes."

"Naturally. We just wanted to get a general picture. What's your own guess?"

"As to the cause?"

"Yes. For the moment we're just piecing together the facts. Nothing you say will be binding; any hypothesis, however shaky, may prove valuable."

"I see. My guess is that something went haywire with the computer. *What*, or even *how*, I couldn't say. I wouldn't have believed it myself if I hadn't witnessed it with my own eyes and ears. The computer aborted the maneuver and signaled a meteorite alert. It sounded like 'Meteorites—attention, full power ahead in the axis.' But with no meteorites around . . ." Pirx shrugged.

"The *Ariel* was an advanced AIBM 09," observed Boulder, an electronics engineer with whom Pirx had rubbed elbows at Syrtis Major.

Pirx nodded.

"I know. That's why I said I wouldn't have believed it if I hadn't seen it with my own eyes. But it did happen."

"Why did Klyne hold back, in your opinion, Commander?" asked Hoyster.

Pirx felt his insides go cold; before answering, he cast a glance around the table. It was a question that had to be asked, though he didn't relish being the first to face it.

"I don't know the answer to that."

"Of course not. But you're an old-timer; put yourself in his place. . . ."

"I did. I would have done what I tried to make him do."

"And?"

"No response. A madhouse. Yelling, maybe. The tapes will have to be checked and rechecked, though I'm afraid it won't do much good."

"Commander," said Hoyster, in a soft but painstaking voice, as if struggling to choose his words, "you realize the situation, don't you? As we're speaking, there are two more superfreighters, equipped with the exact same guidance system, on the Aresterra line. The *Anabis* isn't due for another three weeks, but the *Ares* is nine days away. No matter what our obligations to the dead, we owe more to the living. I'm sure in the past five hours you've given some thought to the case. I can't force you, but I'm asking you to speak your mind."

Pirx blanched. He'd read Hoyster's mind from his opening words, and a sensation, opaque, born of his nightmare, gripped him: an intense, desperate silence, a faceless enemy, and a double killing—of himself and the other. It came and went. He collected himself and looked Hoyster in the eye.

"I see," he said. "Klyne and I belong to two different generations. When I was getting my wings, servo-mechanisms were more error-prone. Distrust becomes second nature. My guess is . . . he trusted in them to the end."

"He thought the computer was in control, had a better command of the situation?"

"Not so much in control. More like, if the computer couldn't handle it, a man would be even less likely to do so."

He sighed. He'd spoken his mind without casting a shadow on his younger, now deceased, colleague.

"Was there any chance of saving that ship, Commander?"

"Hard to say. There was so little time. The *Ariel* dropped to zero velocity."

"Have you ever soft-landed under such conditions?"

"Yes. But in a ship with a smaller mass, and it was on the Moon. The longer and heavier the ship, the harder it is to regain stability when you're losing speed, especially if it goes into a list."

"Did Klyne hear you?"

"I don't know. He should have."

"Did he ever override the controls?"

Pirx was about to defer to the tapes, but answered instead:

"No."

"How do you know?" It was Romani.

"The monitor showed 'automatic landing' the whole time. It went off only on impact."

"Could it not be, sir, that Klyne didn't have time?" asked Seyn. Why was he "sirring" him when they were buddies? Hm. Keeping his distance, maybe. Out to get him?

"The chances of survival can be mathematically deduced." Pirx was aiming for objectivity. "I just don't know offhand."

"But once the list exceeded forty-five degrees, stability was irretrievably lost," insisted Seyn. "Right?"

"Not on the *Cuivier* it wouldn't be. One can increase the thrust beyond the accepted limits."

"An acceleration over twenty g's can be fatal."

"It can be. But a fall from five kilometers up *has* to be."

That ended their brief exchange. Tobacco smoke hung under the lights, which had been switched on despite the daylight.

"Do you mean that Klyne *could* have manned the controls but didn't?" This was the chairman, Hoyster, picking up the thread.

"It looks that way."

"Do you think you might have rattled him when you butted in?" asked Seyn's assistant, a man from Agathodaemon, a stranger to Pirx. Was the home team against him? He could understand it if they were.

"It's a possibility. There was a lot of shouting in the cockpit. Or at least that's what it sounded like."

"Panic?" asked Hoyster.

"No comment."

"Why?"

"You can listen to the tape. The voices were too garbled to be hard data. Too easy to misinterpret."

"In your opinion, could ground control have lent further assistance?" asked a poker-faced Hoyster. The committee was obviously divided; Hoyster was from Syrtis Major.

"No. None."

"Your own reaction would seem to contradict you."

"Not really. Control has no right to countermand a skipper in such a situation. Things can look a lot different in the cockpit."

"So you admit you acted contrary to the rules?" Seyn's assistant again.

"Yes."

"Why?" asked Hoyster.

"The rules aren't sacred. I always do what I think right. I've had to answer for it in the past."

"To whom?"

"The Cosmic Tribunal."

"But you were cleared of all charges," intruded Boulder. Syrtis Major versus Agathodaemon: it was blatantly obvious.

Pirx paused.

"Thank you, sir."

He sat down in an adjacent chair. Seyn was the next to testify, followed by his assistant. They were still at it when the first ground recordings arrived. Telephone reports from the wreckage site confirmed the absence of any survivors, though they had yet to reach the *Ariel*'s cockpit, buried eleven meters below ground. The committee proceeded to audit the tapes and continued taking depositions without a break until seven, then recessed for an hour. Seyn and the Syrtisians drove out to the site of the shipwreck. Romani stopped Pirx in the passageway.

"Commander Pirx . . ."

"Yes?"

"You haven't any—uh—"

"Don't. The stakes are too high," interrupted Pirx.

Romani nodded. "You have seventy-two hours' furlough. We've worked it out with Base."

"Earthside?" asked Pirx, astonished. "I don't see how I can be—"

"Hoyster, Rahaman, and Boulder want to co-opt you onto the committee. You're not going to let us down, are you?"

All three were Syrtisians.

"I couldn't even if I wanted to," he replied, and they let it go at that.

They reconvened at nine. The replay of the tapes was dramatic, but not nearly as much as the film, which recorded each stage of the calamity, from the moment the *Ariel* loomed as a green star in the zenith. Afterward, Hoyster gave a recap of the post-mortem.

"All the evidence points to a computer breakdown. If it didn't signal a meteorite alarm, it must have projected the *Ariel* on a collision course with something. The tapes show that it was three percent over the limit. Why, we don't know. Maybe the cockpit will provide a clue." He was referring to the *Ariel*'s on-board tapes, though Pirx did not share his optimism. "We'll never know the exact sequence of events during those final moments in the cockpit. We do know that the computer's Baud rate was perfect: even at the peak of the crisis, it was fully operative. The sub-routines performed flawlessly till the end, too. That much has been established. We've uncovered nothing to indicate any external or internal interference with the prescribed landing procedure. From 0703 to 0708 hours, all systems were go. The computer's decision to abort the landing cannot, at present, be explained. Mr. Boulder?"

"I don't get it."

"A programming error?" asked someone.

"Impossible. The *Ariel* had made landing after landing with the very same program—axially, and at every possible angle."

"But that was on the Moon, under conditions of lesser gravity."

"Of possible consequence for the thrust modulators, but not for the informational systems. Besides, the power didn't quit."

"Mr. Rahaman?"

"I'm not very up-to-date on this program."

"But you're familiar with the model?"

"I am."

"Failing any external cause, what could have interrupted the landing procedure?"

"Nothing."

"Nothing?"

"A bomb planted under the computer, maybe . . ." said Rahaman.

Out in the open at last; Pirx was all ears now. The exhaust fans whirred as smoke clustered around the ceiling vents.

"Sabotage?"

"The computer functioned till the end, though erratically," observed Kerhoven, the only locally stationed intellectronics engineer on the committee.

"Well, I only mentioned it for what it may be worth," said Rahaman, backing off. "In the case of a normally functioning computer, the landing and lift-off maneuver can be aborted only by something out of the ordinary. A power failure . . ."

"Power there was."

"But, theoretically, can't a computer abort the procedure?"

The chairman knew well enough that it could. Pirx understood that his question was not addressed to them, but was for the benefit of Earth.

"In theory, yes. In practice, no. Not once in the history of astronautics has a meteorite alarm been sounded during a landing. When a meteorite is sighted, the landing is simply postponed."

"But none was sighted."

"No."

A dead end. There were a few moments of silence. The fans purred. Darkness showed through the round ports. A Martian night.

"What we need are the people who constructed that model, the ones who test-loaded it," Rahaman said at last.

Hoyster nodded. He was distracted by a message handed him by the telegraph operator. "They'll be reaching the cockpit in an hour or so," he said. Then, looking up, he added: "Macross and Van der Voyt will take part in tomorrow's session."

There was some commotion. Macross was the chief engineer and Van der Voyt the managing director of the shipyard whence the hundred-thousand-tonners came.

"Tomorrow?" Pirx couldn't believe his ears.

"Not live, of course—but by video, thanks to a direct relay. Here's the cable." He waved the telegram.

"Hold on—what's the time lag?" asked someone.

"Eight minutes."

"What's the big idea? We'll have to wait a lifetime for every answer," someone asked, in a clamor of several voices at once.

Hoyster shrugged.

"We'll have to comply. Granted, it'll be a nuisance, but we'll work out something. . . ."

"Does that mean we're adjourning till tomorrow?" asked Romani.

"Right. We'll reconvene at 0600 hours. By then we should have the on-board tapes."

Pirx gladly accepted Romani's offer to put him up for the night. He wanted no part of Seyn. Though he understood the man's behavior, he couldn't condone it. Accommodations were found for the Syrtisians—not without some difficulty—and by midnight Pirx was left all alone in the tiny cubicle that served as the coordinator's reference library and private study. He lay down, fully dressed, on a cot set up between several theodolites, and, with his arms under his head, stared up at the ceiling, eyes fixed, barely breathing.

It was odd, but, being among strangers, he had been viewing the accident as an outsider, as one of the many witnesses not really involved, even when he had detected the hostility, the irritation in their questions—an unspoken accusation directed at the intruder out to show up the local boys—and when Seyn had turned against him. This was another realm, fixed in the natural dimension of the inevitable: under the circumstances it had had to happen. He would defend what he'd done, on rational grounds; he held himself in no way responsible for the disaster. True, he'd been shaken, but he'd kept his head, always the observer, never entirely overwhelmed by events because of the way they lent themselves to systematic analysis: for all their inexplicability, they could be sifted, categorized, posited according to the method dictated by the solemnity of the investigation.

Now all that was giving way. His mind was a blank, he evoked nothing, the images reasserted themselves on their own, from the beginning: the monitors, the ship's entry into the Martian atmosphere, the deceleration from a cosmic velocity, the shifts in thrust; he was everywhere at once—in the control tower, in the cockpit; he knew the muffled strokes, the rumbling along the keel and ribs when the atomic drive gave way to the pulsating boron hydrides; the deep, reassuring bass of the turbo-pumps; the reverse thrust, the axial descent, stern first, majestically slow; the slight lateral corrections, and then ignition, the thunderous roar accompanying the sudden shift in thrust when full power was restored to the nozzles; the vibrations, the destabilization, the frantic effort to keep on an even keel, swinging pendulously, teetering like a drunken tower, before going into a dive, inert, rudderless, blind, a stone, disintegrating on impact— and he was everywhere. He might have been the struggling ship itself, and, though painfully aware of the hopeless inaccessibility, the finality of what had happened, he returned to those fragmentary seconds with a silent, unremitting question in search of the cause.

Whether or not Klyne had tried to man the controls didn't matter any more. Ground control? Clean. Only someone very superstitious or trained in soberer times could have begrudged them their fun. Reason told him there was nothing sinful about it. He lay there, flat on his back, but at the same time he was standing by the window pitched toward the zenith, watching as the flickering green boron star was consumed by that awesome solar blaze—with its pulsation so typical of atomic power—in the nozzles, which had already begun to cool (hence the restrictions against sudden shifts to full throttle); still watching as the ship swung like the tongue of a bell rocked by a madman's hands, listing with the entire length of its behemoth body, its very dimensions, the very force of its magnitude making it seem immune to danger—a century ago, the passengers of the *Titanic* must have felt similarly comforted.

Suddenly it receded; he was awake. He got up, washed his face and hands, opened his grip, got out his pajamas, slippers, toothbrush, and for the third time that day eyed himself in the washbasin mirror. He saw a stranger.

In his late thirties, pushing forty: the shadow line. Time to accept the terms of the unsigned contract, there without the asking; the knowledge that what binds others applies to you, too, that there are no exceptions to the rule: though it was contrary to nature, one had to grow old. So far, only the body was secretly obeying, but that wasn't enough any more. Now one had to assent to it. Youth made its own unalterability the rule, the basic premise: I was childish, immature, but now I am my true self, and that's the way I'll stay. This was the joke at the very heart of existence, whose discovery was more a cause of amazement than of alarm—a sense of outrage born of the realization that the game we've been forced to play is a hoax. The contest was to have been different; after the initial shock, the anger, the resistance, came the slow negotiations with one's self, with one's body: no matter how smooth and imperceptible the aging process, we can never reconcile ourselves to it rationally. We brace ourselves for thirty-five, then forty, as if it were to last, and with the next revision, the shattering of illusion is greeted with such resistance that the momentum makes us overstep the bounds.

That's when a forty-year-old begins to adopt the mannerisms of an old man. Resigned to the inevitability of it, we carry on the game with grim determination, as if perversely bent on upping the ante: all right, if it's to be dirty, if this cynical, cruel promissory note, this IOU, has to be honored, if I really have to pay, then even though I never agreed to it, never asked for it, never knew, there's your debt, and more! Comical as it sounds, we try to outbluff our opponent: I'll grow old so damned fast you'll be sorry. Stuck at the shadow line, or almost across it, in the phase of abandoning and surrendering positions, we keep up the fight, keep on defying reality, and because of the constant scrimmaging we grow old psychically by leaps and bounds. Either we exaggerate or we underrate, until one day we see, too late as usual, that this fencing match, all these suicidal thrusts, retreats, and sallies, were also a joke. We are like children, withholding our approval of something for which our assent was never required, where there can never be any protest or struggle—a struggle, moreover, rooted in self-deception. The shadow line is not a *memento mori* but is in many respects worse, a vantage point from which to see our prospects diminished. That is, the present is neither a promise nor a waiting room, neither a preface nor a springboard for great hopes, because the terms have been imperceptibly reversed. The so-called training period was an irrevocable reality; the preface—the story proper; the hopes—fantasies; the optional, the provisional, the momentary, and the whimsical— the true stuff of life. What hasn't been achieved by now will never be; and one has to reconcile oneself to this fact, quietly, fearlessly, and, if possible, without despair.

This was an awkward age in an astronaut's career—for him more so than for anybody else, since in the space profession anyone less than perfectly fit was automatically expendable. As the physiologists attested, the demands made by astrocology were too severe, even for the physically and spiritually fittest; to be demoted from the front ranks was to forfeit all. The medical boards were ruthless, devastatingly so, but necessary: no one could be allowed to collapse or die of a heart attack at the controls. People in their prime went ashore and suddenly found themselves near retirement—the examining doctors were so used to their subterfuges and desperate simulations that they waived disciplinary action. And rare was the pilot who could have his eligibility extended past fifty.

Fatigue is the brain's toughest enemy; a hundred or a thousand years hence, this may change, but for now it is an agonizing prospect for anyone during prolonged space flight— anyone at the shadow line.

Klyne belonged to a new generation of astronauts; Pirx, on the other hand, to those called "anti-computer"—thus he was a "reactionary" and a "fossil." Some of his contemporaries had already retired; depending on their talents and effectiveness, they became lecturers or members of the Cosmic Tribunal, took cushy jobs in the shipyards, joined adminis-

trative boards, tended their gardens. On the whole, they held
their own; they simulated acceptance of the inevitable; but
how it cost some of them!

There were also aberrations born of protest, of obstinacy,
of pride and fury, of the sense of a wrong unjustly incurred.
Although it was a profession that did not allow for madmen,
certain individuals came dangerously close to madness, only
to stop short of crossing the line. Under the mounting pressure of the inevitable, people did the wackiest things—bizarre things. Oh, he knew all about those quirks, aberrations,
superstitions, to which both strangers and long-time shipmates—whose stability he would have personally sworn by—
were susceptible. Sweet ignorance was hardly a privilege in
a line of work demanding such sure-fire know-how; every
day neurons perished in the brain by the thousands, so that
by thirty a person was already in the midst of it, that pecu-
liar, imperceptible, but incessant race, that contest between
the slackening of reflexes undermined by atrophy, and their
perfection achieved through experience; from which arose
that shaky equilibrium, that acrobatic tightrope act with
which one had to live, to fly.

And to dream. Whom was he out to kill the night before?
The dream obviously signified something, but what? Reclin-
ing on the cot, which squeaked under his weight, he sensed
a sleepless night on the way—though he had never lost a
night's sleep, the insomnia, too, was inevitable. That alarmed
him. Not the prospect of a sleepless night so much as his
body's recalcitrance, signaling a vulnerability, a break in
what was hitherto infallible, the mere thought of which, at
this moment, connoted defeat. He was not content to lie there
wide-eyed against his will, and so, even though it was silly,
he sat up, stared vacantly at his pajamas, then shifted his
gaze to the bookshelves.

Not expecting to find anything of interest, he was all the
more startled to discover a row of thick-bound volumes above
the compass-pocked plotting board. There, neatly arrayed,

stood practically the entire history of areology, most of the titles being familiar to him from his reference library on Earth. He got up and ran his fingers along their solid spines. Herschel, the father of astronomy, was there; so was Kepler's *Astronomia Nova de Motibus Stellae Martis ex Observationibus Tychonis Brahe*, in a 1784 edition. Then came Flammarion, Backhuysen, Kaiser, and the great dreamer, Schiaparelli—a dark-brown Latin edition of his *Memoria terza*—and Arrhenius, Antoniadi, Kuiper, Lowell, Pickering, Saheko, Struve, Vaucouleurs, all the way up to Wernher von Braun and his *Exploration of Mars*. And maps, rolls of them, inscribed with all the canals—Margaritifer Sinus, Lacus Solis, even Agathodaemon. . . . He stood before the familiar, not really having to open any of these books with their burnished, plywood-thick covers. The musty effluvium of old linen bindings and yellowed pages, bespeaking both dignity and decrepitude, revived memories of long hours spent in contemplation of the mystery that had been attacked, besieged for two centuries by a horde of hypotheses, only to have their authors die, one by one, unrequited. Antoniadi went a lifetime without observing any canals, and only in the twilight of old age did he grudgingly acknowledge "some lines bearing a likeness to same." The "canalists," meanwhile, charted their observations at night, whiling away hours at the eyeglass for one of those fleeting moments of stationary atmosphere, at which time, they averred, a hairthin geometric grid emerged on the fuzzy gray surface. Lowell made it dense, Pickering less so, but he was in luck with his "gemination," as the incredible duplication of canals was called. An illusion? Why, then, did some canals *never* double?

He used to pore over these books as a cadet—in the reading room, of course, since they were too rare to be circulated. Pirx—need it be said?—sided with the "canalists." Their arguments rang infallibly. Graff, Antoniadi, Hall— those incurable doubting Thomases—had their observatories in the air-polluted cities of the North, whereas Schiaparelli worked in Milan, and Pickering on his mountain overlooking the Arizona desert. The "anti-canalists" conducted the most ingenious experiments: they would chart a disk with randomly inscribed dots and blotches that, viewed from a distance, took on a gridlike pattern, and then ask: How could they escape the most powerful instruments? Why were the lunar canals visible with the naked eye? How could the earlier observers have missed them, and everyone after Schiaparelli take them as self-evident? And the "canalists" would counter: The lunar canals went undetected in the pretelescopic age. Earth's atmosphere wasn't stable enough to permit detection with high-powered telescopes; the drawing experiments only sidestepped the issue. The "canalists" had an answer for everything: Mars was a giant frozen ocean, the canals were rifts in its meteor-impacted ice mass or, rather, wide fluvial valleys watered by the spring thaws and graced with vernal efflorescence. When spectroscopy revealed an insufficient water content, they decided the canals were enormous troughs, long valleys covered with cloud masses borne by convex currents adrift from the pole to the equator. Schiaparelli never publicly acknowledged these as figments of a foreign imagination, playing on the ambiguity of the term "canal." This reticence on the part of the Milanese astronomer was shared by many others, who never named, only charted and displayed, but in his papers Schiaparelli left behind drawings explaining the origin of the doubling phenomenon, the famous gemination process: when the parallel, hitherto arid rills were inundated, the water suddenly caused the helices to darken, like wood grooves filled with ink. The "anti-canalists," meanwhile, did not just deny the existence of the canals and amass a body of counterargument, but over time became increasingly vindictive.

In his hundred-page pamphlet, Wallace, after Darwin the second architect of the theory of natural evolution, hence not even an astronomer by profession, a man who probably never even glimpsed Mars through the lenses, demolished the canal hypothesis, and any thought of life on Mars as well: Mars, he wrote, was not only not inhabited by sentient beings, as Lowell claimed, but was actually uninhabitable. None remained neutral; all had to proclaim their credos. The next generation of canalists began to speak of a Martian civilization, thus deepening the split: a realm bearing traces of sentient activity, some said; a corpselike desert, countered others. Then Saheko observed those mysterious flashes—volatile, extinguished by cloud formations, too fleeting to be volcanic eruptions, arising during the period of planetary conjunction, thus ruling out a solar reflection on the planet's high glacial range.

Not until the unleashing of atomic energy was the possibility of nuclear tests on Mars broached. One side had to be right. By the mid-twentieth century, it was unanimously agreed that, although Schiaparelli's geometrical canals were chimerical, there was *something* up there to suggest the presence of canals. The eye may embellish, but not hallucinate; the canals were observed by too many people, in too many places on Earth, to be an allusion. So: no glacial water, no cloud streams borne along the valleys, and most likely no zones of vegetation, either; yet *something* was up there— who knew, perhaps even more mind-boggling, more enigmatic—that only awaited the human eye, the camera lens, and unmanned space probes.

Pirx knew better than to divulge the thoughts inspired by these readings, but Boerst, bright and ruthless as befitted the class brain, soon discovered his true sympathies, and for a few weeks made him the laughingstock of the school, dubbing him "Pirx the canalist," promotor of the doctrine "*Credo, quia non est.*" Pirx knew full well the canals were a fiction; worse, that there was nothing even faintly suggestive of them. How could he *not* have known, what with Mars having been colonized for years, and his having passed his qualifying exams, when he was obliged to orient detailed photographic maps under the vigilant eye of his TA, and even, in his mock-ups, to soft-land in the simulator on the same Agathodaemon floor where he now stood, under the project's dome, by a bookshelf containing two centuries of astronomical discoveries and antique museum pieces. Yes, he knew, but it was a knowledge of a different order, remote, *distanced*, not to be verified by tests, by those exercises seemingly based on a hoax. It was as if there existed yet another, inaccessible, geometrically patterned, and mysterious Mars.

There is a stretch on the Ares-Terra line, a zone from which one can really see—continually, for hours on end—with the naked eye what Schiaparelli, Lowell, and Pickering were able to observe only during brief interludes of atmospheric stability. Through the ports one can see the canals, for up to twenty-four, sometimes forty-eight hours, vaguely outlined against the drab, inhospitable shield. Then, as the globe begins to swell on approach, they commence to fade, to dissolve, blurring one by one into a blank nothingness, leaving only the planet's disk, purged of any sharp contours, to mock with its tedious gray nullity the hopes and expectations it had aroused. True, weeks later, certain surface details, fixed and well defined, begin to re-emerge, but these turn out to be the serrated rims of the largest craters, the wild accretions of weather-beaten rocks, a riot of rock scree buried under deep layers of drab sand, in no way evocative of that pristine, impeccable geometry. At close range, the planet yields its chaos, meekly and irrevocably, incapable of shedding that glaring image of a billion-year erosion; of a chaos not to be reconciled with that memorably lucid design, whose symmetry connoted something compelling, moving, which bespoke a rational order, an unintelligible but manifest logic, that required just a trifle more exertion to be grasped.

Where was that order, and whence came this mocking illusion? Was it a projection of the retina, of human optical processes? A figment of the cerebral cortex? The questions remained unanswered as the problem went the way of all hypotheses phased out and crushed by technological progress: It was swept into the trash. Since there were no canals—not even any topographical features to foster the illusion—the case was closed. A good thing that neither the "canalists" nor the "anti-canalists" lived to hear these sobering revelations, because the riddle was never really solved, merely phased out. Other planets had nebulous shields, and not a single canal was ever sighted on them. Unseen, uncharted. Why? Anyone's guess.

Here, too, hypotheses could be advanced to explain this chapter of astronomy: the combination of distance and optical enlargement, of objective chaos and a subjective craving for order; the residual traces of something that, emerging from the blurred patch in the lens, just beyond the border of perceptibility, momentarily came within the eye's grasp; the faintest visual suggestion combined with subconscious wishful thinking.

Requiring all to choose sides, entrenched in their respective positions, forever joined in noble conflict, generation after generation of astrophysicists had gone to the grave firmly believing that the issue would one day be resolved by the appropriate tribunals, fairly and irrevocably. Pirx was sure that all—each in his own way, each for a different reason—would have felt cheated, disillusioned, if they, like he, had been made privy to the truth. For in this refutation of both pro and con, in the total impropriety of any concept vis-à-vis the enigma, was contained a bitter but dire, cruel but salutary lesson which—it suddenly dawned on him— bore directly on the present, on this brain-teaser of a calamity.

A link between the old astrography and the crack-up of the *Ariel?* But how? And what to make of this intuition, so vague and yet so compelling? A teaser, all right. But whatever the missing link between them, however distant and tenuous the connection, he knew it would no more be revealed now, in the middle of the night, than it would be forgotten. He would have to sleep on it.

As he switched off the light, it occurred to him that Romani was a man of much broader intellectual horizons than he had given him credit for. These books were his own private possession, and one had to fight for every kilo of personal gear shipped to Mars—special notices, appealing to the work crew's loyalty and warning against the dangers of overloading, were plastered all over the Base, Earthside. Everywhere they were crying for expediency, and here was Romani, coordinator of the Agathodaemon project, who, in flagrant violation of the rules, had imported dozens of kilos of uttlerly useless books—and for what? Surely not for bedtime reading.

In the dark, already half asleep, he smiled as he realized the motive that justified the presence of these bibliophilic antiquities under the project's dome. Granted, these books, these passé gospels, these discredited prophecies, had no business being there. But it seemed only fair—necessary, even—that these minds, which had once been the bitterest of enemies, which had given their best to the mystery of the red planet, should find themselves, now fully reconciled, here on Mars. They deserved it, and Romani, who understood, was a man worthy of his trust.

At 0500 hours, he woke from a deep sleep, as alert as if braced by a cold shower. Savoring a few minutes' leisure— exactly five; it was becoming something of a habit—he thought of the commander of the shipwrecked *Ariel*. He wasn't sure whether Klyne could have saved the ship with its thirty-man crew, or whether the man had even tried. Klyne belonged to a generation of rationalists, men trained to keep pace with their impeccably logical allies, the computers, which became more demanding as one made greater efforts to control them; in a sense, blind obedience was the wiser course. But Pirx was incapable of blind obedience. Distrust was in his bones. He flipped on the radio.

The furor had started. Pirx had been expecting it, but he'd underestimated the extent of it. The press kept hammering away at three themes: the suspicion of sabotage, the risk to the other Mars-bound ships, and, of course, the political fall-out. The big papers tiptoed around the sabotage hypothesis, but the tabloids wallowed in it. The hundred-thousand-ton-ners also took flak: they weren't flightworthy, they couldn't lift off from Earth, and worse, they could neither abort a mission (their fuel supply was inadequate) nor be junked in circum-Martian orbits. It was true: they had to land on Mars. But three years before, unbeknownst to these self-styled ex-perts, a test prototype equipped with a different computer model had successfully soft-landed on Mars, not once but several times. The political promotors of the Mars project were also subjected to a campaign of vilification, their critics badmouthing it as sheer lunacy. There were exposures of work-safety violations on both bases, of the project's rubber-stamping and bench-testing methods, of bureaucratic bumbling among high-ranking administrators—in short, a Cassandralike outcry.

When he reported at 0600 hours, he found himself a mem-ber of a nonexistent committee, their self-appointed panel having just been abolished by Earth: it was to start all over again, now officially and legally reconstituted as an adjunct to Earth's board of inquiry. Thus dissolved, the body reaped certain advantages. It was relieved of any decision-making, and so felt freer to make recommendations to its Earthly superior.

Logistically, the situation at Syrtis Major was ticklish but not critical, whereas a suspension of deliveries would sink Agathodaemon before the month was out. Any effective help from Syrtis was out of the question. Not only were building materials in short supply, but water as well. The situation called for the most stringent economizing.

Pirx listened to the update with one ear only, because meanwhile the *Ariel*'s cockpit recorder had been rescued. The human remains were being stored in containers: no decision as yet on whether they would be buried on Mars. The tapes had to be processed before they could be analyzed, which explained why matters not directly related to the causes of the shipwreck were under discussion—such as whether a mobilization of smaller freighters could save the project from extinction, guaranteeing delivery of at least minimal bio-support cargo. While Pirx saw the wisdom of such deliberations, he couldn't help thinking of the two Mars-bound hundred-thousand-tonners, whose existence had somehow been overlooked, almost as if it was taken for granted they would have to abort. But they had to land. By now, all were keenly aware of the reaction of the American press, and radiograms kept them up-to-date on the latest political diatribes. It didn't look good: spokesmen for the project had yet to issue a public statement, and already the administration found itself caught in a firestorm of accusation, including insinuations of "criminal negligence." Pirx, wanting no part of it, slipped out of the smoke-filled hall around ten, and, thanks to ground maintenance, drove out in a jeep to the site of the shipwreck.

By Martian standards, it was a warm, almost cloudy day, the sky more coral-hued than rust-gray. At such times Mars seemed possessed of its own, un-Earthly, raw, slightly veiled, even soiled beauty, the sort we expected to see fully revealed, crowned with a solar radiance, from the vortex of dust and haze, though this expectation went unfulfilled—Mars's ephemeral beauty was not a promise but the very best the planet's landscape could muster.

Having left the squat, bunkerlike ground control a few kilometers back, they reached the end of the launch-pad area, then got hopelessly mired just beyond it. Pirx wore a lightweight partial, which they were all using up here, bright blue, much more comfortable than the full, with a backpack made lighter by an open respirator. Even so, something was wrong with the air conditioning, because the moment he started sweating from the exertion of wading through the sand drifts, his helmet visor began to fog up. Fortunately, hanging like turkey wattles between his neck-ring disconnect and his breastplate were several hand pouches that he could use to dry the glass from the inside—crude but effective.

An immense crater, teeming with caterpillars: the excavation, lined on three sides with sheets of corrugated aluminum acting as sand barriers, resembled the mouth of a mine shaft. The *Ariel*'s midship—huge, like a trans-Atlantic liner storm-battered and shipwrecked against the rocks—took up half of the funnel; some fifty people bustled below her, both they and their dredging machines looking like ants on a giant's carcass. The ship's eighteen-meter nose section, almost intact, lay elsewhere, hurled a few hundred meters away in the crash. The force of impact had been awesome, to judge by the lumps of melted quartz: the kinetic energy had been immediately converted to thermal, producing a shock similar to that of a meteorite landing, despite a velocity less than the speed of sound. In Pirx's mind, the disparity between Agathodaemon's physical capacities and the enormity of the wreckage was not enough to justify the slipshod excavation; one had to improvise, of course, but the almost willful bedlam bespoke a resignation in face of the inconceivable. Even the ship's water was wasted: with every on-board cistern ruptured, the sand had absorbed thousands of hectaliters before the remainder was turned to ice. This ice made a singularly macabre sight, gushing from the forty-meter gash in the ship's fuselage in dirty, dazzling cascades, resting on the dunes like bizarre festoons, as if the exploding ship had spewed a frozen Niagara Falls—temperatures here reached eighteen below zero Celsius, dropping at night to sixty below. The *Ariel*'s ice-packed, ice-glazed hull made the wreckage look positively ancient, prehistoric.

Access to the ship's interior was either through the ice, by drilling and jackhammering, or through the shaft. Through the latter they reached the salvageable boxes, piles of which littered the funnel's slopes, yet the whole operation bordered on sloppy. The tail section was off limits; red pennons, strung on ropes and marking the area of radioactive contamination, fluttered furiously in the wind.

Pirx made a tour of the site, circling the lip of the embankment, and counted two thousand steps before he stood above the ship's soot-blackened nozzles, rankling as he watched how the salvage crew, their chains slipping each time, tried futilely to pull out the one surviving fuel tank. He was there only a short while, or so it seemed to him, when someone tapped his shoulder and pointed to his respirator gauge. The pressure had fallen; since he didn't have a spare, he had to go back. By his watch, a new chronometer, he'd spent almost two hours at the wreckage site.

The conference hall, meanwhile, had been rearranged: the locals were seated on one side of the long table, opposite six large, flat, freshly installed TV monitors. As usual, there was a glitch in the relay, so the session was postponed until 1300 hours. Haroun, the telegraph operator, whom Pirx had come across at Syrtis Major, and who, for some reason, treated him with great respect, gave him the first dubs of the tapes—the ones bearing the decisions of the power regulator—rescued from the *Ariel's* shatterproof chamber. Haroun had no right to leak them, so Pirx could well appreciate the gesture. He shut himself up in his cubicle and, standing under a tensor lamp, took to examining the still-sticky snake of magnetic tape. The picture was as clear as it was incomprehensible. In the 317th second of the landing sequence, flawless until then, the control circuits showed the presence of parasitic currents, which seconds later turned up as a wiggle of beats. Twice extinguished once the load had been shifted to the grid's parallel, back-up components, they came back intensified, and from then on, the "sensors" functioned at a rate of three times the norm. What he held in his hands was not the computer's register, but that of its "spinal cord," which, obeying the commands of the servo-system, coordinated the received instructions with the condition of the power routines. This system sometimes went by the name of the "cerebellum," by analogy with the human cerebellum, which, acting as the control station between the cortex and the body, governed the correlation of movements.

He studied the "cerebellum's" load chart with the utmost attention. The computer seemed to have been hard pressed, as if, without disturbing the operation in any way, it had demanded from the subsystems increasingly greater input per time unit. This created an informational glut and the appearance of reverberating currents; in an animal this would have been equivalent to a radically intensified tonus, a susceptibility to the motor disorders termed clonic spasms. A blind alley. True, he was missing the most important tapes, those with the computer decisions. There was a knock at the door. Pirx stashed the tapes in his grip and met Romani at the door.

"The new brass would like you involved in the work of the committee."

Romani looked less drained than the day before, more upbeat. Simple logic told Pirx that even the mutually antagonistic "Martians" of Agathodaemon and Syrtis would close ranks if the "new brass" tried to railroad the proceedings.

The new committee had eleven members. Hoyster stayed on as chairman, if only because the committee couldn't be chaired on Earth. A board of inquiry whose members were separated by eighty million kilometers was a risky venture; the authorities' agreement to undertake it could only have been made under pressure. The disaster had revived a controversy of political dimensions, one in which the project had been embroiled from the start.

They began with a general recap for the benefit of the Earthlings. Among the latter, Pirx knew only the shipyard director, Van der Voyt. The color screen, for all its fidelity, lent his features a certain monumentality—the bust of a colossus, with a face both flaccid and bloated, full of imperious energy and shrouded by smoke rings from an invisible cigar (his hands were off screen) like some burnt offering. Anything said in the hall reached him after a four-minute delay, followed by another four-minute interval for the reply. Pirx took an immediate dislike to the man, or, rather, to his pompous presence, as if the other experts, whose faces flickered occasionally on the other monitors, were merely dummies.

After Hoyster came an eight-minute interval, but Earth momentarily demurred. Van der Voyt asked to see the *Ariel*'s tapes, a set of which lay by Hoyster's microphone. By now, each member of the committee had received a dubbed set. Not that they were much help, since the tapes covered only the last five minutes of the landing sequence. While the camera crew relayed Earth's set, Pirx fussed with his own, skipping the tapes with which, thanks to Haroun, he was already familiar.

The computer had reversed the landing procedure in the 339th second, shifting not to ordinary lift-off, but to an escape maneuver, as if in response to a meteorite alert, though it looked more like frantic improvisation. Whatever the sequence of events, Pirx attached little importance to the wild curve jumps on the tapes, which proved only that the computer had gagged on its own concoction. Of far greater relevance than a post-mortem of the ship's macabre end was the cause of a decision that, in retrospect, was synonymous with suicide.

From the 170th second onward, the computer had functioned under enormous stress, showing signs of extreme informational overload, a piece of wisdom gained easily in hindsight, now that the final results were in. Not until the 201st second of the maneuver had the computer relayed the overload to the cockpit—to the human crew of the *Ariel*. By then, the computer was glutted with data—and kept demanding more. The tapes, in short, raised more questions than they solved. Hoyster allowed a ten-minute break for perusal of the tapes, then opened up the floor to questions. Pirx raised his hand, classroom-style. But before he could open his mouth, Engineer Stotik, the shipyard supervisor in charge of offloading the hundred-thousand-tonners, said that Earth should take the floor first. Hoyster wavered. It was a nasty ploy, beautifully timed. Romani asked for a point of order, declaring that if they were going to disrupt the proceedings by insisting on equal rights, then neither he nor anyone else from Agathodaemon planned to stay on the committee. Stotik yielded the floor to Pirx.

"The model in question is an updated version of the AIBM 09," he began. "I've logged about a thousand hours with the AIBM 09, so I can speak from experience. I'm not up on the theory, only on what I've needed to know. We're dealing here with a real-time data processor. This newer model, I've heard, has a thirty-six percent larger memory than the AIBM 09. That's quite a bit. On the evidence, here's what I think happened. The computer guided the ship into a normal landing sequence, then started overloading, demanding from the sub-routines more and more data per time unit. Like a company commander who keeps turning his combat soldiers into couriers: by the battle's end, he might be extremely well informed, but he won't have any soldiers.

"The computer wasn't glutted; it glutted itself. It overloaded through the escalation—it *had* to, even with ten times the storage capacity. In mathematical terms, it reduced its capacity exponentially, as a result of which the 'cerebellum'—the narrower channel—was the first to malfunction. Delays were registered by the 'cerebellum,' then jumped to the computer. As it entered a state of input overload, when it ceased to be a real-time machine, the computer jammed and had to make a critical decision. It decided to abort the landing; that is, it interpreted the interference as a sign of imminent disaster."

"A meteorite alert, then. How do you explain that?" asked Seyn.

"How it switched from a primary to a secondary procedure, I don't know. I'm not sufficiently at home with the computer's circuitry to say. Why a meteorite alert? Search me. But this much I do know: *it* was to blame."

Now it was Earth's turn. Pirx was sure Van der Voyt would attack him, and he was right. The flabby, fleshy face, simultaneously distant and close up, viewed him through the cigar haze. Van der Voyt spoke in a polite bass, his eyes smiling, benignly, with the all-knowing indulgence of a professor addressing a promising student.

"So, Commander Pirx rules out sabotage, does he? But on what grounds? What do you mean, '*it* was to blame'? Who is *it?* The computer? But the computer, as Commander Pirx said himself, remained fully functional. The software? But this is the very same program that has seen Commander Pirx through hundreds of landings. Do you suspect someone of having monkeyed with the program?"

"I'll withhold comment on the sabotage theory," said Pirx. "It doesn't interest me right now. If the computer and the software had worked, the *Ariel* would still be in one piece, and we wouldn't be having this conversation. What I'm saying is that, going by the tapes, the computer was executing the proper procedure, but in the manner of a perfectionist. It kept demanding, at a faster and faster clip, input on the reactor's status, ignoring both its own limitations and the capacity of the output channels. Why it did this, I couldn't say. But that's what it did. I have nothing more to add."

Not a word came from the "Martians." Pirx, poker-faced, registered the gleam of satisfaction in Seyn's eye and the mute contentment with which Romani straightened himself in his chair. After an eight-minute interval, Van der Voyt's voice came on. This time his remarks were addressed neither to Pirx nor to the committee. He was eloquence personified. He traced the life history of every computer—from the assembly line to the cockpit. Its systems, he said, were the combined product of eight different companies, based in Japan, France, and the U.S. Still unequipped with a memory, still unprogrammed, as "ignorant" as newborn babies, computers traveled to Boston, where, at Syntronics Corp., they underwent programming. Each computer was then immersed in a "curriculum," divided evenly between "experiments" and "exams." This was the so-called General Fitness Test, followed by the "specialization phase," when the computer evolved from a calculator to a guidance system of the type deployed by the *Ariel.* Last of all came the "debugging phase," when it was hooked up to a simulator capable of imitating an infinite number of in-flight emergencies: mechanical breakdowns, systems malfunctions, emergency flight maneuvers, thrust deficiencies, near collisions. . . . Each of these crisis situations was simulated in myriad variations—some with a full load, some without; some in deep space, some during reentry—increasing in complexity and eventually culminating in the most difficult of all: safely programming a ship's course through a multibodied gravitational field.

The simulator, itself a computer, also played the role of "examiner," and a perfidious one at that, subjecting the already programmed "pupil" to further endurance and efficiency tests, so that, although in actuality the electronic navigator had never piloted a ship, by the time it was finally installed aboard ship, it was more experienced, more flightworthy than the sum total of professional navigators. That is, the problems simulated during the bench-testing phase were too complex ever to occur in reality. And just to safeguard against the slightest imperfection, the pilot-simulator's performance was monitored by a human, an experienced programmer with years of flight training behind him; Syntronics didn't bother with pilots, only with astronauts at the rank of navigator or better, only with those, in other words, who had already logged a minimum of a thousand hours. With them rested the final decision as to which test, out of an inexhaustible range, the computer would be made to undergo next. The systems analyst specified the testing level and, by manipulating the simulator, further complicated the "exams" by simulating sudden—and potentially lethal—power blowouts, flare-outs, collision alerts, skin ruptures, communication breakdowns with ground telemetry . . . until the minimum standard of a hundred bench-testing hours had been achieved. Any model showing the slightest fallibility was sent back to the shop, like a flunked student who has to repeat a year.

Having in effect placed the shipyards beyond reproach, Van der Voyt, probably to counteract the impression of partiality, made an eloquent plea for an impartial inquiry. Next, a team of experts from Earth took the floor, thereupon unleashing a torrent of scientific parlance, flow charts, block diagrams, formulas, models, and statistical comparisons; and Pirx was chagrined to see that they were well on their way to turning the whole affair into an abstruse theoretical case study. The senior computer scientist was followed by Schmidt, the project's systems engineer. Pirx very soon switched off, not bothering to stay alert for another round with Van der Voyt, which seemed progressively less likely. Not one reference was made to his own pronouncements, as if he had committed a *faux pas*—and the sooner it was forgotten, the better. By now they had reached the highest pinnacle of navigational theory. Pirx did not suspect them of malice; prudence dictated that they stay close to home. Throughout, Van der Voyt sat and listened indulgently. The strategy had worked: Earth was dominating the hearing. The "Martians" had been reduced to passive spectators; they had no surprise revelations up their sleeves. The *Ariel*'s computer was now electronic scrap, totally worthless as a source of clues. The tapes may have conveyed the *what*, more or less, but not the *why*. Not everything inside a computer can be monitored: one would need another, more powerful, computer, which, to be made foolproof, would again have to be monitored by yet another, and so on *ad infinitum*.

Thus were they cast adrift on a sea of abstraction. The

profundity of the disquisitions only obscured the fact that the tragedy extended far beyond the shipwreck of the *Ariel*. Automatic sequencers had been around for so long that they had become the basis, indeed, the inviolable premise, of all landing operations, and now this was on the verge of being snatched away. If none of the simpler, less foolproof computers had ever malfunctioned, why should a perfected, more sophisticated one fail? If that was possible, anything was possible. If the computer's fallibility was open to doubt, there was no stopping the erosion of faith; then everything became mired in skepticism.

Meanwhile, the *Ares* and *Anabis* were Mars-bound. Pirx felt alone, on the brink of despair. The inquest into the *Ariel* had given way to a classic argument between theoreticians, and it was leading them further and further afield. As he looked up at Van der Voyt's bloated, overblown face benevolently patronizing the committee, Pirx was suddenly struck by its resemblance to Churchill's: the same look of apparent distraction, belied by a slight twitching of the mouth, betraying an inner smile provoked by a thought lurking behind heavy eyelids. What yesterday seemed unthinkable was now a foregone conclusion: a move to shift the burden of blame onto some higher force, onto the unknown, perhaps, or onto some theoretical omission, one that would require more extensive, long-term research. Pirx knew of similar, though less sensational cases, and knew the sort of passions such a disaster could arouse. Intensive efforts were already under way to reach a face-saving compromise, especially since the project, with its very existence now at stake, was ready to make concessions in exchange for support of the sort the shipyards could provide, if only by supplying a fleet of smaller cargo ships on favorable terms. In view of the high stakes—namely, the project's survival—the *Ariel* calamity was an obstacle to be removed, if it couldn't be immediately solved. After all, bigger scandals had been hushed up. But Pirx had one trump card. Earth had consented to his being on the committee

because, as a veteran pilot, he was more at home with astronautical crews than anyone else present. He had no illusions:
they were moved neither by his reputation nor by his credentials. Quite simply, the committee had need of an astronaut,
an active one, a professional, all the better if that astronaut
had just stepped ashore.

Van der Voyt smoked his cigar in a silence that, because
it was dictated by prudence, lent him an air of omniscience.
He might have preferred someone else to Pirx, but they had
no excuse to bump him. If they now brought in an inconclu-
sive verdict, and Pirx were to cast a dissenting vote, the
result would be a lot of bad publicity: the press, having a
nose for scandals, would pounce on it. The Pilots' Union and
the Truckers' Club wielded little power, but pilots made
credible witnesses—they were, after all, people who put their
lives on the line. So Pirx wasn't at all surprised to hear,
during the break, that Van der Voyt wanted a word with
him. This friend of powerful politicians led off with a joke,
calling their meeting a summit conference—at the summit of
two planets. Pirx at times was subject to impulses that took
even him by surprise. While Van der Voyt puffed on his
cigar and lubricated his throat with beer, Pirx ordered a few
sandwiches from the snack bar. What better way to get on
an equal footing than by munching on a snack as he listened
to the shipyard director in the communications room.

Van der Voyt made as if there had never been a sparring
match between them. He shared Pirx's concern for the crews
of the *Anabis* and *Ares*, and even cried on his shoulder. He
was outraged by the press, by all the hype. He suggested
that Pirx draft a short memo on future landings, on ways to
increase their safety. He exuded such confidence that Pirx
briefly excused himself, stuck his head out the door, and ordered some more potato salad. Van der Voyt was still playing the role of father, even fawning on him, when Pirx
suddenly asked:

"You mentioned the people in charge of simulation. Their names?"

Eight minutes later, Van der Voyt's face winced, but only slightly, for perhaps a fraction of a second.

"The names of the examiners?" he said, grinning broadly. "All colleagues of yours, Commander. Mint, Stoernhein, and Cornelius. Gentlemen of the old school. We recruited only the finest for Syntronics."

They had to interrupt; the conference was back in session. Pirx jotted something down and handed the paper to Hoyster, saying, "A matter of the utmost urgency." The chairman read it aloud: "Three questions for the shipyard staff: One, what are the shifts of the simulation supervisors Cornelius, Stoernhein, and Mint? Two, to what extent are the supervisors held responsible in the event of a malfunction or other defect in a computer? Three, which of the supervisors was in charge of bench-testing the systems aboard the *Ariel, Anabis,* and *Ares?*"

There was a commotion in the hall: Pirx was going after some of the most respected—hallowed—names in astronautics! The managing director acknowledged receipt of the questions and promised a reply within a few minutes.

Pirx felt a twinge of remorse. Making such official inquiries was a bad business. Not only did he risk his colleagues' enmity, but he also cast doubt on his own credibility in the final round—in case of a dissenting vote. His attempt to widen the investigation beyond the technical, to introduce the human factor, could be interpreted as bowing to pressure from Van der Voyt. The moment he deemed it in the shipyard's interest, the director would immediately move to squelch him by dropping a few veiled hints to the press. He would toss them Pirx as a bumbling comrade-in-arms. It was a long shot, but it was the only thing he had left. There was no time to make discreet, indirect inquiries. Not that he entertained any actual suspicions. A hunch, maybe. Some vague notions about the dangers arising not from men or machines so much as from their collision, because the reasoning of men and computers was so awfully different. And something else, something he had sensed as he stood before the bookshelf, but which he couldn't even begin to express in words.

Earth's reply was immediate: The simulation supervisors monitored their computers from start to finish, and were held responsible for any malfunctions the moment they signed their "diplomas." The *Anabis*'s computer had been tested by Stoernhein, the others by Cornelius. Pirx couldn't wait to leave the room. Tension was already running high; he could feel it.

The session ended at eleven. Romani signaled to get Pirx's attention, but he pretended not to notice and made a speedy getaway. Shutting himself up in his cubicle, he collapsed on the cot and took to staring up at the ceiling. Mint and Stoernhein didn't count, only Cornelius. A rational, scientific mind would have started with the question: was there anything a supervisor might have overlooked? A negative answer would have barred any further inquiry. But Pirx wasn't blessed with a scientific mind, so the question never occurred to him. Nor did he bother to analyze the testing procedure, as if intuiting the futility of such efforts. No, his thoughts were of Cornelius, of the man he once knew, fairly well in fact, though they had long since gone their separate ways. Their relationship had not been the merriest, which was hardly surprising, given that Cornelius had commanded the *Gulliver* when Pirx was still a rookie. On board, Cornelius was a bastard of exactitude. He was called a brute, a nitpicker, a skinflint, and a fly-swatter (he had been known to mobilize half the crew to hunt down a stowaway fly).

Pirx smiled in recollection of the eighteen months he had spent under the stickler Cornelius. Now he could afford to smile; at the time, Cornelius had driven him nuts. What a by-the-book man! Even so, he was listed in the encyclopedia for his work on planetary exploration, especially Neptune.

Short, pasty-looking, always mean-tempered, he suspected everybody of wanting to con him. When he threatened periodic body searches—to prevent flies from being smuggled aboard—nobody took him seriously, but Pirx knew it was not just an idle threat: Cornelius kept a big box of DDT in his desk drawer. Sometimes, in the middle of a conversation, he would stiffen, raise his finger (God help those who didn't freeze), and strain his ears to pick up what sounded like a buzzing. A plumb line and a steel measuring tape always in his pocket, he made a cargo inspection more like an inquest at the site of an accident that, though not yet materialized, was imminent. Pirx could still hear them yelling, "Here comes Old Sliderule—everybody scram!," thereby evacuating the mess hall while Cornelius's eyes, seemingly blank, scoured the place for any irregularities.

Tics are quite common among veteran rocket jockeys, but Cornelius broke all records. He was allergic to having anyone stand behind his back; if he inadvertently sat down in a chair just vacated, he would jump up in mortal terror the moment he came into contact with the warm seat. He belonged to that species of man impossible to imagine as ever having been young. Visibly frustrated by the imperfection of everyone around him, he anguished over his inability to convert them to his own pedantry. He would tick off one column after another, and he wasn't satisfied unless everything was checked and rechecked at least twenty— Pirx suddenly went numb and then sat down as if he were made of glass. His thoughts, stumbling through a maze of memories, had tripped an alarm.

Couldn't stand anybody behind his back. Hassled the crew. So? But somehow . . . He felt like a little boy with his hand clasped around a bug, who holds his clenched fist up close, afraid to open it. Easy does it.

Cornelius was notorious for his rituals. (Was that it? he wondered.) At the slightest change in regulations, however minor, he would shut himself up in his cabin until the revised rule had been committed to memory. (It was becoming a game of hide-and-seek; let's see, it was nine, no, ten years since they'd last seen each other.) Cornelius had somehow vanished from the public eye, at the height of his Neptune fame. There were rumors that the lecturing was only temporary, that he was going back aboard ship, but he never did. (Another dead end.) An anonymous letter. (Where the hell . . . ?) What anonymous letter? About his being sick and covering up? That he was a heart-attack risk? No. That was another Cornelius—Cornelius Craig—one, a first name; the other, a surname. (A simple mix-up of names.) But that anonymous letter wouldn't go away, wouldn't stop hounding him. The more emphatically he tried to dismiss it, the more adamantly it returned. He sat hunched over, his head in a muddle. An anonymous letter . . . He was almost sure of it now—a play on words, one of those cases of word substitution, a wrong signal, a stand-in for something else, impossible to shake loose or to fathom . . . ANONYMOUS.

He got up. On the bookshelf, he recalled, among all the books devoted to Mars, was a huge dictionary. He opened it at random to *An. Ana. Anachronism. Anaclastic. Anaconda. Anacreontic. Anacrusis. Analects.* (There were so many words he didn't know. . . .) *Analysis. Ananke (Gk.): goddess of destiny* (Was that the . . . ? But what did a goddess have to do . . . ?); *also: compulsion.*

The scales fell from his eyes. He could see the office, the doctor with his back to him, talking on the phone; an open window, sheets of paper on the desk, furling and unfurling in the breeze. A routine check-up. He hadn't meant to read the typed document, but his eyes couldn't resist the printed word—as a boy he had rigorously trained himself to read upside down. *Warren Cornelius. Diagnosis: anankastic syndrome.* He recalled how the psychiatrist, spotting the forms scattered haphazardly on the desk, had bunched them together and stuffed them into his briefcase. Pirx had often wondered about that diagnosis, but he sensed the impropriety of prying, and then he forgot about it. Let's see, how many years ago was that? At least six.

He put down the dictionary, agitated, flushed, but also a little disillusioned. Ananke—compulsion—compulsive neurosis, probably. An obsessive compulsive? Even as a boy— there must have been something in the family history—he'd hunted for definitions, and now his memory—nobody could accuse him of not having a good memory—though not without resistance, began to yield those medical descriptions. Phrases from the medical encyclopedia flashed before him, revelatory, casting Cornelius in a totally new light.

It was a spectacle as mean as it was pitiable. So that's why the compulsion to wash his hands by the hour, to comb the ship for flies; why he flew into a rage when he lost a bookmark, why he kept his towel under lock and key and wouldn't occupy anyone else's chair. One compulsion compounded by another, a whole complex, overwhelming him, exposing him to ridicule. Sooner or later, the doctors had to notice. Finally he was relieved of his command. Straining his memory, Pirx thought he could recall the phrase underlined in the lower margin: *Disqualified for duty.* And since the psychiatrist knew nothing of computers, he gave Cornelius clearance to work at Syntronics. He probably thought it an ideal place for a pedant like him. What better way to show off his meticulousness! It could only do him good. A responsible position and—most important of all—one closely allied with astronautical science . . .

Pirx lay back, his eyes glued to the ceiling. He could imagine Cornelius at Syntronics effortlessly. What was his job? He ran the load-test simulators. In other words, he put the computers through their paces, something that came naturally to him. The man probably lived in constant dread of being taken for a madman, which he wasn't. He never panicked in a real crisis. He was brave, but his bravery was gradually eroded by his obsessions. Torn between his crew and his own twisted insides, he must have felt caught between the hammer and the anvil. He looked like a sufferer, not because he surrendered to his obsessions, not because he was deranged, but because he resisted them, constantly seeking pretexts, a means of justification. He needed those regulations; he used them to vindicate himself, to show it was not his fault, that he was not to blame for that eternal drilling. He wasn't a sergeant at heart; otherwise, he would not have read Poe's eerie, macabre stories. Was he searching for his own private hell in those tales? What must it be like to harbor a tangle of barbed wire, to be always on the defensive, ready to suppress, time and again . . . and underneath it all, the terror of the unpredictable, of that something against which he had always to be on guard. Hence the drilling and the exercising, the test alerts, the inspections, the musters, the surveillance, the all-night prowling fore and aft—good God, he knew how they all laughed on the sly, possibly even saw himself how senseless it was. Was he now taking it out on those computers? If so, then unconsciously. A case of transference. He excused himself on the grounds of necessity.

How uncanny the degree to which another language, that of medical science, could throw what was previously known, personally and second-hand, into a new perspective. With the master key of psychiatry, Pirx was able to plumb the depths, to have a man's personality laid bare, distilled, reduced to a handful of reflexes, as pitiful as they were inescapable. To be a doctor accustomed to viewing people as case studies, even for the sake of helping them, struck him as unspeakably obscene. And yet only now did the thin aura of buffoonery edging the memory of Cornelius begin to dissolve. In this new and unexpected version there was no room for that maliciously schoolboyish, shipboard, barracks kind of humor. There was nothing funny about Cornelius.

One would have thought his post at Syntronics the right job for the right man: a chance to prod, pressure, and challenge to the utmost of endurance, a place to vent all his frustrations. To the uninitiated, it must have seemed a perfect marriage. An old pro, an ex–rocket jockey, transmitting all he knew to the computers—what could be more ideal? He, on the other hand, was freed from all restraints: he was dealing with slaves, not people. A computer fresh off the assembly line was like a newborn babe: full of potential, but helpless.

Learning requires the ability to filter the relevant from an undifferentiated mass. At the test bench, the computer plays the part of the brain, whereas the simulator imitates the body. The brain fed by the body: an apt analogy.

Just as the brain oversees the state of every muscle, a computer monitors a ship's systems. It transmits a barrage of questions to all parts of the ship, and the computer, that metal colossus, translates the responses into a visual display. Intruding on the infallible was a man debilitated by a fear of the unknown and combatting it with his obsessive rituals. The simulator became a tool of his compulsiveness, the embodiment of his anxieties. Cornelius was governed by the law of maximum safety. How laudable! How hard he must have tried! A routine flow was quickly judged to be substandard. And the greater the challenge, the faster the feedback.

Cornelius must have decided that the retrieval speed of the sub-routines had to be correlated with the importance of the procedure. And since the landing maneuver was the most critical . . . Did he reprogram it? It was just like someone who spends hours inspecting his car motor and ends up trying to rewrite the operator's manual. The program couldn't disobey him. He was pushing into areas where the program was defenseless. Whenever an overloaded computer broke down, Cornelius sent it back to the engineering department. Did he realize that he was infecting them with his obsessions? Probably not. He was a man of practice, not theory— a perfectionist, whether in regard to machines or men. He overloaded his computers, but, then, his computers were hardly able to protest. The latest models were designed to operate like chess players and were programmed to beat any operator, provided their trainer wasn't a Cornelius. They could anticipate two or three moves in advance, but they overloaded when the number of variables increased exponentially. In the case of ten consecutive chess moves, a trillion operations would not have sufficed. In a tournament, a player handicapped by such self-paralysis would be disqualified in the first round. Aboard ship, it took longer: a computer's input/output can be monitored, but not its insides. Inside, a massive traffic jam; outside, a routine procedure. For a while, anyway.

Such was the brain, so overburdened with spurious tasks as to be rendered incapable of dealing with real ones, that stood at the helm of a hundred-thousand-tonner. Each of Cornelius's computers was afflicted with the "anankastic syndrome": a compulsion to repeat, to complicate simple tasks; a formality of gestures, a pattern of ritualized behavior. They simulated not the anxiety, of course, but its systemic reactions. Paradoxically, the fact that they were new, advanced models, equipped with a greater memory, facilitated their undoing: they could continue to function, even with their circuits overloaded.

Still, something in the Agathodaemon's zenith must have precipitated the end—the approach of a strong head wind, perhaps, calling for instantaneous reactions, with the computer mired in its own avalanche, lacking any overriding function. It had ceased to be a real-time computer; it could no longer model real events; it could only founder in a sea of illusions. . . . When it found itself confronted by a huge mass, a planetary shield, its program refused to let it abort the procedure, which, at the same time, it could no longer continue. So it interpreted the planet as a meteorite on a collision course, this being the last gate, the only possibility acceptable to the program. Since it couldn't communicate that to the cockpit—it wasn't a reasoning human being, after all—it went on computing, calculating to the bitter end: a collision meant a 100 percent chance of annihilation, an escape maneuver, a 90–95 percent chance, so it chose the latter: emergency thrust!

It all made sense. Logical—but without the slightest shred of evidence. It was something unprecedented. How could he confirm his suspicions? The psychiatrist who had treated Cornelius, helped him, given him job clearance? The Hippocratic oath would seal his lips, and the seal of secrecy could be broken only by a court order. Meanwhile, six days from now, the *Ares* . . .

That left Cornelius himself. Was he aware by now? After all that had happened, did he suspect anything, have any inkling? There was no second-guessing the veteran commander. He was untouchable, as if insulated by a glass wall. Even if gnawed by doubts, he would not admit to them. He would suppress them, that was clear enough.

But it was bound to come out anyway, after the next shipwreck. Assuming the *Anabis* soft-landed, a routine statistical analysis would point the finger of suspicion at Cornelius's computers. Every component would be microscopically analyzed, every clue traced. . . .

But Pirx couldn't just sit around and twiddle his thumbs. What to do? He knew: erase the *Ares*'s memory, transmit the original program, and the computer would be reprogrammed in a matter of hours.

Still, he needed hard evidence. A shred, at least. Or even some circumstantial evidence. But he had zilch. One fleeting recollection, from years past, of a medical chart read upside down, a nickname, a handful of gossip, anecdotes, a catalogue of the man's quirks . . . To stand before the panel and cite this as proof of the man's mental instability, as the cause of the shipwreck, would have been lunacy. Even if he impugned the old man's sanity, there was still the *Ares*. During the entire reprogramming operation, the ship would be, as it were, blind and deaf. The wildest ideas came to him: if he couldn't do it officially, why not lift off and warn the *Ares* from on board the *Cuvier*, and to hell with the consequences. But it was too risky. He didn't know the chief navigator. Besides, would *he* have taken the advice of a stranger? Advice based on mere hypotheses? Without any hard facts? Hm . . .

So it was Cornelius or nothing. Pirx knew his address: Syntronics Corp., Boston. But how to ask someone so distrustful, pedantic, and fastidious to confess to the very thing he'd spent a lifetime trying to prevent? If he could have taken him aside, worked on him a little, alerted him to the plight of the *Ares*, maybe then Cornelius would have consented, would have gone along with it—he was, after all, a man of scruple. But how, on that remote Mars–Earth hookup, riddled with eight-minute pauses, talking not man to man but screen to screen, could he accuse a pathetic old man of such a thing, and urge him to confess to having murdered—however unintentionally—some thirty people? Impossible.

He sat on the cot, hands clasped, as if praying. He felt profound incredulity, disbelief: to be so sure of something— and so powerless! His eyes roamed the books on the shelf. They had helped him—with their failed vision. They had been more concerned with those canals, with some distant and hypothetical thing, telescopically viewed, than with themselves. They had argued about a Mars they couldn't see, the product only of the heroic and fatal visions hatched by their own minds. They had projected their fantasies two hundred million kilometers into space—instead of probing themselves. And those who sought the causes of the calamity in the wilds of computer theory were sadly off target. The computers were as innocent and neutral as Mars, against which he, Pirx, bore an insane grudge, as if the world were to blame for the illusions fostered about it. These antiquated books had done their best. He saw no way out.

On the very bottom shelf, in a row of garishly bound fiction, stood a faded blue volume of Edgar Allan Poe. So Romani was a Poe fan. Not Pirx; he disliked Poe for the artificiality of his language, for the exquisiteness of vision that refused to admit to its dreamlike derivation. For Cornelius, too, Poe was the Bible. Instinctively, Pirx reached for the volume, which flipped open on its own to the table of contents. One of the titles jogged his memory. Cornelius had recommended it to him once, after the watch—a fantastically rigged story of a murderer uncovered. At the time, Pirx had been obliged to sing its praises—a CO, after all, never erred. . . .

At first, he merely toyed with the idea. A schoolboy's prank, or a blow below the belt? Crude, lowdown, mean— yes, but, who knew, maybe the best solution. A telegram consisting of just four words. But what if he was all wrong? Maybe the medical file referred to another Cornelius; maybe Cornelius ran standard computer tests and had a clear conscience. In that case he'd slough it off as a dumb and exceedingly tasteless joke. But if the shipwreck had piqued his conscience, aroused the vaguest suspicion; if he was gradually being awakened to, but still resisting, his own complicity, then those four words would land like a thunderbolt. Then would come the shock of exposure—for something only partially grasped—and the guilt. Then he couldn't avoid thinking of the *Ares*'s impending fate; even if he tried to repress it, the telegram would fester inside him. No more thumb-twiddling, no more sitting back in idle anticipation; the message would get under his skin, gnaw at his conscience, and—then what? Pirx knew the old man well enough to know that he wouldn't turn himself in, wouldn't confess, any more than he would start inventing alibis. Once convinced of his guilt, he would do what he thought proper, without a whimper, in silence.

Pirx knew it wasn't really right. Again he ticked off the alternatives, ready to approach the devil himself—Van der Voyt—if it would do any good. But no one could stop it now. No one. Oh, if it weren't for the *Ares* and the race against time . . . Getting the psychiatrist to break his oath, reviewing Cornelius's testing methods, tearing down the *Ares*'s computer—all that would take weeks. So what was left? Soften him up first with a message? One that read . . . But that would be a tip-off, a dead give-away. Cornelius, with his twisted mind, was sure to plead some excuse, to cite some pretext—not even the most moral person can stifle the instinct for self-preservation. He would go on the defensive, or withdraw into a disdainful silence, and meanwhile the *Ares* . . .

Pirx was overcome by a sinking sensation, a feeling of losing ground, like the character in another Poe story, "The Pit and the Pendulum," defenseless against the force that kept pushing him, millimeter by millimeter, toward the abyss. For what could be more defenseless than to suffer, and because of this suffering to be dealt a dirty blow? What could be meaner?

Scuttle the idea? Nothing would have been cozier than to keep a tight lip. No one would ever be the wiser. They wouldn't figure it out until the next shipwreck, and after they picked up the scent . . .

But if it was just a matter of time, if his silence really couldn't save the old commander, then wasn't he duty-bound . . . ? Suddenly, as if he had shed all qualms, Pirx went into action.

The ground floor was deserted. Only one operator on duty in the laser-communications cabin: Haroun. The message read as follows: "Syntronics Corp., Boston, Mass., U.S.A., Earth. Warren Cornelius: THOU ART THE MAN." And below Pirx's signature, "Member of the board of inquiry investigating the causes of the *Ariel*'s shipwreck. Address of sender: Agathodaemon, Mars." That was all. He went back and shut himself up in his room. Later there was a knock at the door, and voices, but he played deaf. He had to be alone now— alone with the mortification that he knew was bound to come. Nothing to do but ride it out.

Later that same night he read Schiaparelli—to keep himself from conjuring up, in a hundred different versions, how Cornelius, cocking his gray, bristling eyebrows, would pick up the telegram bearing a Mars address, unfold the crinkly paper, and hold it up to his farsighted eyes. He didn't digest a word of Schiaparelli; each time he turned the page, he was suddenly overwhelmed by shocked dismay mixed with an almost childlike pity. Me? Pirx? How could I have done such a thing?

Pirx had guessed right: Cornelius felt trapped. Cornered. The very nature of the situation, dictated by the natural sequence of events, left him no way out, not the slightest elbow room. Taking a sheet of paper, he jotted down, in his neat and legible hand, a few lines of explanation—that he had acted in good faith, that he accepted full responsibility—signed it, and, at 1530 hours, four hours after having received Pirx's telegram, shot himself in the mouth. No reference to any illness, no attempt at self-vindication. Nothing.

It was as if he acknowledged only that part of the message dealing with the *Ares*, and had decided to cooperate in the rescue attempt—but nothing else. His response seemed to convey sober approval of Pirx's action, but also profound disgust with his methods.

Maybe Pirx had been wrong. Ironically, he was bothered by the theatricality of what he had done, a gesture inspired by Poe. He had trapped Cornelius by using his favorite author, whose manner he himself had always found contrived, irritating, whose fake corpses returning from the grave to point a blood-stained finger at the murderer failed to persuade him of life's horror, which, as Pirx knew from experience, was more mocking than precious. This same discrepancy held for Mars, as viewed by two succeeding generations, during which it went from an unreachable red spot in the night sky, displaying semi-intelligible signs of an alien intelligence, to a quotidian terrain of grinding labor, political machination, and intrigue; a world of enervating windstorms, clutter, shipwrecks; a place from which to behold Earth's poetic blue sparkle, but also one that could inflict a killing. The immaculate—because imperfectly perceived—Mars of early astrography had faded, leaving only those Greek and Latin names having the ring of an alchemist's incantations; the actual terrain by now bore the imprints of heavy boots. The epoch of high-minded theoretical debate had set below the horizon and, in perishing, had revealed its true face: a dream nourished by its own futility of fulfillment. All that remained was the Mars of tedious travail, of budgeting, and of such grimy, dun-gray dawns as the one in which Pirx now went, proof in hand, to the final session.